SEE YOU THEN

A NOVEL

SUSAN COVENTRY

Susan Coventry

To my parents for raising a reader.

To my husband for his enthusiastic support of this endeavor.

Chapter 1

Samantha glanced passively through the day's mail. Same old things—bills and advertisements for things she didn't want or need. At the bottom of the stack was a homemade flyer handwritten in bold black letters. Apparently, a college kid in the neighborhood was looking for work this summer. She tried to place the name, Jason Grant, and realized he lived just a few houses down from her on the opposite side of the street. She recalled meeting him and his parents shortly after they moved in a few years ago. Her image of Jason was that of a teenager mowing the lawn for his parents in that resigned way that teenagers do chores for their parents. Another image flashed by of him shirtless, shooting baskets in his driveway. He had the sculpted, smooth body of a young man who played sports and was active, unlike the mostly middle-aged men in the neighborhood who sat on their riding mowers holding a beer in one hand, their bellies bouncing along with the motion of the tractor. Hmm... do I need any work done? Samantha almost laughed aloud at her lewd thoughts. Yes, but it's not yard work! Sam had been a widow for five years now and had become accustomed to doing all the "manly" chores her husband used to handle around the house. Why was she even pondering this?

Later that day, Sam was relaxing on a lounge chair in the backyard reading a novel when she was interrupted by the sound of a lawn mower starting up next door. It can't be Gretchen, she thought sarcastically. Gretchen was the kind of woman who didn't like to get her hands dirty; plus, her husband Don was the only one Sam ever saw outside. She was surprised in the next second when she saw Jason come into sight pushing a mower, shirtless and sweaty. Sam took him in for a moment, noticing the way his biceps flexed as he pushed the mower and the trickle of sweat that ran down his perfectly ripped abs. His sandy brown hair was tousled in that controlled yet messy way that was trendy for young guys. He wore navy blue board shorts that hung low on his hips showing just a sliver of the waistband of his underwear beneath. Just as she realized she was gawking at him like a teenage girl, Jason looked over and waved at her. She smiled and waved back, then quickly averted her eyes.

What is wrong with me, she scolded herself angrily. I must be twenty years older than him at least! It's been too long since I've had a man around, that's the problem. Maybe I should go out with that guy my sister's been bugging me about. Just then she realized that the sound of the mower had stopped signaling the end of her fantasy. Good, she breathed, now I can go back to concentrating on my book. Sam was disrupted again when she saw movement out of the corner of her eye. Oh no, Jason was walking right toward her with a big grin plastered across his handsome face. Sam sat up straighter and tugged the hem of her skirt down a little further over her bare legs.

"Hey, sorry to interrupt your reading," he said.

"No problem, I wasn't really concentrating anyway," she replied, instantly regretting her choice of words.

"Jason Grant," he said, reaching out to shake her hand.

"Samantha Sullivan," she replied, noting his warm, firm handshake.

"I was just wondering if you got my flyer in your mailbox."

Sam liked him instantly. He had a wide, open smile and sparkly caramel brown eyes that looked directly at her. Not to mention the biceps, the tight abs and... she shook herself. "Yes, I got it but I usually mow my own lawn," she replied, sounding disappointed to her own ears.

"Oh, ok, just thought I'd check since I saw you out here. I'm home from college and I'm trying to make some extra cash this summer."

He sounded so sincere that Sam wished she could conjure up something for him to do. She was also surprised (pleasantly?) that he was in college, so at least she wasn't lusting after a high school student. "What year of college are you going in to?"

"Senior year," he replied seeming to be in no hurry to leave. He glanced over at her lemonade glass on the table beside her chair.

Ah-ha, a way to get him to stay a little longer! I'm really sick, she scolded herself inwardly. "You must be really thirsty. Would you like a glass of lemonade, freshly made this morning," she added, thinking how dorky that sounded.

"Sure, that would be awesome," he replied.

Sam could not believe what she was doing. Since when do I invite college guys over for lemonade? Am I that desperate for male attention? Am I trying to remake *The Graduate*? This is really ridiculous but it's too late now. I offered a glass of lemonade and I have to follow through with it. It's only a glass of lemonade, you idiot! He's a thirsty kid, and I'm giving him a drink, that's all.

"Come on in for a minute." She motioned with one hand while carefully standing up from the chair. She didn't want to give him a view up her skirt; it was only lemonade after all!

Jason followed her through the sliding

glass door into the cool open kitchen. Sam quickly procured a plastic cup and poured in lemonade and ice. She could sense him watching her as she moved about the kitchen.

"Thanks a lot, you really didn't have to do this," he said as she handed him the cup. He tipped his head back and swallowed it in one long gulp. Sam never understood how anyone could do that. If she had tried it, lemonade would have been running down the front of her shirt for sure.

"How about another glass?" she giggled. He nodded, looking somewhat guilty, as she poured another cupful. He drank the second one more slowly while she searched her brain for something else to say. What do I talk about to a college kid—assuming he would want to engage in conversation with a forty-year-old woman in the first place.

"Well, I should probably get going. I have a couple other lawns to mow down the street. Thanks a lot for the lemonade."

Was this boy/man the sweetest or what? How polite, how sincere, how gorgeous. Ok, that's it, he's hired! "You know what Jason? Maybe I could use your help after all. There are a few bushes that I want removed, but I probably won't be able to do it on my own. You could help me with that, right?"

Jason gave her another warm, wide grin and said, "Absolutely."

"Great, when would you like to do it?" Oh no, that didn't come out right. He seemed to sense it too, and they both giggled somewhat uncomfortably. She felt her cheeks getting warm and quickly turned away to grab a scrap of paper from the junk drawer. "Here's my number," she said avoiding eye contact. "Just call me when you can fit it in." Oh no, not again! This time Jason laughed even louder, a deep throaty chuckle that sent a tingle up her spine.

"Ok, I'll call you soon. Thanks again for the lemonade," he said, walking toward the door.

"See you soon, then." She was afraid to say anything more and firmly slid the glass door shut behind him.

Over the next few days, Sam found herself wondering when Jason would call her. She glimpsed him coming and going from his house a couple of times and felt mildly like a stalker. This is so ridiculous, she chastised herself angrily. It's like high school all over again; the angst, the desperation, the self-doubt. I am a forty-year-old school librarian, not a fifteen-year-old girl with a crush on a boy who doesn't even know I exist. I have got to get a hobby, other than reading, which only fuels my over-active imagination. In fact, the book she was currently reading was a "juicy" one that kept her up late at night feeling tingly in all the right places. What else can I do to pass the time?

During the school year, Sam kept very busy, but her summers were emptier now that Brad was gone. Sure, she had her sister living nearby and her lady friends from school, but there was still a missing piece that she couldn't seem to fill no matter what. The grieving widows group she joined shortly after Brad's death confirmed her worst nightmare; time would ease the pain but it would never completely disappear. She went to the group meetings for about a year before deciding she could do this on her own. She grew tired of hearing all the sob stories from virtual strangers about how their lives would never be the same again. I get the gist of it, she remembered thinking; just keep moving forward, that's all you can really do. And she had. After taking a few months off from work and friends and life, she realized she needed it all back. She had to rejoin the living, or she would go crazy. After the first couple of years, well-meaning friends and relatives started talking about fixing her up with some "great guy" they knew, but she kept finding reasons to say no. It's too soon, I'm not ready, it's not time yet. She was beginning to wonder if she was ready now. Did Jason spark something inside her that had been lying dormant for the past five years? That could be the only reasonable explanation for how she was feeling. It was like a part of her was alive again only it was misdirected! She wracked her brain trying to remember the last time her sister had tried to fix her up with someone. What was his name again? Where did she know him from? It was at that very moment that her cell phone rang and, looking down at the number, she knew it was him. Jason.

"Hello," she answered, forcing her voice to stay calm and neutral.

"Hey, it's Jason," he said. "Sorry it took a few days to get back with you."

"No problem at all," she lied. "I'm sure you've been busy."

"I was calling to see if you'll be around this Friday. I could come over and help you with those bushes."

She mentally checked her calendar and couldn't come up with anything; no shock there. "Sure, Friday would be fine. What time were you thinking?"

"How about ten o'clock?"

Why did this feel like a date to her? "Ten o'clock is great."

"Ok, see you then."

"See you then." She hung up the phone feeling satisfied. That wasn't so hard, was it? There's no reason to be nervous at all. You're simply hiring him to do a job.

Friday was two days away, and Sam was determined not to give Jason another thought. She threw herself into some housework that she had been neglecting for some time. When she climbed into bed Thursday evening she decided to watch a documentary on the Amazon rainforest instead of reading her juicy book. She wanted to keep her mind clear and clean before Jason came over tomorrow. Plus, she wanted a decent night's sleep.

She woke up at seven the next morning feeling refreshed and energized. The sun was already streaming through her bedroom blinds, and it promised to be a beautiful day. Sam showered, styled her hair the usual way, and applied her make-up. Then the dilemma of what to wear. Was she planning to help him with the bushes or just supervise? Hmm... she decided on a pair of denim shorts and a red t-shirt. Comfortable and casual, perfect.

She went downstairs and made herself scrambled eggs and toast, enjoying every bite while glancing through a People magazine. She loved this time of day; it was peaceful and quiet. Just as she cleaned up the last of the breakfast dishes, the doorbell rang. She panicked for a moment, thinking she had lost track of time, but it was only nine thirty on the kitchen clock. Wondering who it could be, she wiped her hands on a towel and went to the front door. Ever since Brad died, she made it a habit to look through the peep hole, and there stood Jason-- dressed in a college logo t-shirt and shorts, hair slightly disheveled as if he just rolled out of bed, waiting patiently for her to answer the door.

Pushing down the butterflies in her stomach, she opened the door wide and gave him her best smile. "Good morning. You're early."

"I hope its ok," he said, looking apologetic. "I was up early and thought I could get started."

It suddenly occurred to her that he might have a date tonight. It was Friday after all, and he was a young, good-looking guy...

"Sure, c'mon in while I put on some shoes." Was it her imagination, or did the air feel charged between them? It was as if they had some kind of connection even though they barely knew each other.

As he stood in the foyer waiting patiently for her to tie her Nikes, Jason seemed even taller and broader than she remembered. She couldn't be sure if it was the scent of cologne or a manly deodorant she was getting a whiff of. In either case, he smelled good.

"All set." She stood up quickly, meeting his intense gaze.

"Are you ok living here alone?"

"I am now," she answered truthfully. "It took me a while to get used to, but I'm fine now."

He looked at her with genuine concern in his eyes. "If you ever need anything, I'm right across the street. Don't hesitate to ask."

"That's very sweet of you; I'll keep it in

mind." She smiled at him and got lost for a moment in his twinkling brown eyes.

"Ok, so, let's get to work," he said.

Sam led him around to the west side of the house and pointed out a large overgrown bush. "There's another one against the back of the house that I'd also like removed." Talking about bushes felt so insignificant compared to the conversation they had started in the house. "Come with me to the garage, and I'll show you where the tools are."

She entered the security code to the garage door, and when it had opened halfway, Jason gave out a low whistle. "Awesome. I didn't know you had a Corvette."

Brad had bought the red beauty the year before he died because he "didn't want to be one of those guys who waited for their mid-life crisis to buy a sports car." Sam ended up loving it as much as he did and used to drive it any chance she could get. Now it mostly sat in the garage for long periods of time. She just didn't get the same enjoyment out of it without him.

"I've had it for a while. I just don't get around to driving it that much," she said as she searched for the clippers.

"I would love a car like this," Jason admitted. "I'd probably drive it any chance I got."

Maybe it was his enthusiasm, maybe it was the beautiful summer day, who knows...

but Sam found herself replying, "We could take it for a ride sometime." Oops, did that sound forward? She didn't have time to second-guess herself as Jason was already replying, "How about tonight?"

Sam stopped her search for the clippers and slowly turned around to look at him. Jason was circling the car, inspecting it from all angles. She decided he must not have a date tonight given his eagerness to take a drive with a forty-year-old neighbor lady. Jason glanced over at her, "Unless you have other plans."

Her. Have other plans. What a joke! "No other plans," she said with a grin.

"It's a date, then. Well, you know what I mean." He seemed a little uncomfortable about the terminology. "Maybe we could grab a pizza or something."

Sam recalled her sister telling her about a great new pizza place about a twenty-minute drive away. It suddenly dawned on her that she didn't want to run into any neighbors by staying local. What would people think of her and Jason out together? Cradle-robber, cougar, hussy were just a few words that came to mind. "I know a perfect place, she finally said. What time do you want to go?"

"How about six o'clock? I can walk across the street so you don't have to pick me up," he said, chuckling with that twinkle in his eye that she was quickly becoming fond of.

"Sounds great." Jason then insisted that she relax while he took care of the bushes. He grabbed the tools from the garage and set to work leaving her alone with her panicky thoughts. She tried unsuccessfully to read and put the book down in frustration. Her mind kept whirling, re-playing their conversation over and over and wondering exactly how they'd ended up making a date. She alternated between feeling mortified and strangely excited. How long has it been since I've been on an actual date, she thought. Wait a minute, was this really a date or just a chance for a young guy to ride in a Corvette? No, he specifically called it a date. What was it about this guy that caused such a reaction in her? She tried reasoning it out and decided that, right or wrong, there was some kind of chemistry between them. She could hear the arguments now: he's way too young for you; you need to find someone your own age; what could you possibly have in common? But the fact remained that she felt something with him, and she was intrigued enough to roll with it for now. If nothing else, it could be a good meal and some companionship for the evening. She took a deep breath and exhaled slowly. There, I feel better now, she decided firmly. Now, for the important stuff, what to wear...

Sam decided on a black knit skirt and a white fitted t-shirt with black sandals. Not too dressy, not too casual. She stood in front of the full-length mirror in her bedroom and critiqued herself. She had styled her dark brown shoulder-length hair in loose waves with a side-swept bang. Her makeup was simple: black mascara, rosy blush, and clear lip gloss. She tanned easily and was glad for the golden glow of her skin this time of year. She had bright fucshia polish on her toes but left her fingernails bare. Overall, she looked healthy and vibrant, with just a couple of small wrinkles on her forehead that a person would have to be up close to see. She didn't intend on Jason getting that close to her, so no worries there. Yep, this was as good as it gets. "Let's do this," she muttered aloud, just as the doorbell rang.

Chapter 2

Jason stood on the porch, hands tucked in the pockets of his khaki cargo shorts. He had upgraded from his usual sports team t-shirt to a navy blue polo shirt. His hair was artfully messy, and he had a huge grin on his face as she opened the door to greet him. Sam felt her adrenaline spike and an undeniable flutter in her stomach.

"Hey," he said giving her a quick perusal. "You look nice tonight, not that you didn't look nice earlier… um, never mind." He smiled shyly.

He seemed a little nervous, and so was Sam, so she attempted to put him at ease. "It's ok," she assured him. "You clean up nicely too." She grabbed her purse and keys from the entranceway table and followed him out the door. She had already pulled the Vette out earlier, so it was in the driveway ready to go.

"Would you like to drive?" she asked, handing him the keys.

"Are you serious? I mean, of course, I would love to!" Jason followed her to the passenger door and gallantly opened it for her. She slid in carefully, making sure her skirt didn't ride up. Jason shut the door and quickly moved to the driver's side door. She took a deep breath to calm her nerves as he slid behind the wheel. "Which direction are we headed in?" he asked, checking all the mirrors as he backed out of the drive.

"We need to go north on the expressway for about twenty minutes until we reach the Grand Blanc exit," she replied. They settled into a comfortable silence as Jason appeared to be fixated on the road.

After a few minutes, he turned slightly toward her and said, "This is awesome." Sam was sure he meant the car, so she smiled back and said, "I'm glad you're enjoying it." The ride went by quickly, and they were soon pulling into the parking lot of the pizzeria. Sam put her hand on the door handle, but Jason shook his head. "No, no, that's my job. I'll walk around and open the door."

Really? Did all guys his age have these manners? Sam highly doubted it! "What a gentleman you are," she said, grinning as he held the door open for her. He opened the restaurant door as well, and she felt a slight pressure on her lower back as he guided her inside. The hostess seated them at a corner table and took their drink order: a Coke for him and a Diet Coke for her. Sam found herself glancing around the room and felt a sense of relief when she didn't recognize anybody. She chastised herself for worrying about it. What difference did it make? It's not like they were conducting some sort of covert affair. She could simply introduce him as her neighbor, whom she was treating to dinner as a thank you. Yeah, right!

"What do you like on your pizza?" Jason asked while perusing the menu.

"How about ham and pineapple?"

"That works for me." The waitress saw them set the menus down and quickly came over to take their order.

"Should be about fifteen minutes," she said and walked away.

"So, tell me about school," Sam said, clasping her hands together and leaning forward slightly. Seemed like a safe enough topic. "What's your major?"

"Psychology," he replied. Then, after a moment, "That's the same look my dad had when I told him," he said with a chuckle.

"I'm sorry, I guess I just wasn't expecting that."

"No problem. I had a great Psych teacher in high school, and that's when I became interested. What I really want to do is become a school Psychologist. I like the idea of helping kids work through their problems, especially kids who don't get enough support at home."

Sam knew exactly what he meant. It's why she worked with kids too. She admired Jason's sincerity and sense of purpose, especially at his young age. She would have to stop thinking of him as a kid though; he was in his twenties after all.

"Hey, I thought my parents mentioned that you were a teacher. True?"

"Elementary school librarian, actually. I've always loved books, and I like being around kids, so I put the two together, and voila! The rest, as they say, is history."

"Sounds like you love your job."

"I really do." She smiled, feeling a connection between them. Not just because they both liked to work with kids but because everything about being with him felt so easy. The conversation continued to flow throughout dinner. They talked about everything from their families to their tastes in books and music. Meanwhile, they had devoured most of the pizza and two glasses of soda each. When the bill came, Jason offered to pay, but Sam insisted on splitting it with him.

"Ready to go?" he asked.

Not really she thought; she wasn't ready for the night to end. "Sure," she said, standing up from the table.

Jason held the car door open for her again, and they drove home in companionable silence, each lost in their own thoughts. It was a gorgeous evening, and even though it was almost eight o'clock it felt much earlier. Sam was contemplating how she could keep their "date" going a little longer when Jason interrupted her thoughts.

"Well, here we are." He sounded a little disappointed as they pulled into her driveway. "Do you want me to pull her into the garage for you?"

"That would be great. I'll have to get out and punch in the garage code since I don't keep an opener in here." Sam's heart pounded in her chest as she punched the code in. How can I keep him here a little longer? Should I invite him in for a beer? Is he of legal age?

Jason slid out of the car and walked over to her. He seemed in no hurry to leave either. For a moment they stared at each other, as if trying to read the other's mind, until Sam broke the ice.

"Would you like to come in for a drink or something? I think I still have some lemonade."

He grinned in that charming way that made her warm inside and said, "Got anything a little stronger? I'm old enough to drink beer, you know."

Aha! He was of legal age, good to know. She laughed nervously and replied, "I think I have some Bud Light. Come on inside."

She put her purse and keys down and busied herself about the kitchen gathering beer mugs and a bag of pretzels from the pantry. Jason seemed right at home and perched himself on the stool at her kitchen counter. Sam felt his eyes following her every move and decided she kind of liked it. If only she knew what he was thinking...

"I like your house. It's big yet cozy at the same time."

"Thank you. I try to make it that way. I'm not the formal type." Sam poured their beer and climbed up on the stool next to him. Jason held his mug in the air and said, "Let's make a toast."

She smiled broadly and replied, "What are we toasting to?"

"To new friendships."

"To new friendships," she repeated, clinking her mug against his.

After the last swallow of beer, Jason stood up and said, "I guess I better get going. I had a really good time tonight. Thanks for letting me drive your car and for the beer."

They both stood up and started walking toward the back door. "I had a good time too," Sam whispered. It suddenly felt like that awkward moment on a first date where you don't know if the guy's going to try and kiss you or not.

After a slight pause that felt much longer than it actually was, Jason turned toward her and said, "What are you doing tomorrow? Maybe we could go biking at Indian Springs Metropark."

Sam did a quick calendar check in her

head. Hmm, tomorrow was Saturday and, let's see, no nothing that she could think of. Should she hesitate, play hard to get? No, that's ridiculous, she chided herself. It's just a bike ride on a summer day with my new friend. "Sounds fun," she answered.

Jason breathed an audible sigh of relief. "Great, I can swing by around noon and load your bike into my Jeep. We could grab some sandwiches to take with us on the way."

It sounded like a perfect afternoon. "Ok, I'll see you then." Sam smiled brightly. And then, in the blink of an eye, Jason leaned down and kissed her gently on the cheek.

"See you then," he repeated and was out the door.

Chapter 3

Sam woke on Saturday morning to the noisy chatter of birds outside her bedroom window. The sun was streaming in through the cracks of her blinds, and she wondered drowsily what time it was. She stretched her arms above her head and let out a loud yawn. An inkling of a dream popped into her head from the night before. She had dreamed about Jason; he was kissing her slowly, deeply, and tenderly. She felt her breath catch in her throat and shook her head to clear it. No wonder she'd had the dream; she had gone to bed with visions of Jason bending down to kiss her cheek the night before. It was such a sweet and simple kiss, but it ignited feelings inside her that had been dormant for a long time. It made her feel alive and hopeful and a little scared too. Where could this relationship possibly go? This was a college kid who had his whole life before him, while she had already lived half of hers. She had already experienced love and marriage and loss. Jason, she was guessing, probably hadn't even experienced his first true love yet. With his good lucks and easy-going personality, she was sure he'd had lots of dates. There was probably some college girl out there right now who was dying to go out with him. How could Sam compete with that? Why would she want to?

She shook her head again to stop these questions from rattling around inside it. "I need to say something to him, "she said aloud. I need to tell him that this thing between us, whatever it is, isn't a good idea. He should be out there with girls his own age doing the things that college kids do (whatever that is, these days). I need to tell him that being with me won't get him anywhere; I'm like a dead-end street. But why do I desperately want to go on a bike ride with him? Why can't I just have fun and not worry about the future? Why can't I just enjoy the attention of a young guy while it lasts? This is probably just a little flirtation for him, it doesn't really mean anything. I'm sure I'm making a big deal out of nothing, like I always do. Brad used to complain about that all the time. "You always blow things way out of proportion," he used to say. "Why do you do that? Why do you punish yourself that way?" I always suspected that he thought I was punishing him too! He was always the glass half-full to my glass half-empty.

Sam popped herself out of bed and headed for the shower. She decided to "go with the flow" today. She was determined to simply enjoy the gorgeous sunshine and the exercise and not worry about anything else, at least for now.

Sure enough, the doorbell rang right at noon. Jason stood before her in a pair of black, Nike basketball shorts and a charcoal grey t-shirt. His smile lit up his whole face. "Good morning, or should I say afternoon? How'd you sleep?"

Flashbacks of her dream came streaming into her mind. "Great! I'm rested and ready to go." Sam was dressed in a loose-fitting pair of khaki shorts and a striped t-shirt. She grabbed her purse and sunglasses and locked the door behind her.

"I saw your bike in the driveway, so I loaded it up already. There's a Subway on the way to the park, so we can stop and grab some subs if that's ok with you."

"Perfect," she said as she hopped up into the Jeep. It was an older model but very clean inside. She noticed that Jason didn't open the door for her this time. Maybe he didn't look at today's outing as a date. Instead of disturbing her, the thought actually calmed her nerves. Maybe he looked at this as a casual friendship after all, and she had nothing to worry about.

"So, do you want to eat first or go for a ride?" Jason asked, eyes staring straight ahead.

Hmm... go for a ride? Get your mind out of the gutter, Sam. "Why don't we ride first so we can work up an appetite?"

"I was thinking the same thing." Jason

glanced over at her.

"You know what they say… great minds…"

"Think alike."

It was a short drive to Subway, and after ordering turkey subs, potato chips and bottles of water, they were back in the Jeep. Jason had brought along a small cooler with a few Bud Lights inside. They added the subs and waters and were back on the road in no time. Sam settled in and contentedly gazed out the window for the remaining few miles of the drive. Jason paid the park entrance fee and pulled into a small parking lot near the bike trail.

"Do you come here often?" she asked.

"Once in a while to ride my bike or just sit and read. It's really peaceful here."

Sam agreed. There were only a few other cars in the lot and no people in sight. The only sounds came from some noisy birds in the large oak tree nearby. The sun shone brightly, but the air was a comfortable seventy-five degrees. They would probably work up a good sweat riding, but she was anxious to exercise. Jason unloaded the bikes, and she couldn't help but notice his biceps straining against the material of his t-shirt as he hoisted them out of the Jeep. He was definitely in excellent shape. His shoulders were broad, and his arms and legs were muscled but not overly so. She knew his abs were tight and defined beneath his shirt as a flashback of him mowing the lawn bare-chested floated into her mind.

"Sam, are you ready to go?" he asked, breaking her out of her reverie.

"Oh yeah, sorry." Jason was already perched on his bike seat waiting for her. Sam wondered how long she had been standing there lost in thought.

"Ladies first." He motioned with his hand for her to take the lead.

The bike trail started out flat and gradually became hilly. Sam kept a steady pace, and the whir of Jason's bike tires indicated he was right behind her. She didn't dare turn around to look at him for fear of falling. Every so often, he asked if she needed a break. "Nope, I'm good," she called, enjoying the wind in her hair and the strain in her leg muscles. She did yoga and walked for exercise, but she hadn't ridden a bike in a long time. She had forgotten how much fun it was.

The trail was a seven-mile loop, and they stopped only twice for a water break. They passed a few people walking or biking on the trail, but overall it felt like they had the place to themselves. When they got back to the parking lot, they were both breathing heavily, and Jason's shirt was soaked with sweat. "That felt great," she said. I haven't been on a ride like that in a long time." Why did everything out of her mouth sound like an innuendo? If Jason picked up on it, he didn't react.

"That did feel good, but my shirt is soaked through. Do you mind if I take it off and let it dry out while we eat?"

Mind? Really? Of course she didn't mind; she encouraged it. "By all means." She tried not to gawk as he pulled the t-shirt over his head.

His chest and back appeared to sparkle in the sun. Since when did perspiration become so attractive, she wondered, cursing herself silently. The ends of his hair were damp and curled up adorably at the back of his neck. Sam could only hope that she looked as good after their ride, but it was more likely that she resembled Medusa right about now. She self-consciously smoothed her hair down as Jason busied himself in the Jeep getting out the cooler and a blue blanket he must have kept in the back.

"Is there anything I can do?" Sam asked. She watched as he loaded the bikes back into the Jeep, his muscles straining with the effort.

"Yeah, you can carry the blanket while I get the cooler." He chuckled and tossed her the blanket.

"Where are we taking this?"

"Just up this hill, behind that clump of trees, is a nice clearing. It's where I like to sit and read sometimes."

Hmm... or does he bring girls there to seduce them? Sam started to feel panicky again.

She certainly wasn't afraid of Jason; she just wasn't sure that being alone with him on a blanket in the woods was a good idea. Ok, just relax and breathe, she instructed herself. All you're doing is eating a sandwich with him, no harm in that.

"How about right here?" Jason asked, setting the cooler down with a thump. Sam took one end of the blanket, and he took the other, and they spread it out on a fairly flat piece of ground. The temperature had probably climbed to around eighty degrees by now, but there was a slight breeze that it made it bearable. Jason plopped down on the blanket immediately and began wiping the sweat off his face and neck with a Subway napkin.

"Here, let me serve you," Sam offered, "since you were the one who had to do all the hard work today." She brought out the subs, chips, and two beers from the cooler and arranged them neatly on the blanket. She twisted off the first beer cap and handed it to Jason with a slight bow. "My lord," she joked, acting the humble servant.

"My lady," Jason teased back, eyes crinkling up in the corners. He tipped the beer back and guzzled half of it in one swig.

"I don't get how guys do that."

"Do what?"

"Drink something in one gulp."

"It's a gift. Do you want to learn how?"

"No, thanks. I'll leave it to the professionals."

"I can show you, but you have to trust me." Jason inched closer to her on the blanket.

"No way. It'll end up all down my shirt."

"Well, I guess you would just have to take it off, then."

Sam felt the air shift between them. He was close enough now that their knees were touching on the blanket. His caramel brown eyes stared intensely into hers, and she felt like he was looking straight into her soul. Neither of them spoke as he positioned himself even closer to her and set his beer bottle down. Without breaking eye contact, Jason raised his right hand up to stroke the side of her face. His thumb brushed lightly back and forth against her cheek, and he moved his forehead to rest against hers. Was she breathing? She couldn't be sure. Time and sound and everything else seemed to be standing still until Jason finally broke the silence.

"I really want to kiss you right now," he breathed softly.

Sam felt herself nodding, yes, and then she felt his warm, full lips meet hers. The kiss was slow and tender. His thumb continued to brush against her cheek. The contact felt delicious and all-consuming as the intensity started to build. His tongue probed gently along the inner rim of her lips, and he reached his left hand around to support the back of her neck. Sam's breasts were pressed tight against his hard, bare chest, and she could feel the blood pounding in her ears. Wait, what was that? Sounds, like children's laughter, drifted up the hill toward them. They broke apart simultaneously just as two kids, two adults, and a poodle came trudging up the hill straight toward them.

"Oops, sorry to interrupt. We didn't know anyone was up here," said the middle-aged man holding the dog's leash.

"That's ok." Jason stood up. "We were just leaving."

Sam was grateful that Jason replied because she couldn't find her voice. She was still reeling from their kiss and felt a little unsteady on her feet. They began packing up the food, and Jason rolled up the blanket. Sam couldn't bring herself to look at the family, who were busy setting up their own picnic spot. She was sure they could guess what she and Jason were up to just by the flush on her face. Jason hoisted the cooler up with one arm while she grabbed the blanket, and wordlessly, they walked back down the hill to the parking lot.

As they drove slowly out of the park, Jason turned to her with a concerned gaze. "Are you ok?"

Sam cleared her throat and replied, "Yeah, why?" She never had been very good at hiding her feelings.

"Listen, what happened back there, it doesn't have to happen again if you don't want it to. I didn't mean to make you uncomfortable."

Sam knew that now was the time to voice her concerns. They had crossed a bridge today, and she didn't know quite how to handle it. She turned sideways in the seat to get a better look at him. "Jason," she began, "I think you're a great guy..."

"But," he interrupted. "It sounds like there's a but coming."

"But," she continued, "I don't know if this thing between us can really go anywhere. You are a young, good-looking guy with your whole life ahead of you. I've already lived half of mine. I'm sure there are lots of gorgeous college girls who would love the chance to be with you, so I guess I'm wondering, why me?"

"Why you? I'll tell you why. Because you're smart and funny and sexy as hell, that's why. And I don't care how old you are and honestly, I wish you didn't care either. Why not just give us a chance?"

"Because I'm afraid," she admitted.

"Afraid of what?"

"Afraid that someone's going to get hurt." There she said it. She looked down and noticed her hands were trembling.

They had pulled up in her driveway. Jason put the car in park and turned to face her.

"I will never hurt you."

She wanted to believe him, and she saw by the intensity in his eyes that he meant it.

"Do you like spending time with me?"

Uh-oh, he was taking the control away from her little by little. "Yes," she replied truthfully.

"Are you attracted to me?"

Oh boy, here we go. "Yes," she admitted.

"Well, in case you haven't noticed, I feel the same way about you. So, can you do us both a favor?"

"What is it?"

"Can you relax a little and see where this journey takes us?"

Well, when he put it like that..." I'll try to, but you should know that I'm a worrier by nature."

A wide grin broke out on Jason's face. "Well, we'll just have to work around that."

Sam took a deep breath and exhaled, willing her body to relax. It had been quite a day; first the *kiss*, then the *talk*. She was whipped.

"When can I see you next?" He was nothing if not persistent.

Sam made a split second decision to take a day or two off. "I'm meeting up with my sister tomorrow, so maybe one night next week?"

"Ok," Jason said, sounding a little discouraged.

"I could cook for you," Sam offered, brightening up. "What do you like to eat, besides pizza and Subway, that is?"

Her suggestion seemed to perk him up too. "I'm not fussy. Steak, seafood, pasta. Anything but meatloaf. I don't care for the loaf."

Sam laughed out loud, happy to lighten the mood. "What's wrong with the loaf?"

"The loaf is not good. I'm just saying... ground beef is for hamburgers or sloppy joes. It's not meant to be shaped into a loaf and cooked."

Sam was completely cracking up at this point; her laughter dangerously close to snort territory. "Ok, ok," she said, throwing her hands up in the air, "no loaf."

"Great. I'm glad you see it my way." His eyes were sparkling. "I'll call you next week."

Sam put her hand on the door handle. "I'll see you then."

"See you then," he said with a nod, and Sam felt the emptiness as she closed the door behind her.

Chapter 4

Sam decided she needed to talk to someone about Jason, and by process of elimination, decided to call her sister Jaime. If anyone could be impartial, Jaime could. The only problem might be getting a hold of her; she had a husband, two kids, and a dog that took up most of her time, but Jaime wouldn't have wanted it any other way. Since it was Sunday, Sam hoped that her brother-in-law, Steve, would be home to watch the kids so Sam and Jaime could go out to lunch.

"Hey sis," Jaime answered cheerfully. "What's up?"

Now that was a loaded question! "Do you have time to meet me for lunch today?" Sam asked, getting right to the point. "I have something I really need to talk to you about."

"Sounds important. Hold on a minute." She heard Jaime cover the phone and yell, "Steve, can you watch the kids this afternoon while I go out to lunch with Sam?" Steve yelled back, "No problem."

Sam couldn't help but feel a twinge of jealousy every time she was around her sister and Steve. It was obvious how much they adored each other, and it reminded her of how she and Brad used to be. It made her miss the rhythm of marriage and how after a certain amount of years it felt as easy as breathing.

"Ok, it's all set. Where and when do you want to meet?" Jaime sounded slightly out of breath, probably from chasing the kids around the house.

"We could meet at that pizza place you recommended." Even though Sam had just been there with Jason, she figured it would be a convenient place to meet.

"Sounds wonderful, noon?"

"That will be perfect. See you then." Sam spent the rest of the morning getting ready and thinking about what she was going to tell her sister. Would she be surprised, shocked, disgusted? Jaime had tried to set her up on a blind date a few times, but the men had all been around Sam's age and either widowed or divorced. Sam decided that, regardless of her sister's reaction, she had to get it out there, otherwise she would go crazy!

Jaime and Sam arrived at the restaurant at exactly the same time, Jaime in her black SUV and Sam in her Corvette. Jaime jumped out in black yoga pants, a grey tank top, and baseball cap while Sam was dressed in white cropped pants, a navy and white striped tee, and white sandals. Jaime was always teasing Sam that she had the extra time to put herself together while

Jaime didn't. Little did she know that Sam would kill for the bustling family life that Jaime had.

They hugged hello and entered the restaurant. Sam had a flashback of Jason leading her through the door with his warm hand pressed against the small of her back. She shook herself back to the present.

They ordered a pepperoni pizza and two Diet Cokes before Jaime asked, "So, what's this all about?"

"I met a guy," said Sam, jumping right in.

"Oh my God, Sam, that's awesome." Jaime looked genuinely thrilled. "What's his name? Where'd you meet him?"

Sam swallowed nervously, thinking, here comes the hard part. "His name is Jason, and he lives in my neighborhood."

"Have I ever met him?"

"No, you've never met him. Jaime, he's twenty-three years old."

Jaime's eyes doubled in size. "Really?"

"Yes. We've only gone out a couple times so far, but I just felt the need to tell someone."

"Wow, I'm not sure what to say. What else can you tell me about him?"

"Let's see. Number one, he's gorgeous. He's also sweet and funny and smart. When I'm with him, I almost forget that he's seventeen years younger than me, almost."

Jaime leaned back in her seat trying to

absorb the news. "So, what's the problem here? A young, good-looking guy wants to go out with you, and this is a problem, why?"

Sam knew she could count on Jaime to be open-minded, which is why she had chosen her to talk to. "The problem is, I don't see where this relationship can go. He has one more year of college and then what? He'll have to find a job, and he still lives with his parents, for God's sake. I just don't understand why he wants to waste his time on a middle-aged widow when he could be out there having sex with any co-ed of his choice. It just doesn't make any sense."

"Are you done now?" Jaime said with a sigh, frustration evident in her tone and on her face.

Sam looked at her confused. "You don't see a problem here?"

"No, quite frankly I don't. Sam, look at yourself. You're a hot, single, older, but not too old, woman who is also smart, sweet, and funny just like you described him. You ask why would he be attracted to you, and I ask, why not?"

"You're just saying that because you're my sister."

"No Sam. I'm saying it because it's true. You need to step outside yourself and see yourself the way Jason sees you. The way I'm sure a lot of other men see you if you would just take a moment to notice. I understand that after Brad died you needed to grieve, and you've done that, Sam, you've done it for five long years. But it's time to get out there and explore your options."

"Yes, but with a twenty-three-year-old college student?"

"Why not? It sounds like there's some kind of connection there, so why not see where it leads."

"You sound like Jason right now."

"Well, then I like Jason already! When do I get to meet him?"

Sam sat back and smiled, feeling some of the tension drain out of her body. "Do you really think I should pursue this?"

"Yes, absolutely. At the very least you can be friends with benefits."

"Oh my God Jaime, you are so bad," said Sam, although she couldn't help but chuckle.

"Just give the guy a chance. Go out, have fun, and see what happens. If you have things in common, the age difference really shouldn't matter. Has he told anyone yet? His parents?"

"That's a good question. I'll have to ask him at dinner this week."

"Where are you having dinner?"

"At my house. I'm cooking."

"Oh, sounds cozy." Jaime wiggled her eyebrows up and down.

"Ok, enough of this. This conversation is officially over."

"Oh darn, I was just getting started."

Sam and Jaime paid the bill and walked out of the restaurant together.

"Thanks for listening." Sam hugged her sister goodbye.

"Always," Jaime replied and waved as she drove away.

That night around nine o'clock, Sam's cell rang, disrupting her reading. She had given up watching dry documentaries and resumed reading her juicy romance novel. She hurried to retrieve her phone from the kitchen and smiled when she saw Jason's number on the display. "Hey," she answered, smile still in place.

"Hey," he said back. I know we said we'd talk during the week, but I just wanted to hear your voice."

Boy, did he know the right things to say or what? Sam felt warm and fuzzy all over as she curled back into her reading chair. "I'm glad to hear your voice too."

"Did you have fun with your sister today?"

A good listener too. Wow, his list of attributes went on and on... "Yep, we went out to lunch at the Pizza Shack. We had a nice talk."

"Talk about anything interesting?" Jason asked in a teasing voice.

"Maybe," she teased back.

"Well, I hope it was all good things."

"It was, although she said something about us being friends with benefits." Sam regretted the words right after they came out of her mouth. She didn't want Jason to think she was suggesting that arrangement!

"Ha," he scoffed, "that will never work."

She took the bait. "Why not?"

"Because friends with benefits implies that I would be willing to share you with some other guy, and I would never want that."

Sam felt blown away with his admission. The idea of Jason just wanting a fling with an "older woman" went flying out the window. Some college guys may have been all for the friends-with-benefits concept, but apparently not him. Sam was still trying to decide how to respond when he interrupted her thoughts.

"Anyway, I was just calling to find out when we can have dinner this week. That, and I really did want to hear your voice."

Sam was melting fast. Was he this smooth with all the girls? "How about Wednesday?"

"Three whole days from now?" he asked.

"Well, tomorrow night I have a yoga class, and Tuesday I was planning to get together with some of my co-workers... but you know what, I can see them some other time. How about Tuesday night instead?"

Jason seemed pleased that she was willing to change her plans for him. "Tuesday night is better than Wednesday," he said with a chuckle, sounding a little embarrassed. "I'm looking forward to it."

"Me too, Sam admitted. I'm anxious for you to try my meatloaf!"

After a few seconds of silence, they both burst out laughing. After their laughter died down, Jason said, "See you Tuesday, then."

"See you then," Sam said, and he was gone.

Chapter 5

Monday turned out to be another picture perfect summer day, and since she didn't have anywhere to be until her five o'clock yoga class, Sam decided to do some gardening. She put her hair in a ponytail, pulled on an old t-shirt of Brad's and some ratty jean shorts, and went to work. She wondered briefly what Jason was doing today and sighed. She couldn't seem to stop thinking about him and must have replayed their kiss in the park dozens of times. What struck her the most was how gentle and unhurried he was. There was nothing reminiscent of the hurried, fumbling, teenage days about it. She kept reminding herself that he wasn't a teenager; he probably had plenty of experience under his belt (so to speak).

Just as she was bending over to pull up some weeds along her front walkway, the loud, abrupt sound of a honking horn caused her to look up. There he was, grinning from ear to ear and waving to her out his Jeep window. Sam waved and smiled back and was disappointed that he didn't stop to talk. Must be in a hurry to get somewhere, she thought, wondering where he was off to. Oh, well, I'll be seeing him tomorrow, she reminded herself and resumed pulling weeds.

Sam looked forward to her twice-weekly yoga class with her friend and co-worker Leslie Nelson. Leslie, married with a five year old son, was probably her closest friend at Brandon Elementary School. She was a first grade teacher there and had been especially supportive to Sam after Brad died. Next to her sister, Sam would call Leslie whenever she needed an ear. She wasn't sure how Leslie would react to her "dating" Jason, so when Leslie asked "What's new?" Sam responded with, "Not much." Here was an example of how dating a younger man was problematic. Sam didn't feel comfortable enough to tell her best friend about him. If Jason had been closer to her age, she would have shared the news with Leslie immediately. Sam made a mental note to ask Jason if he had told anyone about her yet.

The yoga class helped to clear her mind, and she felt stretched and relaxed afterward. She promised Leslie they'd get together for lunch soon and climbed into her car tired but happy. She drove home looking forward to a warm bath followed by curling up in bed with her romance novel. Just as she was getting out of the tub, her cell phone buzzed on the bathroom counter. It was a text from Jason that read: *Looking forward to dinner tomorrow.*

She wrapped the towel tightly around her

and texted back: *Me too.*

A second later another text came: *Do I need to bring anything?*

She replied: *Just yourself.*

He wrote: *What time do you want me?* And then a second later: *Oops, maybe I should rephrase that.*

She giggled out loud and typed: *It's ok! Dinner will be ready at 6pm but feel free to come earlier.* After she hit send, she realized the innuendo in her phrasing too!

Jason responded: *Ha, ha, you just did it too!*

Sam felt a warm tingle travel up her spine as she realized she was standing there naked under the towel texting with Jason. If he only knew...

She was enjoying their sexy banter and was feeling brave at that moment, so she typed: *I'm standing here in a towel, so I better get going. See you at 5:30?*

Jason wrote back: *What? Nice of you to plant that image in my brain and tell me you have to go!*

She could practically feel his sparkly eyes appraising her through the phone. Daringly deciding to stay on the path they were on, she wrote: *Just giving you a little something to think about tonight.* After she hit send, she said out loud, "I can't believe I just sent that!"

The phone beeped again: *Oh you gave me something to think about all right!*

Sam smiled and wrote: *Ok it's time for me to get my beauty sleep now.* She thought for a minute and then added: *Sweet dreams.*

A couple of seconds later and then: *I will now! Same to you.*

Sam replied with one word: *Night.* She shut off her phone so as not to be tempted to write more, then climbed into bed with a silly smile still plastered on her face. She seemed to be smiling a lot these days, and she knew it was mostly because of Jason. It didn't take long before her eyelids started drooping, and Jason was the last image she saw before sleep overtook her. Little did she know that Jason was lying in bed, staring up at the ceiling, thinking of her too.

Chapter 6

Sam woke up on Tuesday anxious to embark on her day. She had a long list of things to do before Jason came over, starting with a trip to the grocery store. She had decided on the menu last night: penne pasta with homemade sauce, tossed salad, and a loaf of Italian bread to dip in olive oil. She also bought regular Coke and Bud Light with Jason in mind. Dessert would be cream puff sundaes.

After the shopping, she tackled the housekeeping tasks: vacuuming, dusting, and cleaning the bathrooms. She made sure that every room in the house was presentable. Around three o'clock she started on the food preparation. Her goal was to have everything ready to go before Jason arrived so she wouldn't feel rushed while he was there. She prepared the cream puffs first, and while they were baking, she set to making the pasta sauce. Sam found herself humming a popular Maroon 5 song as she worked. Once she felt comfortable that the dinner was well under way, she went upstairs to change. She stood in her closet for a few minutes, perusing the choices. Somehow, shorts and a t-shirt seemed too casual, yet she didn't want to look too dressy either. She finally settled on a short-sleeve flower print dress that nipped in at the waist and flared out over her hips. She touched up her blush, added a swipe of clear lip gloss, and slipped into her nude-tone wedge sandals. Standing in front of the full length mirror, she surveyed herself from all angles. Not too bad, she decided and returned to the kitchen. It was getting close to five thirty, and she felt surprisingly calm waiting for Jason to arrive. She felt pleased with her efforts and was anxious to get the evening started. Sure enough, he rang the doorbell right on time. Apparently punctuality was on the list of his many attributes!

Jason entered the house looking like he'd just left a Tommy Hilfiger photo shoot; khaki pants, striped polo shirt, and boat shoes rounded out his look. Not to mention the artfully messy hair and sexy grin. I swear he gets better looking every time I see him, she thought, inviting him into the kitchen.

"I like your dress," Jason said while giving her an appreciative once-over.

"Thanks, I like your ensemble too." Ensemble, really Sam?

Jason chuckled. "Well, this is about as dressy as I get unless I'm going to a wedding or a funeral!"

"Would you like a beer before dinner?" Sam offered.

"Only if you join me," he replied with that sexy grin lighting up his face.

Jason perched casually on the bar stool as she got out the mugs and poured them each a glass of beer. "It smells great in here. I hope you haven't been toiling away all day just for me."

Sam smiled up at him. "Actually, I really enjoyed it. It's a lot more fun to cook for someone else rather than just myself."

"Did you cook a lot... when your husband was alive?" Jason shifted on the stool uncomfortably. "Sorry, we don't have to talk about that if you don't want to."

"No, no, it's ok," she assured him. "I did cook quite a bit, but we went out to eat too. What about you, do you cook?"

"Me, ha! Not unless you count scrambled eggs or a grilled cheese sandwich."

Sam took a swig of her beer then turned to face Jason. "Do your parents know you're here tonight?" Right after she said it, she realized her mistake.

Jason's face turned serious as he answered, "No, why?"

"I just wondered. I was just curious if they knew we were (she searched for the right words), hanging out together."

"No, they don't, Sam, but it's probably not for the reason you think. I'm not embarrassed to tell them that I'm seeing you. I just don't want any judgments right now. I'm not ready to share this just yet."

Sam felt as if she had disappointed him in some way, and she was eager to change the tide of their discussion. "It's no big deal, seriously. I just thought they might ask about your comings and goings that's all."

Jason's eyes narrowed in thought as he took a long swallow of his beer. "They don't really ask a lot of questions any more. They probably think that I'm a big boy and I can handle myself. Besides they're out of town this week anyway."

Sam decided to turn the conversation back to herself. "I know what you mean about not wanting judgments. I saw my friend Leslie at yoga last night, and I didn't tell her either. I'm just not sure how people would react."

"You told your sister, though."

"That's different. I basically knew she'd be ok with it."

"I'm not really worried about what people think Sam. I just enjoy being with you," he said, his voice suddenly softening.

Sam felt her face flush as his last sentence hung in the air. How was it that he always knew just the right thing to say?

"Well." She stood, breaking the spell. "Are you ready to eat?"

The grin instantly returned to his face. "Absolutely." Jason carried the dishes to the table as she lit an aromatic candle that sat in the middle.

"Do you want another beer or a Coke?" she asked before sitting down.

"No, I'm good for right now. Let's just eat." They talked easily throughout dinner about various topics, just like they had that first night at the pizza place. Sam asked questions about his family and discovered that his dad was a divorce attorney and his mom helped out at the practice part time. He had an older sister, Kathy, who lived in Chicago with her new husband Mark. She learned about Jason's two best friends from high school, Scott and Bryan, and his college roommate, Max. She, in turn, told him a few details about her family and friends. Every so often, he would interrupt to tell her how much he was enjoying the food. She thanked him, basking in his praises. When they were finally finished, Jason offered to help clear the table. He handed the dishes to Sam one at a time while she rinsed them and placed them in the dishwasher. The domestic chore suddenly felt very intimate. There were several times when Jason's fingers brushed against hers and she felt a little jolt at their contact.

As Sam wiped down the kitchen counters, she wondered what they would do next. It was only seven o'clock, and she wasn't ready for the evening to end.

"Do you want to go to a movie or

something?" Jason asked as she dried her hands on the kitchen towel.

Sam couldn't think of a current movie that she really wanted to see. "I have a decent DVD collection," she suggested. "We could just watch one here."

Jason clapped his hands together. "Ok, let's see what you've got."

Sam led him into the living room and walked over to the entertainment cabinet. Jason followed right behind her, and she caught the scent of his cologne as they moved across the room. She opened the cabinet doors and started searching the movie titles. "Let me guess, you probably like action movies right?"

Jason leaned over her right shoulder to get a better look inside. She could feel the heat of his body against her back and squirmed a little.

"It doesn't have to be action. I can handle a chick flick once in a while."

"Who said I like chick flicks?"

"Gee, let me see... The Notebook, Sleepless in Seattle, When Harry Met Sally..." Jason read off the titles over her shoulder.

Sam raised her hands in the air. "Ok, you got me. I like chick flicks. However, I can also sit through a James Bond movie if I must." There were several action films in the cabinet that had been part of Brad's collection. Sam hadn't had the heart to remove them and planned to give them to her brother-in-law someday.

Jason continued to peruse the titles and said, "What is *When Harry Met Sally* about anyway?"

Sam glanced over her shoulder to see the mirth in his eyes. She loved when his eyes crinkled up at the edges. "It's basically about whether or not men and women can be just friends."

"Hmm." Jason appeared to seriously contemplate this. "What do you think? Can they?"

There it was again, that spark in the air between them. Sam felt sure at that moment that Jason felt it too. She was definitely enjoying the fun and flirty Jason!

"I'm not sure they can. I've never really had a male friend, unless you count co-workers, but even then…"

Jason studied her for a second. "I think that if a guy spends a lot of time with a woman, chances are pretty good that he wants to be more than just friends."

When he looked at her like that, she swore he was seeing straight into her soul. Was he talking about them? If their kiss at the park was any indication…

"Let's watch it," he said suddenly, bringing her back to the present.

"Are you sure? There's plenty to choose

from in here."

"I'm sure," he said, chuckling deeply. "Just put it in."

Uh-oh, here we go with the innuendos again, thought Sam, as she slipped the DVD into the player. Jason must have walked away from her because all of a sudden the lights clicked off.

"Just trying to duplicate the movie theater experience." He plopped down casually on the couch and spread his arms out across the back of it.

Oh great, where am I supposed to sit, Sam fretted. If I sit on the chair, he'll think I'm afraid of him, but if I sit on the couch he might think I'm being presumptuous. Jason sensed her indecision and patted the couch cushion next to him. "I won't bite, I promise," he teased.

She let out a breathy laugh and sat down on the seat next to him, keeping a respectable distance between them. Once the movie started, she actually relaxed and propped her feet up on the ottoman next to his. Occasionally she would sneak a peek at Jason to try and read his expressions, but it was dark, and she couldn't make out much. He laughed out loud at several of the scenes, especially the one where Meg Ryan pretends to have an orgasm in the restaurant. Instead of feeling uncomfortable, Sam found herself laughing right along with him. About halfway through the movie, Jason shifted around in his seat so that their arms were slightly touching. Again, Sam felt the familiar shiver of warmth pass through her, and she made sure not to move away. After another fifteen minutes or so, Jason slowly reached over with his left hand and took her right hand in his, moving their intertwined fingers to rest on his pant leg. It happened so smoothly and felt so natural, that Sam just settled into it. Jason's thumb brushed back and forth across the back of her hand, sending tingles up her spine. Did he notice the effect he was having on her? He didn't seem to miss a beat and went on laughing at the appropriate points in the movie. Sam could have sat that way forever. Her eyes moved away from the screen to focus on the movement of Jason's thumb on her hand. At some point, he realized that she was looking at him because he turned toward her and asked, "You ok?"

Sam cleared her throat, which suddenly felt very parched, and nodded. "Yeah, I'm good." Jason untwined their fingers and reached up to brush her bangs off to the side.

"You're so beautiful, Sam. Do you know that?"

Sam was mesmerized by his hands, his eyes locked in place with hers, his scent, his nearness. The only light in the room came from the television screen, making the moment even more intimate and intense. She swallowed nervously. "Thank you," she whispered.

The corners of his mouth turned up in what was becoming his trademark grin. "Sam, I really want to kiss you right now, but I need you to tell me what you want. I don't want to be the only one…"

His words fell away as she leaned into him and placed her lips on his. She wound her arms around his neck and pulled him closer. She felt the warmth, the wet, his hands tightening around her waist. It was as if they couldn't get close enough, each wanting to erase any space between them. Their lips became more demanding, mouths opening to invite further exploration. Jason leaned back against the headrest of the couch, pulling her down on top of him. Her dress rode up as they jostled into place, and she felt a whoosh of cool air on the back of her thighs. Jason had one hand in her hair, and the other began to stroke the back of her leg, inching closer and closer to her panty line. Sam felt his belt buckle pressing into her abdomen and the hardness of his chest against her rapidly beating heart. The sharp ringing of a cell phone broke the spell, bringing their frenzy to an abrupt halt.

"Damn it," Jason swore while moving them both back to a seated position. "Why do we keep getting interrupted?" He ran his hand through his disheveled hair while Sam straightened her dress.

"Sorry, I meant to silence my phone,"

Sam said. "I better check my messages to make sure nothing's wrong at my sister's house." She left Jason as he was tucking his shirt back in and went to retrieve her phone from the kitchen. It was Jaime, as Sam suspected. "Hi, it's me. Just checking in to see how your dinner went tonight. Call me." Just as she laid the phone back on the counter, Jason came up behind her and circled his arms around her waist. He dipped his head down to nuzzle her neck, placing soft kisses there.

"Jason?"

"Mmm-hmm," he answered, continuing to kiss her neck.

"Can we... I mean... I'm feeling a little overwhelmed right now. Can we just talk for a little while?" As much as Sam was enjoying the feel of him up against her, she wasn't sure she was ready to go any further (at least not tonight).

"Ok, sure." He pulled away, a look of confusion and disappointment etched on his face. "I didn't mean to..."

"No, please, don't apologize. I enjoyed everything tonight. I just don't think I'm ready..."

"To make love."

"Wow, you certainly don't beat around the bush, do you?" She half giggled, half coughed.

"I don't believe in playing games, Sam. I know a lot of guys my age do, but that's not me.

I want to be up front with you about my feelings. All of my feelings."

He gave her that intense stare again, the kind that made her toes tingle and her heart skip a few beats. "I appreciate your openness, I really do. I want to be open with you too, which is why I'm letting you know that I'm not there yet."

"That's ok. I can wait because I know you're worth it." Before she could respond further, he added, "Now, how about dessert?"

"Oh my God, I forgot all about it. Sit down and I'll get it for you." Sam was glad for the distraction as she busied herself dishing out cream puffs, ice cream, and hot fudge. She could feel Jason's eyes following her every move, and finally she looked up and said, "What?"

"I just like to watch you sometimes," he grinned. "You're like a busy little bee, always in motion."

"I'm glad to entertain you." She laughed, feeling the mood lighten between them. They sat at the kitchen island eating cream puffs amid Jason's sounds of approval.

"This is delicious. I've never had one before."

"I'm glad you like it." She smiled, pleased that her culinary skills were still intact.

"I like everything about you." Jason leaned toward her and wiped a drop of chocolate off her chin. "Thank you for a terrific evening."

Why is it he always knew just what to say? Once they finished their dessert, Jason stood up and said, "I should probably get going."

Sam glanced at the kitchen clock, which read ten o'clock. Part of her didn't want Jason to leave, but another part of her thought it was for the best. If he stayed any longer they might end up back on the couch finishing what they had started, or maybe they would end up in her bedroom...

"When can I see you next?" he asked, interrupting her thoughts.

Sam mentally went through her calendar and replied, "How about Friday night?"

"Friday night huh? Is it ok if I call you once or twice before then?"

Sam smiled and nodded, "Of course." She walked Jason to the door, feeling a sense of loss already. He put one hand on the doorknob, turned, and pulled her to him with the other. She anticipated his lips on hers, but was surprised when he bent down and brushed her cheek instead.

"I'll see you then," he said gruffly.

"See you then," she whispered as he walked out the door.

Chapter 7

Wednesday and Thursday were fairly uneventful for Sam. She spoke to Jaime on the phone and gave her a summary of her dinner with Jason, leaving out a few of the intimate details. She wasn't ready to share everything with her sister just yet. Of course, Jaime badgered her until Sam admitted that they had kissed and, yes, it was good, wonderful, in fact.

She didn't hear from Jason at all on Wednesday, which surprised and concerned her a little. Was he mad about the other night? Maybe he felt like she rejected him. She went over and over their evening together until she couldn't stand it anymore. She almost gave in and called him, but stopped herself. You are not a teenager, she scolded herself angrily. It's been twenty-four hours since you last saw him, and you can wait another day. Maybe he's out with his friends or busy doing yard work for the neighbors. She found herself glancing out the front window every so often thinking she might catch a glimpse of him, but to no avail. She went to bed that night frustrated and mad at herself.

On Thursday, Sam met up with Leslie for lunch at a local bar and grill where they chatted over hamburgers, fries, and a beer. Leslie sensed that something was different about her, but Sam didn't let on about Jason. His words rang true about wanting to keep their relationship safe from judgment. Finally, on Thursday evening, just as she was settling in for the night, her phone rang. It was him.

"Hello," she answered cautiously.

"Hey," he said, followed by an awkward stretch of silence.

"I...," they both said at the same time.

"Ladies first."

"I missed you," she breathed.

"I missed you too. I wanted to call yesterday, but I didn't want to seem too pushy."

"You're not pushy, Jason. I always like talking to you." And she meant it.

"I was just trying to give you some space. I wasn't sure if the other night was too much, too soon..."

Talking to him on the phone, in bed, in the dark, bolstered her courage. Sam wanted to set his mind at ease and erase the discomfort between them. "I don't need space, Jason. I've had lots of space over the last several years. What I need is for you to be patient and know that I want to be with you."

"I want to be with you too, and I'm glad to hear you say it."

His voice still sounded hesitant to her ears. "It's been a long time for me. I'm a little out of practice with all this."

"I know, and I want it to be perfect for us, for you. I don't want to rush you."

Sam scooted down a little further under the covers. "I wish you were here right now," she whispered.

"Are you in bed?" His voice sounded husky and deep.

"Yes."

"Then I wish I was there too."

"That could be dangerous."

"We could just cuddle," he said, chuckling as though fully aware that cuddling was not what they had in mind.

"Do you like to cuddle?" She was genuinely curious now.

"Sometimes, but it can be kind of frustrating too, for a guy anyway."

"I'll try to remember that."

"Right now, I would take cuddling with you over not being able to touch you at all."

Sam loved their playful banter. "Ok, Mr. Smooth. That's about enough for tonight!"

Jason laughed, "I'll be glad to continue this discussion tomorrow."

"I'm sure you will. Sweet dreams."

"Guaranteed."

"Call me tomorrow," she whispered, feeling the sleepiness taking over.

"I will."

They disconnected, and Sam felt herself

smiling as she drifted off to sleep.

Chapter 8

Sam was woken abruptly Friday morning by the sound of her cell phone vibrating on her nightstand. She opened one eye and groggily wondered what time it was and who would be calling her so early. Her other eye flicked open, and she peered grumpily at the alarm clock — seven a.m. She reached for her phone and smiled at the name on her display — Jason.

"Do you know what time it is?" she answered, trying to sound irritated while stifling a laugh.

"Well, good morning to you too," he teased. "I'm guessing I disturbed your slumber."

"You guessed right." She sat up and leaned back against the headboard. "Is this about our date tonight?"

"Yes, and who said it only had to be tonight?" The playfulness in his tone was contagious.

"Ok, what great idea have you concocted that can't wait until a more reasonable hour in the morning?"

"Pack your bag and come away with me this weekend."

Whoa—she hadn't been expecting that one! "Away where, and how…," she sputtered.

"Never mind all the details right now. Just say you'll do it."

Sam couldn't seem to get her thoughts in order, and truthfully, she hated surprises. "Before I answer, can you at least give me some clue as to where we're going?"

"Ok, ok," he sighed. "I thought we could spend the weekend at my parents' cabin on Lake Charlevoix."

Sam had been to Charlevoix several times over the years and knew it was only a few hours away. She tried to think of a reason why she shouldn't go but was unsuccessful. Plus, it was a great little town on the water with lots of quaint shops and restaurants.

"Hello? Sam, are you still there?"

"Ok. I mean yes. Yes, I'll go with you." There, it was settled!

"Awesome!" Jason's relief was palpable. "How long do you need to get ready?"

She'd have to shower, eat breakfast, pack… "Can you give me until 8:30?"

"Sure, see you then."

"See you then."

Sam's mind was working overtime as she went about packing. What to bring? Why did I agree to this? Am I really ready? This was quite a jump from dinner dates and picnics, going away for the weekend together. Should she call her sister just to let her know? No, she quickly dismissed that idea. If she was going to do this, she was doing it without any outside influence.

She packed bathing suits and cover-ups, shorts, tees, a knit dress, sandals, and sneakers. When she reached in her pajama drawer, her fingers lingered on a black lace baby-doll set that was shoved in behind the tank and short sets she usually wore to bed. What to do? She hesitated a moment more and grabbed both the baby doll and a tank/short set. Just in case. Which brought about the question, what would the sleeping arrangements be? Did the cabin have multiple bedrooms? Most likely it would, in order to accommodate Jason's family of four. Her heart was racing now, and she decided to take a break to do some of the deep-breathing exercises she learned in yoga. She sat cross-legged on her bedroom floor, clothes scattered all about, and took a deep breath in, then out, then in and out again. She cleared her mind and chanted to herself, it will be ok, it will be ok. After ten minutes, she felt much more relaxed and resumed packing. She made a determined decision to let go and enjoy the weekend, come what may. If nothing else, it would be a fun summer getaway.

She had her bags ready and waiting by the back door as Jason pulled in the driveway. She took him in as he stepped out of the Jeep and sauntered toward her. He looked gorgeous as usual in his cargo shorts, t-shirt, and Nikes. He walked with an easy stride, giving the impression of a man who was comfortable in his own skin.

"Morning," he called, grinning at her. "Ready to go?"

"I think so," she said, grinning back.

Jason placed her bags in the back seat alongside his and opened the passenger door for her. "I'm glad you said yes," he said as she hopped into the seat.

"Me too."

Jason's enthusiasm was infectious as he dove in with his ideas for the weekend. "It'll take us about three hours to get there, which puts us there around lunchtime. We can either eat in town or grab some sandwich fixings and take them to the cabin. We'll want to stop at the grocery store at some point, regardless, so we can stock the fridge with some basics. The cabin is right on the water, so we can swim or take the boat out during the day and build a bonfire on the beach at night. There are a lot of cool shops in town, so we'll probably want to hit those too." Finally, he took a breath and glanced over to see her smiling at him. "What? Am I talking too much? I'm talking too much aren't I?"

"No," she said with a laugh. "It's not that. It's just you sound so excited, almost like you've never been there before."

"Well, I've never been there with you."

There it was again, that warm, gooey feeling that rushed over her. "It all sounds great," she said seriously.

"Have you ever been there before?"

"Yes, several times, but not since Brad…"

"Was that the last time you've been there, with him?"

She nodded yes, unable to find her voice suddenly. Jason understood her need to compose herself, so they drove in silence for a while. She hated when this happened. Some simple word or sentence or thought could trigger all of the sadness and hurt that she carried with her every day. Sometimes it was his name or mention of a place they had been or something they had done together, and all of the grief came flooding back, sharp and biting in the pit of her stomach. Days and weeks would go by without any incident, and then, out of the blue, something would dredge it all up again. She didn't want this to happen now with Jason, especially when he was so obviously excited about the weekend. She concentrated on her breathing and the hum of the tires on the road while desperately willing her thoughts back to the present.

"Do you want to talk about it?" Jason broke the silence.

"I don't know. Yes and no, it doesn't always help."

"Is it because of me? Should I not bring

him up?"

"No, it's ok most of the time. There are just moments when it feels as painful as the day it happened. I never know when those moments will come, but they throw me for a loop. Still, after all this time."

"I think you're doing really well with it, actually. Better than a lot of people would."

"I don't know about that. Don't forget, you didn't know me five years ago. I was a mess for quite a while."

"How did you climb out of it?"

"I just finally decided to rejoin the land of the living. I remembered something that my dad taught me when I was ten years old and it really stuck with me. We were at a funeral dinner for my Grandma. I looked around and noticed a lot of the guests were smiling and laughing as they were enjoying their meal. Something about the scene made me angry, and I asked my dad how people could laugh and carry on as usual while at a funeral. It didn't make any sense to me."

"What did he say?" Jason urged her on.

"He said it's because life is for the living. Just because someone dies doesn't mean the world stops turning. People still need to laugh and love and eat and so on... Of course, I was only ten at the time, and I still didn't get it. It wasn't until Brad died and I went through my initial grieving period that I remembered my dad's words. Life is for the living. It was at that point, that I started to resume my usual activities: work, friends, yoga, etc. It still took a long time for things to feel somewhat 'normal,' but I forced myself to do it all. Life is for the living."

"Your dad sounds like a very smart man."

"He's gone now. When I looked around at his funeral and saw people laughing and smiling, I didn't get angry. I found a way to laugh and smile too."

"That's why I said you're handling things well, Sam. You have a great attitude, and it shows."

"I'm glad you think so. Now, enough of the deep stuff. Tell me more about your parent's cabin…"

And he did. In fact, Jason talked for the duration of their drive to Charlevoix. Sam settled back and reveled in the deep feeling of contentment that washed over her as they made their way "Up North."

Chapter 9

They rolled into town right around noon and decided to eat at a deli rather than wait to get to the cabin. Sam was anxious to get out and stretch her legs; they were so busy talking they hadn't stopped along the way. The summer crowds were out in force, gliding along the streets in their shorts and sunglasses, toting shopping bags from the local stores. Sam took a quick scan around and immediately felt at home. Charlevoix was one of those towns she never tired of. Jason guided her through the door of the deli, and they stood packed in with the crowd, waiting to order. Nobody seemed to mind though; this is what summer was all about in Northern Michigan.

They found a table for two in the corner by a window overlooking the bay and ate ham and cheese sandwiches as boats travelled in and out of the harbor. The water glistened in the sun as Sam admired the bright colors of the sailboats and the relaxed faces of the passengers. Jason studied her intently as they finished their lunch. "Ready to go? If we leave now, we can take the boat out this afternoon."

"Sure, let's go." Sam was still anxious

about the sleeping arrangements at the cabin.

Jason seemed to sense her discomfort and said, "Don't worry, there are plenty of bedrooms there."

"I wasn't thinking about that."

"Oh, yes you were. It's written all over your face."

Sam was unnerved that he could read her so well after such a short time. "I was actually just thinking how nice it sounds to be out on the water," she stated somewhat adamantly.

Jason just chuckled and shook his head. "Well, we'll be there soon enough," he said, pulling out into the busy traffic.

About twenty minutes later, they pulled onto a dirt road with a sign out front that read "Water's Edge." Homes of various sizes lined both sides of the road, and Sam caught glimpses of the lake through the tall pines. The houses seemed to grow in size the further down the lane they went, and those on the lakeside boasted large decks with beautiful views. Finally, they came to a dead end, and Jason turned left onto a downward sloping asphalt drive. At first, she couldn't see the house through the trees, but as the driveway curved to the right, a sprawling, two-story log cabin appeared.

"It doesn't look like much from the front, but the views from the deck are awesome." Jason pulled up in front of the garage and hopped out to get their bags. He led her up a stone path to the wrap-around covered porch and set their bags down while he unlocked the front door. Sam took in her surroundings, breathing in the fresh, unspoiled air. The only sounds she could hear were some birds squawking in a nearby tree and the muffled sound of childrens' laughter coming from the lake.

"Home sweet home," Jason sighed as he pushed the door open.

Sam sucked in a breath as she took it all in. They were standing in a small foyer with a white-washed wood bench against one wall and a matching table against the opposing wall. In front of her sprawled a large, open living room with floor-to-ceiling windows overlooking Lake Charlevoix. The nautical-themed décor added to the ambiance of the space, lending a bright and airy feel. Sam glanced down the hall to her right and could see a glimpse of a bright yellow kitchen. She assumed the staircase to her left led to the bedrooms.

"This is beautiful," she said. "How long have your parents had this place?"

"Since I was about five years old," he replied. "Let's take these bags upstairs."

Sam followed him up the staircase, her attention on the many framed photos that hung on the wall. Someone, probably his mom, had hung every school picture of Jason and his sister in chronological order. "Aww, you were so cute." She stopped to study a picture of Jason at age six or seven, his hair sticking up in places with that sweet smile on his face.

"*Was, was*, so cute? So, I'm not anymore."

"That's not what I meant. Cute is for first graders, now you're…"

"Hot? Sexy? Strapping?"

"Strapping?" Sam laughed loudly. "Who uses that word, strapping?"

"Gaston used it in *Beauty and the Beast*. Don't you know your Disney movies? What kind of teacher are you anyway?"

"First of all, I'm not a teacher, I'm a librarian. Second, I do know my Disney movies, thank you very much."

At the top of the stairs, he stopped and locked eyes with her. "You still haven't answered my question."

"What question?" Sam knew what he wanted to hear; she was just stalling for time.

"Hot, sexy or strapping?" Jason's eyes sparkled mischievously.

"All of the above." She returned his intense gaze, smiling seductively.

"Good answer," he said with a chuckle, breaking the tension. "Now, let's show you to a room."

There were three bedrooms upstairs to choose from. Two faced the lake, and one had a view of the front yard. The two rooms on the lake side shared a bathroom, while the third room boasted a private bath. "Which one do you usually sleep in? I mean, I don't want to take yours." Sam felt herself flushing.

"I usually take a lakefront room, and I figured you might like that too. If you want more privacy, you can take the one across the hall."

Was that a challenge? His expression was neutral, but Sam sensed that he wanted her to take the adjoining room. I'm a grown woman. I can handle this, she assured herself. "The adjoining rooms will be fine."

"Great," he said, setting her bag on the floor. "Let's get into our bathing suits, and I'll meet you down at the boat dock. I'll use the bathroom across the hall, so you can use this one. I'm guessing you might take a little longer than me, so I'll go down and get the boat prepared. Don't forget your sunscreen, and there are beach towels in the linen closet if you need one."

"Yes, sir." She mock saluted him. "I'll try not to take too long." Sam dug in her bag and pulled out the two swimsuits she had brought: a conservative one-piece and a moderately conservative two-piece. Hmm... which to choose? She would probably feel more comfortable in the one-piece, but she took an educated guess that Jason would prefer the two-piece. "Oh, what the heck, I'm on vacation," she explained to the empty room. She went into the connecting bathroom to change, and put her hair up in a quick ponytail. She took the time to slather on a healthy amount of sunscreen and stood back to critique herself in the full length mirror on the back of the bathroom door. Yoga class had definitely paid off; her body was trim with gentle curves. Her friends always teased her about not having a baby pooch, which she regarded as a double-edged sword. She would have loved to have had children with Brad. However, at this moment, she was glad for her smooth, flat belly.

She went back into the bedroom to grab her cover-up and flip flops before heading downstairs. There were two sets of French doors leading out to the deck, but she took a moment to explore the rest of the house before heading out. She discovered a huge master suite to the left of the living room, complete with an oversized Jacuzzi tub. To the right she found an open kitchen/dining area with top-of-the-line appliances and a granite-topped work island in the center. The home was spacious, yet warm and inviting at the same time; just like Jason, she mused. She sized him up as she walked down the sloping back yard to the boat dock. He wore navy and white striped board shorts and was bare chested. She could see beads of sweat gathering on his back as he bent over to hoist a cooler into the boat. His aviators were perched on top of his head, and his hair curled up around them. Just then, he looked up and caught her gaze. He waved at her, flashing his sexy grin, and gave her an approving once-over. Suddenly, she was glad for the cover-up, although she had left the front hanging open given the warmth of the day.

"You look great!" he said as she joined him on the dock.

"Thanks."

"I brought some water and snacks that I found in the pantry," he said, pointing to the cooler. "Let me help you in." Jason reached out his hand and clasped hers with a warm, firm grip. He unwound the rope from the wooden post and shoved the boat away from the dock before hopping in himself. The lake stretched ahead of them wide and long, dotted with boats of various sizes. Jason revved the engine, and off they went.

Sam sat back and enjoyed the view while the wind whipped her ponytail around. After a few minutes, she noticed Jason staring at her. "What?" she yelled over the sound of the engine.

"You have a huge smile plastered on your face," he yelled back.

"I'm enjoying this; it's so relaxing!" She felt invigorated by the fresh air, the warm sun, and, of course, his company. He had that effect on her, making her feel energized and relaxed at the same time.

After a few spins around the lake, Jason

stopped the boat near a sandy beach and threw the anchor over. "Do you want to go up on shore and sit out for a while?" She nodded her agreement.

Jason stuffed their beach towels, sunscreen, and waters into a tote bag and jumped over the side into the shallow water. Once again, he held out a hand to help her over, and this time she didn't let go as he led her up to the beach. She noticed a few appraising glances as they walked toward shore and wondered briefly what people were thinking. Surely, the young girls were admiring Jason's physique. Were they wondering why he was with an "older woman?" At least he didn't seem to notice; his eyes were directed straight ahead to a section of sand away from where the majority of the sunbathers were gathered. He spread out their towels, and they plopped down.

"Ahh, this is the life!" Jason leaned back on his elbows and lifted his face to the sun. Sam took off her cover-up and lay flat on her back. She was proud of herself for wearing the bikini and hoped she could pass as his girlfriend rather than his sister or aunt! She closed her eyes and let her thoughts drift, hyper-aware of Jason's presence on the towel next to her. They relaxed silently for a time until Jason sat up abruptly.

"Time to flip. We don't want to burn on one side." He reached for the sunscreen and held it out to her. "Do my back?"

Sam took the sunscreen and motioned for him to face away from her. She studied Jason's broad back and shoulders, noting the sprinkling of light brown freckles across his smooth skin. He really is a fine specimen, she mused, squeezing some sunscreen onto her hands.

"Hey pokey, whatcha doing back there?" Jason twisted his head around to tease her.

"Sorry! I was just getting the cap off." She began massaging the lotion on his neck and shoulders, feeling the tautness of his muscles under her hands. His head tipped forward, allowing her greater access. She slowly and methodically worked her way down his back and along his sides, feeling his body relax beneath her fingers. She carefully applied the lotion along the waistband of his swim trunks and swore she felt him flinch when she touched him there. She could tell he was enjoying the attention; his breathing had slowed, and he lay still and silent. He was good and covered, but she hated to break the spell between them. She let her hands slip back up to his shoulders and leaned over to whisper in his ear, "You're all set."

"Oh no I'm not." He turned to face her. "It's your turn now." His voice had turned husky, and she could feel the waves of desire flowing out his pores. She handed over the lotion and turned her back to him. He started with her shoulders, rubbing the lotion in gentle, circling motions. He gently moved her straps partway down her arms so as not to miss a spot. The feel of her straps slipping down sent a shiver of anticipation surging through her body. He slid his hand under the strap around her back and down her spine to the waistband of her bottoms. She was mesmerized by the hot sun on her face and the hot hands on her back. Every sense was heightened, and she didn't want the moment to end.

"Lay down so I can get the back of your legs," he mumbled, his breath moving the hair on the back of her neck. She silently obeyed and lay face down on her beach towel, arms and legs slightly apart. Jason continued massaging the lotion into her thighs and calves, all the way down to her heels. He purposely slid one fingertip up the inside of her right leg, tickling her with his light touch. She giggled like a school girl. "You did that on purpose!"

He chuckled and plopped back over on his towel. They faced each other, just inches apart, sparks flying between them. Who knew applying sunscreen could be so erotic?

"I love being here with you," Jason said earnestly.

Sam was at a loss for words, so she just smiled and nodded in response. She chastised herself for being so out of practice at this.

After a time, Jason asked, "Are you ready to go back? Are you hungry?"

She was definitely hungry, and it was for more than just food. He must have read the answer in her eyes as he pushed himself up and started gathering their things. Sam felt a little shaky when she finally stood and took his outstretched hand as they walked back to the boat. Jason grasped her hand tightly and quietly led her along. This is it, she thought, I finally feel ready. The blood pounded through her veins and her heart beat strongly in her chest. Did Jason feel it too?

They climbed into the boat and took off across the lake, the cool breeze a welcome relief against her overheated skin. She sneaked a few glances at Jason, but he seemed deep in thought and kept his eyes straight ahead. They hadn't eaten for a few hours, but right now, Sam didn't even care about food. She just wanted to get back to the cabin before the logical part of her brain kicked back in. She guessed that Jason might be feeling the same given the intensity with which he was driving the boat. At the dock, he hopped out quickly and then helped her out. He hastily tied up the boat, and they walked hand in hand up the hill to the house. The air crackled between them. He unlocked the door, and they entered through the kitchen. "Do you want to eat now?" he asked, but she was already shaking her head no. "What do you want to do?" he asked, swallowing nervously.

Sam closed the distance between them

and reached her arms up around his neck. "This," she whispered, bringing her lips to meet his. The kiss started out slow and soft but quickly became more urgent and demanding. Jason pulled her tightly against him, and she felt the hard muscles of his torso push into her breasts. His hands wandered from her waist down to her backside, where he cupped her firmly to him. They were leaning against the kitchen island with Sam on her tiptoes to better reach his mouth. Suddenly, he pulled his lips away and took in a shallow breath.

"Let's go somewhere more comfortable," he said, part question, part statement.

She nodded her head in agreement, and he grabbed her hand and led her upstairs. As they entered his room and moved toward the bed, Sam felt the first nibble of panic bubble up in her stomach. It was the middle of the day, and she was about to make love with a twenty-three-year-old man in his parent's lake house. First part of the panicky thought—middle of the day. She and Brad had made love any time—day or night, whenever the mood struck. After being with him for so many years, it felt natural and comfortable being naked in broad daylight. This was different though! In her fantasies, she and Jason made love at night in the cover of darkness surrounded by blankets! She wasn't exactly comfortable with him seeing her naked for the first time at four o'clock on a sunny afternoon.

Second, she was about to make love to someone other than her husband, which she'd never thought possible. When she had married Brad, she had felt sure in her heart that he was the one for her, and she had never looked back. She may have been attracted to other men at certain points during their marriage, but she had never acted on it. Even after the initial passionate feelings had subsided, she'd still been in love with her husband and had intended to stay that way. Her friends had teased her about being oblivious to other men, and she'd wondered if some of them were jealous. She'd always put her husband and their marriage first, and it showed. Sam realized now that she'd never even entertained the idea of sleeping with someone else until Jason came along. It still nagged at her that she was so much older than him. On the other hand, here was a handsome young man who wanted her, and she was tired of pretending that she didn't want him too. The connection between them was powerful and real, their attraction to each other undeniable. She wanted to be held and caressed and kissed and…

"Sam, are you ok?" They stood next to the bed. His eyes searched hers for reassurance.

She nodded her head, not trusting her voice to cooperate. She held out both of her hands to join with his, and that seemed to be all the encouragement he needed. He pulled her closer and kissed her slowly and tenderly, letting the feelings build between them again. She let her hands glide up and down the ridges of his back and into the soft curls at the back of his neck. He moved his lips to her neck and placed soft, warm kisses down to her collarbone. She tilted her head back and gave a moan of pleasure. In one fluid movement, Jason picked her up and placed her on the bed, sidling up next to her. Face to face, bodies pressed tightly together, they began exploring each other with their hands and mouths.

"You are so beautiful, Sam," he breathed against her neck.

"You are so hot and strapping," she giggled.

He pulled up on his elbows, and she felt a draft of cool air as their bodies separated. Was something wrong? Why was he stopping?

"I want to see all of you."

Aha, the moment of truth. All that was between them were their bathing suits, but that still counted for something! Oh well, Sam thought determinedly. We've come this far, and I'm not stopping now! She sat up, maintaining eye contact, and slowly slid the straps of her bikini top down her arms, pulling the material away from her breasts until they were bare before him. She reached around, unhooked her top, and tossed it off the side of the bed, smiling softly at his reaction. Jason was frozen in place, eyes hooded with desire, giving her the courage she needed to continue the seduction. She leaned back, hooked her fingers in the sides of her bikini bottoms, and slipped them down over her hips. The hunger in his eyes warmed her as he perused her nakedness.

"Wow." His enthusiastic reaction gave her the courage she needed.

"Now it's your turn, "she urged, eyes sparkling.

"I don't think I can pull off the striptease the way you just did." He stood up next to the bed, fingers on the drawstring of his trunks.

She leaned up on one elbow, feeling every bit the seductress. "Give it a try," she dared.

He smirked at her and teasingly pulled his waistband down slightly, showing a glimpse of the trail of hair leading to... uh, oh. In one quick flash, he whipped his trunks down and stood there in all his glory, amusement lighting up his face.

Sam didn't realize she had put both hands over her mouth and gasped. She wasn't expecting such a quick unveiling! She composed herself and felt a flutter low in her belly at the sight of him. He really was gorgeous, standing before her, hard and muscular, with ruffled hair and a smug smile. He was confident without being cocky—no pun intended. His physical beauty combined with his many other attributes were a heady combination. She motioned for him to come closer, anxious to feel the warmth of his body against hers, this time with no barriers between them.

They made love slowly and deliciously, touching, teasing, and tantalizing each other, reveling in the fire between them. Sam felt as if every cell in her body was alive with pleasure. She lost herself in the wet, warm sensations that pulsed through her. Jason was just as considerate in bed as he was out of it; he concentrated on her pleasure first before taking his own. The world fell away, and it was just the two of them in the cocoon they created, safe and sensuous. Finally, their bodies spent, they lay side by side, only their fingertips touching, lost in their own thoughts, still naked atop the covers.

Jason lightly ran his fingertip up and down her arm. "Sam…"

"Shh… don't say anything. We don't need to talk right now, really. Everything was wonderful, and I'm not worrying, I'm just lying here enjoying the moment."

He smirked at her. "I was just going to ask if you were hungry."

"Oh," she smiled back. "Yes, as a matter of fact, I'm starved."

"Me too. I have an idea; how about if I run out to the store and grab some steaks for us while you enjoy a luxurious bath in the Jacuzzi?"

"That sounds perfect." She loved that he was always thinking of ways to please her.

"Ok, I'll be back in about twenty minutes or so, but take your time. I'll throw the steaks on the grill as soon as I get back." Jason slid off the side of the bed and walked around to where his swim trunks were discarded on the floor. Sam enjoyed the view and didn't avert her eyes when he caught her looking. He picked up the trunks but didn't put them on. Instead, he leaned over and gave her a quick kiss on the lips. "Now, now, you can enjoy me again later. First things first, we need to eat!"

She swatted him playfully and said, "Get out of here."

"Enjoy your bath," he called over his shoulder, strolling naked from the room.

For a few minutes, Sam just lay there, enjoying the total relaxation of her mind and body. Making love with Jason was even better than she had dreamed it would be. There was no awkwardness between them, and any inhibitions she'd had at the beginning had quickly melted away. He was passionate, yet gentle, giving and taking in equal measure, always tuned in to her responses. Did he have a lot of experience? Is that what made him such a great lover? Or was it their chemistry that made it so good? They'd never really talked about his past relationships, and now was probably not the time, but she was curious. Whatever the case, the day had been just perfect. She felt happy and content and invigorated from the experience. Even if it never happened again, she would always savor the memory of this day. Although, why wouldn't it happen again? He had all but promised it would as he left the room. She smiled at the thought while she forced herself to get up and prepare the tub.

She dug through her bag, wondering what to wear afterward. Would they be going anywhere after dinner or staying in? She was secretly hoping they'd stay in. Feeling bold, she chose a leopard print cami, matching thong, and her black silk robe. She padded naked down the stairs to the Jacuzzi tub, anxious to immerse in the warm water. She poured in some rose-scented bubble bath, twisted her hair into a quick knot, and sank down in the water. She closed her eyes for what felt like just a few minutes until she heard the sound of the front door opening and closing. The next thing she knew the bathroom door flung open, and Jason poked his head in.

"Hey. Just letting you know I'm back."

"I see that," she said somewhat shyly. The bubbles covered most of her body, but somehow, she felt vulnerable.

"I'll fire up the grill. Come out and join me when you're done."

Something about the situation suddenly felt very intimate to her. It was no wonder; they had transitioned from "hanging out" to being lovers. Sam wasn't exactly sure how to process it all. "I'll be out in a few minutes," she said as he closed the door gently behind him. She wished she had chosen her conservative pajamas instead of the sexy lingerie, but it was too late. She didn't want to go back upstairs and alert him to her discomfort. Why can't I get a handle on this? It's because everything has changed and it's all brand new, she reasoned. Just relax and enjoy dinner. She dried off, put on her clothes, and went out to join Jason on the deck.

He was bent over the grill, shaking seasoning on the steaks, when she slipped out the door and sat down at the table. "I got us a baked potato and a salad to go with this, plus a chocolate cake for dessert." He still hadn't looked up as she pulled her robe tighter around her.

"Sounds delicious," she replied. The slight waver in her voice seemed to tip him off that something was wrong. He looked up then and reacted to her appearance with a low whistle.

"You look delicious," he sighed, coming toward her.

"I should have worn something else. I didn't think about us eating outside." She shifted uncomfortably in her chair.

"Sam, no one is going to see us. We're surrounded by trees."

"I know. It's just that…"

"What is it? I can tell that something's bothering you. Tell me what it is." He sat down in the chair across from her and took her hand in his.

The comforting feel of his strong hand sent a flood of relief through her. He had the uncanny ability to relax her no matter what the situation. "I guess I'm just wondering what happens next. I mean how does this change things between us? Where do we go from here?"

Jason tilted his head down while gathering his thoughts together. "I knew you would do this." He didn't sound angry, just resigned.

"Do what?"

"Analyze the crap out of what just happened."

Now it was her turn to hang her head.

"I was just hoping that you wouldn't," he continued.

"I'm sorry," she whispered.

"Let me ask you a question. Did you enjoy yourself with me today?"

"Yes," she said, nodding vehemently.

"So did I, so why can't that be enough for now?"

Sam finally raised her head to meet his eyes. "You're right. I probably enjoyed myself too much, and that's the problem. I'm afraid …"

"Stop right there. That is your only problem, Sam—fear. Nobody knows what tomorrow will bring, nobody. It doesn't matter what age you are or who you're with or any of that. I don't have all the answers either, but I'm not afraid. I'm just so damn happy that you're here with me right now, right here, in this moment. I wish you could be in this moment too."

He hadn't let go of her hand the entire time, and she felt him loosen his grip as he leaned back in the chair. She was at a loss for words. He spoke so earnestly and with such conviction she was blown away. On the outside he appeared to be a casual, easy-going guy, but his words reflected the depth of emotion inside of him. He will make an excellent psychologist someday, she mused.

"I wish I could be more like you," she admitted, rubbing the back of his hand.

"You don't have to be like me. Just be *with* me."

Sam got up from the chair, walked over to him, bent down, and pressed her lips to his. He pulled her onto his lap and held her close as she leaned against his chest. "Are you ready to eat now?"

"Yes, let's eat." They decided to eat inside after all. Jason lit the vanilla-scented candle that sat in the middle of the kitchen table, and they ravenously attacked the steak, potato, and salad, washing it down with cold beer. When the last dish had been cleaned and put away, Jason took her hand and led her into the living room. The sofa was U-shaped, affording a great view of the lake from every angle. The sun was slowly setting, but they didn't turn any lights on. They sat down in the middle of the sofa, holding hands, and watched as the last boats hurried in before dark.

"This is a great place," she finally said. "I can see why you love it here."

"My parents bought it when I was five years old. We've come here every summer since then as often as we could. They let my sister and I bring one friend each unless my dad designated a 'family only' weekend. I used to bring my buddy Scott, who is still one of my best friends."

"That must have been so fun for you. I can see how two boys would have plenty to do around here. Girls too, for that matter. Did you ever bring girls here?" She tried to sound casual and flippant, but she wasn't sure it came out that way.

He glanced away from the window and met her eyes. "Yes, a few times. Why?"

"I just figured you probably had a few girlfriends along the way, what with you being so 'strapping' and all." She gave him her best flirtatious smile.

"Sam, if you want to know something

about me just come out and ask. Your little ploy with the compliment isn't necessary."

He wasn't scolding her; he was just being straightforward, which was something she admired in him. "Ok, then, tell me about your girlfriends."

"Starting at what age?"

"There's that many?" she chided. "How about starting with high school?"

"Let's see. In tenth grade, I didn't really care much about girls. I was too busy playing football and hanging out with my buddies. It wasn't until my junior year that I really started dating."

"Was there someone special?"

"Do you really want to do this right now?" He shifted uncomfortably while searching her eyes for the answer.

"I want to know more about you, Jason. I've talked quite a bit about Brad, but we've never talked about any of your relationships."

"Ok, ok." He threw his hands up in mock surrender. "My first serious relationship was with Jessica in my junior and senior year. I thought I loved her, but we broke up over the summer before college."

"How come?"

"She was going to Northern Michigan, and I was going to Central. She thought it would be too hard to maintain a long distance relationship. I think that she just lost interest in me but didn't want to admit it."

"Ouch... that must have been difficult."

"No, not really. I had lost interest too. I think we just outgrew each other."

"Was she one of the girls you brought here?"

"It's not like I had a string of them, Sam! But yes, she came up here a few times."

It disturbed her to think of Jason making love to someone else in the very same bed that they had been in this afternoon. She quickly realized how ridiculous it was to be jealous, but not before Jason had a chance to read her mind.

"What I had with her was nothing compared to what I feel now," he assured her. "We were just teenagers pretending we had a real relationship."

"So who came after Jessica?"

"My freshman year in college, I kind of played the field a little bit. I didn't want anything serious after Jessica, and I didn't always make the best decisions. I had a few drunken encounters with girls, but it never amounted to anything."

It was hard for Sam to imagine Jason as a player, even with his good looks and confidence. He was too serious a person to play around. It was the same story for a lot of people she knew in college, so she tried not to judge him for it.

"In my sophomore year, I met Rebecca."

Uh-oh, she could tell this was going to be

an important story just by the way he shifted around and averted his eyes.

"We met in a psychology class when we were placed in the same group for a project. I was instantly attracted to her, and we spent a lot of time together for the class. We saw each other exclusively for two years before she dumped me for my roommate."

Wow, Sam hadn't see that coming. "What a slut!" she exclaimed, the words tumbling out of her mouth before she could stop them.

Jason laughed loudly into the darkened room. "That's one way of putting it."

"What ended up happening?"

"Last I heard they're still together and planning to get married."

"Wow, Jason, I'm so sorry." She could tell that Rebecca had really meant something to him and instantly branded her a foolish girl to give him up.

"It's ok. I'm over it. Can we be done with this conversation now?"

She felt bad about badgering him, but she also felt closer to him, knowing about his past. She wanted to ask more questions about Rebecca, but she could tell it wasn't the right time. "Thanks for sharing all that with me."

Jason nodded and leaned his head back against the couch cushion. Sam felt an overwhelming need to comfort him and decided to put her newfound sexual prowess to the test. "I know all that talking was difficult for you, so tell me what I can do to relieve your stress?" she offered with a seductive smile.

"Hmm...let me think. How about a massage?"

"A massage? Really? Out of all the possible options..."

"You didn't say I could only pick one thing. The massage is just the beginning. I have other ideas too."

"I see. I guess I kind of left it wide open."

"I guess so!" Jason turned over and sprawled across the couch on his stomach. "Whenever you're ready," he announced in a mocking tone.

She perched on the edge of the couch and began massaging his neck and shoulders.

"Don't be afraid to apply pressure," he said. "I won't break."

In response to his request, she dug her fingers in a little deeper, and he sighed with pleasure. She made her way from his shoulders, down his arms, and then to his back. She alternated between kneading him with her fingertips to using her palms in a circular motion. Jason was completely still and silent for a few minutes. "Don't fall asleep on me," she scolded.

"Believe me, I won't. I'm just enjoying it." Jason flipped back over and pulled her down on top of him so their faces were just inches apart. "Take off your clothes," he demanded.

"I'm sorry, sir, but I don't give those kinds of massages," she teased. Jason wasn't teasing back as he reached down and hastily untied the belt of her robe.

"Wait," she said, standing up. "Let me make this easier." The only light in the room came from a sliver of moonlight that cast shadows and made it difficult for her to see his face. She slowly removed her robe, letting it fall to the floor, followed by her cami and thong. She turned in a little circle and whispered, "How's this?"

"You're getting really good at this stripping thing. I'm starting to wonder if you had another career in the past."

She giggled as she approached him on the couch. "Lay on top of me again," he pleaded.

"No fair. You're fully dressed, and I'm naked." But she stretched out against his length, nuzzling her nose into his neck. He put his arms around her waist and hugged her close, turning his head to the side to give her greater access. She could feel the heat building between them and settled into it. His hands started roaming up and down her back, before reaching down to squeeze her buttocks.

"Your body is beautiful," he breathed against her hair.

"Your body is pretty great too. I'd like to be able to see it, though."

He stood up and moved to the patch of moonlight in the center of the room. He slowly pulled his t-shirt up and over his head, adding it to her pile of discarded clothes. Next came his shorts, which he made quite a show of, revealing small glimpses of his boxer-briefs and then covering up again. She grinned at him, encouraging him to continue. Finally, his boxers hit the floor, and he stood there, tall and proud in the moonlight.

Sam motioned him over with her finger, and he tumbled back to the couch, placing her beneath him this time. As big and broad as he was, she didn't feel crushed beneath him. He kissed her passionately and without reserve, starting at her lips and working his way down her body until every fiber in her being was lit with desire. As Jason placed delicate kisses around her belly button, she whispered, "I was supposed to be doing things for you, remember?"

"You are, he whispered back and continued kissing her. "By letting me pleasure you, that's giving pleasure to me."

Wow, really? Her friends would never believe those words had come out of a man's mouth! Most women she knew complained that their husbands were selfish in bed or quick and hurried when making love. Jason was in no rush, taking the time to enjoy every nuance right along with her. Her sighs and moans just encouraged him to continue his leisurely exploration.

He was pushing her to the edge, but she wasn't ready to give in just yet. "It's your turn," she demanded. "Lay down." Jason obeyed and watched as she eagerly nipped, licked, and kissed her way down his hard body. After a few minutes his husky voice said, "I can't take it anymore." They were both breathing heavily, a thin glaze of sweat between them, as Sam straddled him, and they found sweet release together. Sam collapsed on top of him, head resting against his beating heart, as their breathing returned to normal, and she felt the first chill of the night air.

Jason leaned up and said, "Stay here while I get us some blankets." Like she was going anywhere! Sam's body was limp as could be; she had no intention of moving. Jason was back in a flash, loaded down with cozy blankets and pillows. They wrapped up together, creating the perfect cocoon and, within minutes, were sound asleep.

Chapter 10

Sam was wakened by the blinding sunlight streaming through the living room windows. She glanced over at Jason's sleeping form and wondered groggily what time it was. She realized that she was still naked and marveled that last night was the first time she had ever slept without clothes on—ever! Something about being with Jason made her feel so free and uninhibited. Brad had tried to convince her many times to sleep nude, but she never did. She gave a little sigh of regret thinking that her husband would have loved it. Surprisingly, she didn't feel any remorse about being with Jason last night. Somehow, it felt right as rain. Sam sat up carefully, trying not to wake him. She grabbed her robe from their discarded clothes pile and tiptoed across the room. She felt an urgent need for a hot shower and some breakfast. Maybe I can get cleaned up and make him breakfast in bed... or on the couch, as the case may be.

The shower felt wonderful, and she hummed as she washed her hair and body thoroughly. As she squeezed the water out of her hair, it dawned on her that she hadn't hung a towel within reach. The glass door was all fogged up, so she cleared a spot to see out and was startled to see Jason standing there.

"I suppose you'll be needing this." Jason held out a towel with an amused look on his face.

"I thought you were sleeping," she replied, suddenly feeling shy.

"I was, but I must have sensed you were missing, so I came to investigate. Looks like I found you just in the nick of time."

He looked disarmingly adorable standing there, his hair sticking up in every direction, bare chested wearing only his boxers and an enormous grin.

"Why am I always the one without clothes on?" she muttered. "This is definitely not fair!"

"You shouldn't have snuck out on me, so this is your punishment. Come out and get your towel." He dangled the towel teasingly in one hand.

"Game over, you win," she conceded, stepping out of the shower. "Now give me that." She reached her hand out for the towel, dripping water onto the bath mat.

Jason sauntered over and began toweling her off. "This is for being such a good sport," he said with a laugh, patting her down.

There was something so intimate about him drying her off that Sam couldn't tear her eyes away. He was always taking such good care of her.

"Here, you can do your hair." He handed her the towel. "I know women can be fussy about that."

"Thanks," she said, wrapping the towel around her head. With that, she pranced out of the bathroom, feeling his perusal on the way out.

"Damn shame. You could have taken a shower with me," he called.

"Next time," she replied and headed into her room to get dressed. She heard the water come on and pictured it running over Jason's nude body. Wow, she had it bad! What had happened to her? Was it only a few weeks ago that she was alone with no man in sight? Now, here she was spending a weekend with a sexy college guy, prancing around naked like it was a perfectly normal thing to do. And the weekend wasn't over yet! Sam felt herself smiling as she pulled on a pair of shorts and a t-shirt. She combed her hair, deciding to let it dry naturally, and dusted on a bit of blush and some lip gloss. Just then, she heard the water shut off and decided to give Jason a taste of his own medicine. She hurried back to the bathroom and grabbed the clean towel off the rack just as he opened the shower door.

"Aha, two can play this game," she teased, holding the towel close to her chest.

"Fine with me but prepare to get wet."

He started toward her, water dripping off him in rivulets.

Would she ever tire of seeing him this way? The defined biceps and abs, the tight calves, and…

"Ok, ok, here you go." She handed the towel to him and watched in fascination as he dried himself off. He ran the towel over his hair a few times and hung it back on the rack.

"Is that it? You're all ready?" How did guys do that?

"Usually, I put some gel in my hair and dry it with a blow dryer, but today I'm going au naturel, like you."

"Oh, well, I wasn't sure what we're doing today, so I didn't want to get all dressed up."

"You're fine, just like that." He reached over and ran a finger down her cheek. "You look perfect, as always."

"Jason?"

"Hmm?"

"I'm really hungry," she replied tentatively. She could see the glaze of desire in his eyes, but right now her stomach was demanding she eat.

"Me too," he admitted. "Let me get dressed, and I'll meet you in the kitchen."

Sam gave him a quick kiss on the cheek and left the room. She entered the kitchen and started rummaging through cupboards looking for breakfast foods. There were a few boxes of cereal, but she wanted something heartier. She found pancake mix, syrup, and eggs in the fridge, that Jason must have picked up yesterday. Sam set to mixing the pancake batter and scrambling some eggs. By the time Jason joined her, pancakes were sizzling on the griddle, and she was stirring the eggs in a fry pan.

"Smells awesome." He came up behind her and placed a soft kiss on her neck.

"So do you," she said, breathing in the masculine scent of his cologne.

"What can I help with?"

"You can pour us some juice and get out the plates and forks," she replied, flipping the pancakes over. Jason set the table, and she loaded their plates with pancakes and eggs.

"You really are hungry this morning."

"You worked up my appetite."

They ate in contented silence for a few minutes, savoring every bite. "I have some ideas about what we can do today." Jason set down his fork and leaned back in his chair.

"I bet you do."

"Besides that." He winked at her. "There's a summer festival downtown, and I thought we could check it out, maybe grab some lunch and then head back here for some boating."

"Sounds great," Sam said, smiling. It didn't take long to clean up, and they were out the door. It was another gorgeous summer day, pleasantly warm with a light breeze. The festival was just getting underway when they arrived in town. They found a parking spot and hopped out, Jason reaching for her hand as they strolled along. Some of the streets were closed off, and there were carnival rides and games. All of the shops along Main Street had their doors propped open to welcome the many visitors they would have today. Vendors' booths lined the streets, selling everything from hot dogs to tacky souvenirs. When they approached a store called Charlevoix Sportswear, Jason suggested they go in.

"I like their t-shirts and hats," he explained, leading her around the store. When they came to a table of hats, Jason started trying them on. "You have to try one too." He handed her a pink baseball cap that read Charlevoix in bold white letters across the front.

"I don't wear hats," she said, shaking her head. "I don't have the right kind of head for it."

"What?" he said, laughing loudly. "What is the right kind of head for a hat?"

"You know, nicely proportioned, like yours."

"Let me see that hat on you," he insisted.

"Ok, fine, but no laughing." Sam stepped in front of a full-length mirror and put the hat on her head, tucking her hair behind her ears.

"That looks adorable on you!"

Sam surveyed it from various angles and decided it wasn't half bad. "I guess it's ok."

"We have to get it for you. Where did you get the idea that you don't look good in hats?"

She didn't want to tell him that it was Brad. Early on in their relationship, they had gone to a Tigers game, and Brad had suggested they buy baseball caps. He'd placed one on her head and declared that she wasn't "a hat person." From then on, Sam never wore hats. It was as if Brad's statement was the absolute truth, and she'd bought into it. He'd been pretty easygoing when it came to how she dressed, but if he didn't like her in a hat, she decided she didn't need to wear one. Rather than explain the whole story to Jason, she just shrugged and said, "I just never thought I looked good in one."

"Well, you do, and I'm buying it for you. I'm buying this blue one for me."

There was no point in arguing with him; he was already making his way to the front counter hats in hand. As they waited in line to pay, Sam glanced at the front door, and her heart stopped. Leslie saw her at the same time and broke out in a wide smile. "Sam, what are you doing here?" She walked over and gave Sam a warm hug. Jason was standing just ahead of her in line, and Leslie obviously didn't think they were together. Sam swallowed nervously and said, "I'm here for the festival."

"I'm surprised to see you. You never mentioned it at yoga."

There are a lot of things I haven't mentioned at yoga, she thought, but smiled at Leslie and said, "It must have slipped my mind." Just then, Jason cleared his throat as if to remind her he was standing there. Sam was caught; she couldn't pretend she wasn't with him, but she dreaded Leslie's reaction that was sure to come. She inhaled and hurriedly said, "Leslie, this is my friend Jason." Jason gave her a sideways glance and then stuck his hand out. "Nice to meet you Leslie." Surprise was written all over Leslie's face, but she took his hand and mumbled, "You too."

Sam felt the heat prickling up her chest to her neck and knew she was flushed with color. To fill the silence, she stated, "Jason's parents own a cabin on Lake Charlevoix."

"Oh, how nice. Are they here with you too?" She looked from Sam to Jason and back to Sam again.

"No," Jason answered, a slight grin on his face. "They decided I'm old enough to come here on my own now."

He looked like he was actually enjoying this, Sam thought with a shudder. All she wanted to do was escape, but of course, the line to pay had hardly moved. "Are Jed and Grayson here with you?"

"Yeah, they're around here somewhere. We split up so I could shop and they can wander around doing whatever it is men do." She gave a nervous giggle and glanced in Jason's direction. Sam could tell that Leslie was sizing him up, trying to figure out how old he was, most likely. Just then, the line moved forward, and it was Jason's turn to pay. Leslie must have realized that she wasn't going to get an explanation at that moment, so she finally said, "Well, have a good time. I'll see you at yoga next week?"

"Yes, and you have a good time too." Sam hugged her friend and watched as she walked hurriedly out of the store. Jason finished the transaction and started to walk out too, without a word to Sam. She could tell he was mad by the way he carried himself, stiff-backed and tense, arms locked down at his sides. Sam hurried to keep up with him as he led them across the street to the harbor front. When they found a spot that offered some degree of privacy, he turned to her and spat, "That was bullshit."

"What do you mean?" Her eyes pleaded with his not to be angry.

"You know exactly what I mean. The way you treated me in front of Leslie was bullshit. Your *friend* Jason. Is that all I am to you?"

His voice was rising in anger, and a few

passersby glanced curiously in their direction. She had never seen him this mad but found herself getting angry too. "You haven't told anyone about us either, Jason. What's the difference?"

"The difference is I wouldn't have acted like you were a stranger or some casual friend. I would have at least introduced you as my girlfriend."

She could tell he was backing down some. "Jason, I was caught off guard. Who would have thought that I'd run into someone I know in Charlevoix this weekend? I didn't know what to say, and it was awkward trying to talk in the middle of a busy store." Her reasoning sounded weak to her own ears. She hung her head with sadness. "I'm so sorry."

Jason reached out and pulled her in for a tight hug. "I'm sorry too. It just hurt when you called me your friend, after all we've shared this weekend. I feel like we're so much more than that."

"Of course we are, but you said yourself you don't want anyone's judgment."

"I did feel like that a few days ago, but not now. I'm not ashamed of us, and I don't want to hide anymore."

She looked up at him, still locked in his embrace. "I did tell my sister about you already. That counts for something, right?"

"Yes, but Sam, if we want people to take

our relationship seriously, we can't be afraid to present it to them."

"It felt too soon before, but you're right, things are different now." Sam couldn't shake the sense of trepidation inside her. Despite all his assurances, she was still afraid of how people would react. She wondered if and when she would ever get past it.

"When we get back, I'm going to tell my parents about us."

"When I see Leslie at yoga next week, I'll tell her too. I'm sure she's already figured it out, but I'll explain that she caught me off guard and…"

"It's ok, Sam. If you need more time to feel comfortable with everything, then take it." He could probably sense her hesitation, and she felt guilty for it. If only she could be as confident as he was and not be so worried about what other people thought.

"One day at a time, ok? We've been having a wonderful time here, so let's not spoil it." He took her face gently into his hands and bent down to kiss her. "No pressure," he whispered against her lips.

She nodded her head and attempted a smile, but it didn't reach her eyes. Switching gears, Jason said, "I don't know about you, but I'm hungry. Do you want to look for something to eat?"

Sam didn't feel overly hungry, but it was

a good distraction. "Sure. What sounds good?"

"I was thinking about a burger, fries, and a shake."

"Wow, thank God for yoga! I'm in." Jason led her to a bar and grill on one of the side streets, and because it was before noon, they were able to get a table right away. They sat by the window and watched the crowds stroll by. Sam felt her spirits lift as she bit into quite possibly the best burger she had ever eaten, not to mention the smooth and creamy chocolate shake.

"Do you want to hang around town some more or go back to the house?" he asked between bites.

"I'm fine to go back," she said, wiping the grease off her chin. They finished their meal, paid, and headed back to the Jeep. The crowds were thickening, and Sam was relieved that they were leaving. For some reason, she felt more comfortable when she and Jason were alone. The thought disturbed her because of his earlier comment about hiding from people. Is that what she was doing? She interrupted her thought pattern before it could spin out of control. Jason was right; they had been having fun up to this point, and she didn't want to spoil it. They still had the rest of today and tomorrow before heading home, and she was determined to enjoy it. There would be plenty of time to ruminate when she returned home!

Jason was unusually quiet on the drive back to the house. He kept his eyes straight ahead and never even glanced in her direction. Sam came to the conclusion that he was still upset over what had happened when they'd run into Leslie, and she was determined to make it right between them again. She came up with her plan as they drove in silence down the winding dirt road and pulled up to the house. They walked silently up the sidewalk, and Jason let them in the front door. He set his keys and wallet down on the hall table and moved toward the living room, but Sam grabbed his hand and pulled him toward the stairs.

"Where are you taking me?" he asked with a blank expression.

"Just follow me," she said and led him upstairs to her bedroom.

When they entered the room, Jason looked uneasy and leaned up against the dresser while she approached the bed. He definitely wasn't making this easy for her. She would have to drum up her best art of seduction to lighten the mood. Sam walked over to the bed and sat on the edge of it, beckoning to him with her index finger. Jason hesitated for a moment and then slowly moved across the room to sit beside her. Sam reached over and laid a hand on his thigh. "I brought you up here so I can show you how much you mean to me," she breathed shakily.

"You don't have to do this," he responded, his head down and watching her hand move back and forth along his thigh.

"I know that, but I really want to. I want you to feel how important you are to me." Sam could feel him thawing toward her but knew she had more work to do. She leaned into him and whispered softly in his ear, "I want to be with you." She bent down to place a series of kisses from his earlobe down his neck and heard him sigh with pleasure. "Lay back," she directed. Jason shifted so his entire body was atop the bed, and she sidled up next to him continuing to place kisses along his neck and throat and then up to his mouth. When their lips finally met, she felt the warmth and relief flood through her body as he responded to her with equal passion. Suddenly, they couldn't get close enough, their hands grasping desperately at each other, their lips working furiously to kiss, nibble, and lick. Clothes were whipped off and thrown carelessly on the floor as they melted together with complete abandon. The room was alive with the sounds of their lovemaking and the rest of the world slipped away as they got lost in a fog of pleasure. Afterward, they lay wrapped in each other's embrace, unwilling to break the connection that soothed them both.

"Thank you," he said, turning on his side to gaze directly into her eyes.

"You don't have to thank me," she

giggled.

"I know, but I feel better about us now, and it's because of you."

"I'm glad."

He smiled broadly, and it seemed like a beam of light shone from his eyes.

"Uh-oh, I know that look."

"What look?"

"That devilish look that means you're up to something."

Jason sat up and pulled her up with him. "Have you ever been skinny-dipping?" he asked.

Sam's eyes widened, "Um, no, but I'm guessing you have."

"Yeah and it's very liberating, trust me!"

"And where do you propose we do this at?" She couldn't help but grin at his overflowing enthusiasm.

"In the lake, where else!"

Sam sputtered, "The lake? What about all the boats full of people?"

"I know a private spot. Believe me, I don't want anyone to see your gorgeous naked body but me. It'll be fun."

"I don't know about that. If someone sees us, I will be mortified."

"I promise no one will see us. Do you have a bathing suit that's easy to take on and off?"

Sam thought of the one piece she had

brought with her. "Ok, fine," she said, feigning exasperation. "You win."

"Awesome." He leaned over and lightly kissed her lips. "Let's get suited up, and I'll meet you down at the dock." He waltzed out of the room, stark naked, and she admired the view. "I can feel you looking at me," he called over his shoulder.

"Was not."

"Were too."

Sam chuckled as she went into the bathroom to clean up and don her swimsuit. She studied her reflection in the mirror and noted the glow in her cheeks and her mussed up hair. She looked like a woman in love, she thought and then stumbled on that word in her head. Love? Really? Could it be? This was the first time she'd really given it a name, this thing with Jason. But wait a second, Love was a serious word. It wasn't something to be tossed around lightly. Maybe the correct word was Lust. No, she quickly dismissed that word as it didn't adequately describe her feelings for Jason. Although, she felt that too! Here I go again, always trying to define things! Whatever this is, it feels damn good, she decided and quickly pulled on her swimsuit. One thing was certain; she'd never felt this uninhibited in her entire life. Sure, she'd felt comfortable with Brad, but that wasn't the same thing. He hadn't sparked that sense of freedom in her like Jason did. Jason made her feel like nothing was off limits, that she could do anything and he would be right there beside her every step of the way. Brad had been very content to keep things status quo; he'd never pushed her to try new things, sexually or otherwise. What would he think of me going skinny dipping? Sam grabbed her cover-up and flip-flops and headed downstairs, leaving her memories of Brad behind her.

Jason navigated the boat away from the dock and out into open water. There was less traffic on the lake today, maybe because the clouds were gathering into what could become a storm.

"It looks like it might rain," Sam yelled over the sound of the motor.

"Not for another hour or so," he answered over his shoulder.

"How can you be so sure?"

"Because I checked the weather forecast on my phone. You're not getting out of this, so just enjoy it."

Easy for him to say, she thought, giving him a resigned smile. A few minutes later, Jason shifted to a lower gear and steered the boat closer to the shoreline. Sam couldn't see where they were going; there were tall grasses along the water's edge blocking her view. Suddenly Jason turned the boat into a narrow opening among the grass, the reeds rubbing against its sides as they drifted into a secluded cove.

Jason cut the engine and threw the anchor out. "Here we are," he said smugly.

The cove was surrounded by trees with low-hanging branches. The only sounds came from the birds and insects nearby. "Wow, this is really private," she said, feeling some of her anxiety drain away.

"I told you. I doubt many people know about this place. We're safe here." Jason stood up and started untying his swim trunks.

"What are you doing?" Sam stuttered, her nerves reappearing.

"I'm getting naked. How else do you go skinny-dipping?" He stood smiling down at her and continued to untie his shorts. She was rooted to the spot as she realized what she had agreed to. Private or not, someone could still come upon them, and it was broad daylight! Jason took her silence as encouragement to put on a strip show and teasingly removed his trunks, twirling them around on his index finger before tossing them on the seat. "Your turn."

Sam glanced nervously around her as she stood up. Finally convinced that there was no immediate danger, she started to slide down her bathing suit straps. Jason stood transfixed as she slowly removed her suit and tossed it on the seat atop his. As often as they had seen each other naked, it was still a sensory delight. Jason's excitement was obvious, and Sam could feel her own body swell in response. In one swift movement, he swung himself over the side of the boat, sending a spray of water onto her bare skin.

"Ahh...," she cried as the cool water hit her warm skin.

Jason laughed and held his arms out toward her. "Jump in."

Sam quickly calculated the best way to get in given her current state of undress. Unfortunately, she couldn't think of a delicate way to enter the water without showing all her bits and pieces!

"Just come over to the edge and swing your legs over. I'll catch you."

Sam did as she was told, and the next thing she knew she was immersed in the cool water up to her chest, Jason's arms snugly around her. "There you go. That wasn't too bad, was it?"

The water was cool, but the sun was warm, and being in Jason's arms gave her the extra warmth she needed. "No, not bad at all," she said, smiling up at him. They swam around the boat, surrounded by the reeds, trees, and sounds of nature, basking in their private world. Sam became braver with every minute and even floated on her back, kicking her legs playfully.

He was right; it did feel liberating! Sam was floating and staring up at the clouds when she realized that Jason had disappeared. All of a sudden, he erupted out of the water and wrapped her in a tight hug.

"You scared me," she scolded as he set her back down.

He flicked his wet hair back off his forehead and wiped the water droplets off her nose. "I'm sorry. Come closer and let me make it up to you."

"Oh no, you don't," she teased and tried to get away from him. He was much quicker and grabbed her around the waist.

"You can't get away from me that easily," he said with a chuckle, gripping her tightly against him. She was suddenly very aware of their naked bodies pressed close together, the water lapping gently against them. Her breasts rubbed up against his bare chest, and she could feel her nipples hardening. His hands slid down from her waist to grasp her bottom firmly as he bent to kiss her lips. Sam pressed harder against him, sliding her hands up his arms to interlock around his neck. His tongue probed into her mouth, and she felt her heart rate quicken. "I want to make love to you here," he whispered against her lips.

Sam nodded in agreement, her breath coming in ragged gasps. "I'm going to lift you up so you can wrap your legs around my waist," he instructed urgently. She simply did as she was told. Jason carefully guided himself into her as she clung to him. She could feel his muscles tighten and tense beneath her and marveled at his ability to keep them upright in the water. It wasn't long before all thoughts were banished and she was riding the waves of passion with him, crying out with pleasure in the quiet of the empty cove.

Chapter 11

Their last night at the cabin was heavenly. Sure enough, the rain came down in torrents after they had safely returned from their boat trip. They scrounged up some sandwiches for dinner and ate in front of the "fake fireplace," as Jason referred to it. Sam felt like their relationship was on solid footing again, enabling her to relax into the evening. After dinner, they chose a DVD from the entertainment cabinet. Sam let Jason choose this time since she'd picked last time. He slipped in a James Bond film, and they settled back on the couch. At some point much later, Sam was vaguely aware of being carried up the stairs and tucked into bed. The next thing she knew she was awakened by some very noisy birds outside her window. She stretched contentedly and glanced over at the clock on the bedside table. Just then, Jason walked in carrying a tray of pancakes and juice.

"Rise and shine, beautiful. Your breakfast is served!"

"Wow, what service!" She smiled up at him.

"I was beginning to wonder if I would have to wake you. You were snoring when I peeked in on you a half hour ago."

"Snoring? I don't think so."

"Oh yes, you were. I have an audio recording of it on my phone if you want proof."

Sam looked at him aghast. "Are you serious? You recorded me snoring?"

Jason struggled to keep a straight face. "No, I didn't record you, but you were snoring a little. In the most feminine way, of course."

Sam chuckled and scooted over, allowing Jason to join her. "This looks delicious. What time did you get up this morning?"

"I was up at eight, and when I saw you were still asleep, I decided to shower and make breakfast." They dug into their pancakes heartily. "It was a tough choice, though."

"What was?"

"I had to decide whether to wake you with a kiss or make breakfast."

"And you chose breakfast?" she asked with a mock accusatory tone.

"I figured it would be best to get your energy up first, if you know what I mean." He winked at her as she took a big bite of syrupy pancake.

"I do know what you mean, but I should probably shower first. It's not fair that you're already cleaned up and I'm still dirty." There goes the innuendo again, she mused.

"I'll take you any way I can get you," he replied, sending a warm rush through her body.

They hurried through the rest of their breakfast, set the tray down and tumbled into each other's arms. A little while later, as Sam was catching her breath, she said, "That was the best wake-up call ever."

Jason placed a kiss on the tip of her nose and replied, "I agree, but sadly, we need to get ready to leave."

"I know," she said. "I wish we didn't have to, though. This was so wonderful, I hate for it to end."

"Our good times don't have to end when we get home. Once we tell our family and friends, we can date openly. We won't have to hide anymore."

Sam wished she could feel as confident as he did, but she still felt a prickly sense of nervousness at the thought of telling people. She swallowed her fear and headed to the bathroom. "I better get showered so we can get going."

Her back was to him, but Jason could sense her discomfort. "I promise it will be ok, Sam."

"I know," she said, softly closing the door behind her. Sam took her time in the shower and concentrated on breathing evenly to steady herself. The thought of going home sounded ominous to her. Here, they were able to hide from criticizing stares, except for the one from Leslie, that is. They had built their own little oasis where Sam felt safe and comfortable. She wanted the relationship to continue, but she was also keenly aware of the obstacles in their way. Aside from the opinions of family and friends, there was the fact of Jason returning to school in the fall and Sam returning to work. Central Michigan University was only a couple of hours away, but she was sure they wouldn't be able to see each other as often. He would have classes and studying, and she would be busy with her lesson plans each week. Would he want to come home every weekend just to be with her? Would she visit him at school? How awkward would it be for him to introduce her to his college friends? How would a forty-year-old woman fit in with a group of college students? While she appreciated Jason's idealistic view of the world, Sam considered herself a realist. She could clearly see the obstacles they faced, and he simply refused to acknowledge them. It's true they had a couple more months of summer left, but Sam wanted to get his take on what would happen during the school year. While she dressed and dried her hair, she thought about the best time and place to broach the subject.

Sam came downstairs with her luggage in tow and found Jason in the kitchen, waiting for her. "I would have brought that down for you," he said.

"I'm used to doing things for myself."

"Well, you don't have to anymore. I'm

going to load up our stuff. Can you take a look around and make sure we didn't forget anything?"

"Sure." Sam wandered through the rooms, wondering if she would ever see this place again or if it would just be a pleasant memory. She wished she could shake her melancholy mood, but it didn't seem possible at the moment. She passed through each room they had been in and was back in the foyer as Jason came through the door.

"Ready?"

"Yes, but no," she sighed.

"This isn't the end for us, Sam; it's only the beginning." There it was again, his cheerful optimism. He grabbed her hand and led her out the door, locking up behind them. They hadn't been driving very long before both of them started to speak at once.

"Ladies first."

"I was just wondering what you think will happen with us once you go back to school."

"I think we'll continue to see each other as much as possible. I'll try to come home on the weekends and holidays, and you can come to visit me too. What are you worried about?"

"I'm worried that we won't get to see each other as much as you think. I'll be back in school, and so will you. It won't be like it is now, where we can see each other every day."

"Lots of couples don't get to see each other every day. That doesn't mean we're doomed, Sam."

He was making sense, as always. "That's true."

"But? I can tell there's a but in there."

"But we won't be having as many shared experiences. It's easy for people to grow apart under those circumstances."

"Only if people let themselves grow apart. Did you have to work at your marriage?"

"Yes, of course." She could see where this was going.

"It's no different for any relationship. I, for one, intend to work on our relationship, whether I'm at school or at home. What about you?"

How long would he continue to bolster her up? She marveled at his infinite patience and felt guilty for constantly questioning him. She would have to get a grip on her emotions or risk losing him altogether. "You're right, all relationships require work. Sometimes I just get carried away with my worries."

"I know," he said, grinning at her. "We're going to work on that too."

Sam decided to change the subject. "Now it's your turn. What were you going to tell me?"

"I talked to my dad while you were in the shower this morning. He invited us over for dinner tonight."

Sam's eyes practically popped out of her head. "What? You told him already?" She tried to choke down the panic in her throat.

"Well, sort of. I told him there's someone I want them to meet, but I didn't tell him who."

"Oh, well, that was fast." She shook her head in disbelief.

"It seemed like the right time when he called to ask how I was enjoying the cabin. He knew I wasn't there alone."

"What time is dinner?"

"Six o'clock. My plan is to tell them before you show up, so they won't be shocked when you walk in the door."

"Good idea." She knew this was coming, but she didn't expect it to happen so fast. Maybe it was better this way, less time for her to fret about it. Surely his parents were mature adults who would treat her with respect. How bad could it be?

She found out a few hours later when Jason answered his parent's door with a strained expression on his face. This was not going to be good. He ushered her inside to the kitchen where his mom was busy preparing a salad at the counter. Sam glimpsed his dad's back through the sliding glass door where he stood tending the grill. "Sam, this is my mom, Janet. I think you may have met before." Jason's discomfort was obvious as he shot his mom a warning look. Sam could feel the tension hovering over the room like Eeyore's gloomy cloud.

"Hello Janet. It's nice to meet you again." Sam would have extended her hand but Janet was tossing the salad with such force that bits of lettuce were flying out of the bowl. Janet glared at Sam with pursed lips and muttered a hello. Sam had never been a big hit with her boyfriends' moms. She had come to the conclusion long ago that some moms had trouble sharing their son's attention with another woman. It had been the same with Brad's mom, although, she had thawed out toward Sam after his death, better late than never. Luckily, Jason's dad walked into the room wielding a spatula and a warm smile. "Hello, Samantha, nice to see you again." He set the spatula on the counter and reached out with his large masculine hand to shake her trembling one. "Jason tells us you enjoyed our place on the lake."

Whoa, what else had Jason told them? "Yes, very much so. It's a beautiful home."

"We agree. The steaks are almost ready. How do you like yours cooked?"

His friendliness was in stark contrast to the icy cold draft coming from behind the kitchen counter. Sam didn't dare look in Janet's direction as she engaged in conversation with Dan. "Medium is fine with me."

"Can we get you anything to drink? A

beer, wine, soda…"

"I'll take care of it Dad. Just go back to being the grill master." Jason didn't have to ask; he brought Sam an ice cold beer and grabbed one for himself. Janet was silent as she went about setting the table with gruff efficiency.

Sam decided to try another tack, the old kill em' with kindness method. "Janet, both of your homes are so lovely. You really have a knack for decorating."

"I hired an interior decorator," she replied, refusing to meet Sam's eyes.

"Mom, that's enough," Jason shouted, causing Sam to jump. The room fell eerily still. "It's obvious you don't agree with us dating, but you better get used to it because it's not going to change. I'm not a kid anymore, and you can't dictate what I do or who I do it with."

His dad must have heard the commotion and came in holding a plate of steaks in one hand. "What's all the ruckus about?" He looked from one to the other of them standing dead still in the kitchen. "Steaks are ready. Let's eat."

Like father, like son. Dan's easy-going attitude saved the evening from being a complete disaster. He guided the conversation to neutral topics and asked Sam several questions about her job. Janet concentrated on eating and hardly said a word while Jason squeezed Sam's hand under the table. When they were finished, Sam offered to help clean up, but Jason made an excuse about them being late for a movie and whisked her out of the house as quickly as possible. Dan thanked Sam for coming as he shut the door behind them.

"Well, that was interesting," Sam said as they hurried across the street to her house. Jason gripped her hand so tightly it hurt. Luckily, they didn't have far to walk. Once inside, he let loose with a tirade that included a fair share of obscenities. Sam didn't dare say a word until he was finished.

"I'm sure it was just a shock to her. Give her some time to get used to the idea." What a turnaround; Sam was trying to reassure him this time.

"I hated the way she treated you," he growled, the veins in his neck pulsing with anger. "She had no right to treat you like that."

Sam felt surprisingly calm, probably because Janet's reaction hadn't really come as a surprise to her. What mother wouldn't question their son if he brought home a much older woman? She tried to put herself in Janet's shoes. "I can't really blame her, Jason. She just wants what's best for you." Oops, not the right thing to say, judging by the grimace on his face.

"What if you're who's best for me?" he asked, eyebrows raised.

The last thing she wanted was for him to get mad at her too. "Let's just put this aside for the rest of the night. What do you say?" She walked over to where he was leaning against her kitchen counter and wrapped her arms around his waist. She leaned her head against his warm chest and felt the tension start to drain from his body as he pulled her tighter against him. He ran one hand gently over her hair and soothed her as she was soothing him.

"I'm so sorry, Sam. Sorry you had to go through that."

"Shh... no more talking." She raised her head up to him, lips parted slightly, inviting his kiss. He placed his lips on hers and gently probed her mouth. The heat instantly flared between them, and she welcomed it, relished it. His hands stroked her back, and she shivered with expectation. When his fingers traveled beneath the waistband of her knit skirt, he pulled back in surprise at the feel of her bare skin.

"No panties?" he breathed huskily.

"I must have forgotten to put them on," she teased, feeling the full power of her femininity. His eyes were hooded with desire, and she reveled in his reaction. Jason returned both hands to her bare skin and tugged her against him again.

"You are so sexy," he said, his voice heavy with hunger.

"Right back at ya," she said with a grin, tilting her head back as he placed wet kisses down her neck. "Jason?"

"Hmm?" he replied, continuing to nibble on her neck.

"Do you want to go upstairs?"

"Yes," he answered and scooped her into his arms. He carried her upstairs as if she weighed no more than a feather and laid her carefully on the bed.

"That was very he-man of you," she giggled.

"Think so?" he smirked as he lifted his t-shirt over his head. She leaned up on her elbows to watch, admiration glowing in her eyes. She loved the hard planes of his chest and arms and the taper of his waist above his belt. He maintained eye contact as he unzipped his khakis and discarded them with his boxers in one fluid motion. Her pulse throbbed (along with other parts of her) as he moved over her on the bed. She was still fully dressed except for her panties and squirmed in sweet anticipation. He brushed the back of his hand across her cheek and whispered, "What do you want me to do to you?"

"Undress me," she replied, emboldened. Jason sat back and gently tugged her skirt down, ravaging her with his eyes as he went. Any shyness she once had was completely gone, and she basked in his open admiration.

"Arms up," he ordered as he wriggled her shirt over her head. He unhooked her lacy pink bra and discarded it with the rest of their clothes.

For a moment he did nothing but stare at her longingly, making her squirm all the more.

"Touch me," she demanded and reached out to place his hand on her breast. Jason flicked his thumb over her nipple and watched as it peaked in response. He brought his other hand to her other breast and matched his torturous movements. She was in such a state of heightened arousal that his touch set off a rocket of flame inside her. Jason locked his eyes on hers as he slowly trailed a finger down her stomach and further. He took his time probing, stroking, and caressing until she felt ready to burst, and she hadn't even touched him yet. Finally, he slid up to meet her hip to hip, pressing himself firmly against her.

"Are you ready for me?" His rich warm voice vibrated through her.

"Yes," she said, nodding urgently. It was the only word he needed as they entwined together as one. It wasn't long before they reached the peak together and glided back down on their release. Jason sprawled out on her king-size bed, a look of complete satisfaction plastered on his face. Sam curled up on her side and gazed contentedly at him. "I wish you could stay with me tonight."

"I do too, but it might be kind of awkward now that my parents know," he admitted reluctantly. She didn't want to say, "I told you so," but the thought crossed her mind.

The little bubble they had built around themselves was broken, and it wouldn't be as easy for him to stay now.

"My parents will have to get over it. I'm not going to tiptoe around them every time I come over to see you."

She pulled her hand through his messy hair in an attempt to keep him calm. "It's ok, we can see each other again tomorrow."

He turned on his side to face her and traced a finger over her soft curves. "We might have to wait until Tuesday. I have a few jobs lined up tomorrow, and then I promised to play basketball with my buddies in the evening."

She tried to hide her disappointment and said, "Ok, no problem. I was thinking about calling my sister anyway."

Jason pulled her over on top of him. "I hate to have to leave you."

She could feel the proof of his statement pressing hard against her thigh. "I believe you," she giggled, placing a quick kiss on his full lips. "I'll still be here on Tuesday, though."

He rested his big masculine hands on her backside, trapping her against him. "It'll be hard for a 'strapping' guy like me to wait until Tuesday."

"I think you'll survive," she teased. If they stayed like this much longer, it would be another hour before he left, and it was already approaching eleven o'clock. "You should probably get going."

Jason agreed, but he was reluctant to break their connection. "Think about me tonight." It was more of a statement than a question.

"I will. You think about me too."

"Guaranteed." He sat them up and went about dressing while Sam stepped into the bathroom to retrieve her robe from the hook on the door. She tied it tightly around her waist before rejoining him. They held hands as they walked to the back door.

"Thank you for a wonderful weekend."

He pulled her close and kissed her sweetly. "No, thank you. I'll call you tomorrow, ok?"

"Ok," she nodded, reluctant to let him go.

"See you then," he said, one foot already out the door.

"See you then." She smiled and closed the door gently behind him.

Chapter 12

The next day, when Sam entered Jaime's house, she was immediately struck by how quiet it was. "James?" she said, calling out her sister's nickname.

"In the kitchen," her sister yelled back.

"Where are the kids?" Sam asked, plopping down on a stool at the kitchen island.

"They're at the neighbor's house, having a play date," she replied, arranging some sandwiches on a plate. "How's it going?"

Now that was a loaded question. "Pretty good," Sam said with a touch of hesitation in her voice.

"Let me re-phrase the question; how's it going with your young stud?" Jaime laughed at her description of Jason.

"Well, me and my 'young stud' just got back from a weekend together in Charlevoix."

"Get out," Jaime exclaimed banging her hand on the counter. She was nothing if not expressive. "Tell me everything."

Sam chuckled. "I'm not telling you everything, but I will say we had a wonderful time."

"I bet you did. What all did you do?"

"We stayed at his parents' cabin, which was really more like an estate on the lake. We went boating and shopping and…"

Jaime cut her off impatiently. "I don't want to hear the PG version. Did you do it or not?"

"Oh my gosh, James," Sam said with a smirk. "Yes, we did it."

"Yeah!!" Jaime did a little jump in the air and clapped her hands. "I'm so happy for you."

"I was happy too, until he insisted I meet his parents last night."

"Uh-oh, didn't go so well?"

Sam shook her head. "His dad was fine, but his mom spit fire at me the entire time."

"To be expected," Jaime sighed, waving her hand in the air dismissively.

"I know, but it was uncomfortable. Jason yelled at her, and we left in a huge rush."

"Wow, Sam. This is a lot to take in. I knew you liked him, but I didn't know you were that cozy all ready. How do you feel about it?"

"I love being with him. He treats me like a queen, and I haven't felt this alive in years. Our weekend together was incredible."

"I sense a 'but' coming."

Sam looked down at her hands. "He says that all the time too. The 'but' is I don't think other people will accept our relationship that easily. I think it's going to be hard for us going forward. He'll be going back to school in the fall, and I'll be back to work and..."

Jaime cut her off clearly exasperated. "Stop right there. Stop listing all the reasons why this relationship can't work. Focus on the reasons it can. He sounds like a great guy, and you need to give him a chance."

"I am giving him a chance. I went away with him didn't I?"

"Well then, stop worrying about the future. Just roll with it." Jaime's words were similar to Jason's. Sam sighed in defeat. She wondered why she couldn't be more easygoing like them.

Jaime softened her voice and placed a hand over her sister's. "I understand that you're overwhelmed by all this. For five years, you were alone, and all of a sudden, you meet this guy who happens to be a lot younger than you. Even if he was your age, you'd probably be questioning things. I just don't want you to push him away because of fear—at least, not until I get the chance to meet him."

Sam rolled her eyes at her sister. "Do you really want to meet him?"

"Of course I do. When and where?"

"What if we came over here for dinner one night? You wouldn't have to cook; we can just order pizza."

"Sounds fun. Check with your stud and let me know when."

"You're not going to call him 'stud' when

you meet him, are you?"

"Of course not. I have a lot more class than that. I'll be on my best behavior, I promise."

"Yeah, right," Sam giggled before digging in to one of the sandwiches sitting in front of her.

Later that day, Sam entered the door of the yoga studio with trepidation, knowing she would have to face Leslie's interrogation about Jason. Sure enough, Leslie was waiting for her in the locker room with an inquisitive look on her face. "So, how was your weekend?" she asked with mock innocence.

Sam decided to cut right to the chase. "Yes, I'm dating him, and yes, he's younger than me."

"Well, I could see that. How much younger?"

"Does it really matter?"

"I don't know, does it?" After Jaime, Leslie probably knew her better than anyone. Sam could hear the concern in her voice but was determined not to let it get to her.

"Les, I'm as shocked as you that this happened. I never expected to meet someone, let alone someone who's younger than me."

"Can you at least tell me a little bit about him? How did you meet?"

"He trimmed my bushes." Wait a minute, that hadn't come out right. "He was looking for ways to earn money this summer, and he offered to do some yard work for me. The next thing I knew he asked me out and…"

"So is he in college?"

"Yes. He's a really great guy, Les, and I enjoy spending time with him."

"You don't have to sell him to me, Sam. It's really your business. I'm just a little surprised."

"So am I, but I haven't felt this good in years—not since Brad. I'm trying to just go with it right now." She glanced at her watch. "We better get out there. Class is about to start."

"I want you to be happy Sam, I really do. I just don't want you to get hurt again. "

Sam nodded her head as they walked out to join the class. Yoga helped to clear her mind, and she felt more at peace as she waved goodbye to Leslie and climbed into her car. She'd made it a habit to check her phone before driving off, and sure enough, there was a message from Jason. "Hey, beautiful, it's me. I just remembered that you're probably at yoga right now. Sorry I missed you. I'm on my way to meet up with my friends, and I'm not sure what time I'll be home. I don't want to interrupt your beauty sleep, so I'll probably wait and call you tomorrow. Can't wait to see you. Bye."

Sam realized she was smiling as she set her phone back down. She liked knowing that someone cared about her and knew her schedule. It had been so long since anyone had checked in on her, and she'd forgotten how nice it felt. That night, she ate a light dinner, took a long bubble bath, and climbed in bed with her book. She must have fallen asleep with the light on because the next thing she knew she was being awakened by a tapping sound against her window pane. She glanced over at the alarm clock and registered that it was eleven o'clock as the tapping noise persisted. She clicked the lamp off so she could see outside and slowly pulled back the curtain. Standing below her window, lit by the moonlight, was Jason holding what appeared to be a handful of pebbles. She unlatched the window and slid it open. "What are you doing?" she called down, still a little groggy.

"I came to kiss you goodnight," he called back.

"Oh my gosh," she giggled, "come around to the garage door before you wake the neighbors."

She shut the window and hurried downstairs to let him in, pulling her robe on as she went.

"Sorry if I woke you," he said, entering the kitchen with a rush of warm summer air. "I felt a strong urge to kiss you goodnight, and when I saw your light on, I figured you were still awake."

Sam smiled sleepily. "I must have fallen

asleep with the light on."

Jason stepped forward and gathered her in his warm embrace. For some reason, she felt smaller and more vulnerable in his arms than usual. She needed this as much as he did, and she breathed him in. They stood like that for several minutes until he pulled away. "Ok, you can go back to bed now."

"What?" she said, laughing in disbelief. "You're serious? You came over just for that?"

"Yep, pretty much. It felt strange not talking to you today, so I just needed to see you."

She stepped into his arms again, reluctant to let go. "You're crazy."

"Crazy for you," he replied and hugged her tighter. "Now go back to sleep. I don't want you to be crabby for our date tomorrow."

"What date?"

"I'm not exactly sure yet, but I'll think of something."

Sam added spontaneity to his ever-growing list of attributes. She loved that he was constantly thinking of things they could do together. "You're not going to whisk me away again, are you?"

"I wish, but no. I have too many jobs lined up this week. Just go back to bed, and I'll call you in the morning." He bent down and placed a chaste kiss on her forehead.

"Oh no you don't," she scolded. "You

don't get to come over here, wake me up out of a sound sleep, and kiss my forehead like I'm a little girl. If you're going to kiss me, kiss me like you mean it."

He didn't need further prompting. This time, he tilted her chin up, and with his sparkly brown eyes firmly locked on hers, bent down to kiss her passionately. When their lips parted, she felt somewhat unsteady on her feet. "I wish you could stay," she whispered.

"Me too, but I didn't say anything to my parents about staying out all night. I don't want them waking up panicked in the middle of the night because I'm not there."

"I understand."

"However, they said something about going up north this weekend, so..." he wiggled his eyebrows up and down suggestively.

A shiver of anticipation ran through her at the thought. "I can't wait."

He kissed her again, gently this time, and turned to leave. "See you tomorrow."

She nodded her head. "See you then." She padded back to bed and drifted off again, wondering briefly if it had all been a dream.

Chapter 13

The next morning, Jason called just after breakfast. "Good morning," he said energetically. "How'd you sleep?"

"I might have slept better if a peeping Tom hadn't woken me up last night."

"Ok, first of all, I wasn't peeping, and second, my name is Jason, not Tom."

She loved their playful banter. "I actually slept really well, although I missed waking up with you beside me. Aside from that, what did you cook up for our date today?"

"First, I need to know if you like Mexican food?"

"Love it, why?"

"There's a great Mexican restaurant in Oxford that I'd like to take you to."

Sam was slightly disappointed even though she loved Mexican food. She would have to tame her expectations. He couldn't whisk her away somewhere exciting every day. "That sounds nice."

"You're a horrible liar, Sam," he teased. "Eating out isn't all I have planned. Second question, have you ever ridden on a motorcycle before?"

Now this sounded more like Jason. "No, I've always been kind of scared of them."

"I guessed that, so today you're about to conquer your fear of motorcycles."

Surely, he didn't expect her to drive one. "Um, you're driving right?"

"Absolutely. I have a couple of errands to run this morning, but how about if I pick you up at noon?"

"Wait a minute, cowboy. I didn't even know you owned a motorcycle."

He chuckled at the uncertainty in her voice. "It's my dad's, actually. It'll be fun, Sam. Really, all you have to do is hang on tight and enjoy the ride."

Funny how his innocent statement conjured up a much different meaning in her head. "We're not going on the expressway, are we? I mean, we can take the side streets to get there, right?"

"Goodbye, Sam. Gotta run. Dress in long sleeves, jeans, and a jacket. Oh and put your hair in a ponytail. It's just going to blow around anyway." He hung up before she could say another word.

Great. She should have just accepted the idea of going to a restaurant the old-fashioned way—in a vehicle with four wheels! By the time she got herself dressed and completed some minor house cleaning, it was time to go. She heard the loud, rumbling sound of the motorcycle before he even pulled up in her driveway, so she went out to greet him. Wow! The sight of hunky Jason on a motorcycle made her breath catch in her throat. She always found him attractive no matter what he wore (or didn't wear as the case may be), but this was something else entirely. He hauled himself off the motorcycle and sauntered over to her in ripped jeans, a white t-shirt, and a black leather jacket. He also wore chunky black boots and his aviators, topped off by his trademark grin. She couldn't help but smile right back at him.

"Well, what do you think?" He gestured toward the Harley. "How do you like her?"

"Why do men insist on referring to cars and motorcycles as women?"

"I honestly have no idea." He laughed, bending down to give her a quick kiss. She found herself glancing from side to side to check if any neighbors were lurking about. Not a soul in sight. Jason didn't seem to notice; he was too busy admiring the Harley. He extracted two helmets from the side compartments and handed one to her. Hesitantly, she put it on, and Jason helped her fasten the chin strap before donning his own.

"We're taking the surface streets, right?"

"Yes, Sam, there's nothing to worry about." Jason casually hopped on the bike and patted the seat behind him. "Hop on and sit as close to me as you can get."

Now that shouldn't be a problem, she thought giddily.

"You need to put your arms around my waist and squeeze really tight the entire time, ok? Don't worry about hurting me, I can take it."

Sam pressed her chest to his back and crossed her arms around his midsection. "Like that?"

"Even tighter."

Ok, head out of the gutter, Sam. Concentrate! "How about that?" She squeezed as hard as she could.

"Good. If at any point you get scared or want me to stop, just pinch me or something. It'll be hard to talk while we're riding."

"Ok." Sam was anxious to get going now. The longer they sat there, the more nervous she became. "Let's go."

Jason slowly pulled out of her driveway, and they were off. It took them just a few minutes to turn out of the subdivision and onto the two-lane road heading toward Oxford. At first, Sam was concentrating so hard on holding tight that she didn't look around. After a few minutes, she relaxed enough to actually enjoy herself. As Jason accelerated, she felt the wind whipping her ponytail around, nothing but open air around her, which she found exhilarating. She felt the power of the machine humming beneath them and sank into it. She loved the sensation of freedom combined with the pressure of Jason's muscular back against her chest. When they pulled up to a stoplight, he turned to ask if she was having a good time.

"It's awesome," she said with enthusiasm. Before long, they pulled into the parking lot of Senorita's Mexican Cantina. "Wow, that was really fun," she said as he helped her off the bike.

"I'm glad you enjoyed it." They held hands as they entered the restaurant. Sam wasn't sure if it was the thrill of the ride or if the chicken quesadillas were truly the best she'd ever tasted. They ate on a small patio outside and heartily delved into their food.

"Have I ever told you that I like the way you eat?" Jason stared at her with a forkful of food suspended in mid-air. "I love how you savor every morsel and that you order real food instead of just a salad."

"So I eat like a man, is that it?" she tilted her head to study him.

"No, not at all. Men attack their food. You eat like you're making love to it."

Sam almost choked on her quesadilla. She glanced around them to make sure no one had overheard. "I'm not quite sure how to take that." She raised her eyebrows inquisitively.

"It's a good thing, trust me." Jason's cheeks turned pink with embarrassment.

"I'll take it as a compliment, then," she

replied, hoping to put him more at ease. Sam had the distinct impression that something was bothering him, but she couldn't imagine what it might be. They finished their lunch in silence, paid the bill, and left the restaurant. Jason gave her a tight smile as they got back on the bike and accelerated out of the parking lot. Once again, she wrapped her arms around his waist and pressed her body against him. She put her worries aside and let herself relax as they rode home. When they got off the bike, she immediately felt the discomfort edge between them again.

"Is everything ok? Do you want to come in for a few minutes?" she asked as he packed the helmets away. Sam was sure that a few of their neighbors had seen him coming and going from her house, and she would feel better talking away from prying eyes.

"I only have a few minutes, and then I have some more lawn jobs to do," he replied flatly, as he followed her into the house.

She led him into the living room and settled on the couch, patting the space beside her. "What's going on, Jason? I thought we were having a great time, and then all of a sudden, you clammed up. Did I say something or do something…"

"No," he cut her off abruptly. "You didn't do anything wrong. There's just something I've been meaning to ask you, but I'm not sure how to."

"The best way is to come out and ask me. We've shared a lot at this point, don't you think? Whatever it is, I'm sure I can handle it." He was making her nervous; she just wanted him to come out with it.

Jason swallowed noisily and looked up at her. "I was wondering how you felt about our lovemaking. I mean, you've had a lot more experience than me, and I'm not sure how I measure up to…"

Now it was her turn to cut him off. "Stop, don't say his name. Please," she urged, shaking her head vehemently. "I loved my husband, and yes, we had many 'experiences' over the years, but I don't compare you to him — ever. All you need to know is that I fully enjoy making love with you. Can't you tell by the way I respond when we're being intimate?"

Jason shifted around to face her. "I know, it's dumb, but I just want everything to be really good for you."

Sam let out a big sigh. "Jason, believe me when I say it's good for me. In fact, it's more than good, it's wonderful. You are a very loving and generous man, and I've enjoyed every moment we've spent together, in bed and out."

"Promise me something," he pleaded. Promise me that if there's anything I need to do differently, you'll let me know. I mean anything."

"I promise," she replied, holding her fingers up to indicate scout's honor.

The look of relief on Jason's face washed her tension away. "I hate to do this, but I have to go." He stood up reluctantly, and she followed him to the door. "Are you free later tonight?"

"Actually, I need to take care of a few things too. How about if we talk tomorrow?"

"Ok," he said with a nod. He pulled her toward him. "Sorry for being an insecure wuss."

Sam chuckled at his choice of terms. "No need to apologize. It happens to the best of us."

"Thanks for going on the bike with me today."

"Thank you. I really, thoroughly enjoyed it."

"I could tell."

Sam had a sudden urge to be close to him, so she tugged on his t-shirt to pull him toward her. She wrapped her arms around his neck and reached up on her tiptoes to draw him into a deep kiss. She took charge this time, gently probing his mouth with her tongue while pressing her breasts against him. His hands slid down her sides, reaching back to cup her behind. She could feel the sexual tension building between them but was acutely aware that he had to leave. She finished off the kiss with soft sweeps against his lips before breaking contact. "Nope, I didn't enjoy that at all," she said, smiling up at him, eyes wide with mirth.

"Ok, ok, I get it." He grinned back at her, and his smile lit up the room. "If I didn't have to go, we could *not* enjoy things a little more."

"I guess we're going to have to *not* enjoy things tomorrow, then."

"I'll try to gear myself up for it," he replied with an eye roll.

"Me too. Now go. Get out of here." She swatted him on the behind as he put his hands in the air and said, "I'm going, I'm going."

Sam watched him straddle the Harley and didn't take her eyes off him until he disappeared into the garage across the street.

Chapter 14

That night, since Sam had some time on her hands, she decided to call her mother. Sadly, they didn't have as close a relationship as they used to, in part because her mom lived in Florida. Eight years before, her mom, Elise, had gone to Tampa with some of her lady friends, and while there, she'd met Ted, a property manager at the condominium complex where they'd been staying. Six months later, Elise had packed up all her belongings, moved to Tampa and married Ted. Jaime and Sam had found it difficult to accept their mom's hasty decision, and even now, it was hard for Sam to wrap her head around it. Elise claimed that she was happier than she'd ever been, which angered Jaime, who dubbed her the "neglectful grandmother." Sam had been angry at first, but when Brad had died, she'd become consumed with her own worries and had quickly forgiven her mother. Now she only saw Elise a couple of times a year and only called a few times in between. Despite everything, though, Elise was still her mom, and Sam wanted to tell her about Jason.

Elise answered on the second ring, in her

signature cheery voice. Sam thought her mom sounded like she was permanently on vacation.

"Hi Mom, it's Sam."

"Hi Sweetie. How are you?"

"I'm good, how about you?" Her question prompted a long discussion about the happenings in the condo complex. Sam waited for a lull to share her news. "I just called to let you know that I'm dating someone."

"Oh Sammy, that's wonderful. Tell me all about him."

Sam hated the use of her childhood nickname but didn't bother to correct Elise. "His name is Jason, and we've been seeing each other for a few weeks now. He lives in my neighborhood."

"Well, that's convenient," she said with a laugh. "What does he do?" Elise often measured the worth of a man based on what line of work he was in. She was forever citing Ted's title as Property Manager as if he was the governor of Florida!

"He's in college right now. Well, not exactly right now since it's summer break, but he'll be returning in the fall." Sam realized she'd probably just given away Jason's age, but her mom didn't miss a beat.

"So, you found yourself a young one, huh? My daughter the cougar." She laughed with delight. Elise had a whole new attitude since meeting Ted. She was, in her own words, much more "open-minded" than she used to be. Life was short, and she intended to "live it up" before she was in the grave.

"Mom, I'm not a cougar. It just sort of happened. He's a great guy, and we're having a lot of fun together."

"Oh, I bet you are," she said knowingly. Sam could almost sense her winking through the phone. "Well, I'm happy for you Sammy. It's about time you put yourself back on the market." Sam rolled her eyes; like she was a slab of meat! "Hey, if you want to bring your young stallion down to Florida to visit, you're welcome any time. Ted can fix you up in one of the rental units for a real good price. It's pretty quiet down here in the summer."

"I'm sure it is. What's the temperature today—one hundred degrees?" Sam didn't mean to be sarcastic, so she followed up with, "Thanks for the offer though." It had been six months since she had seen her mom, and she felt a twinge of regret at not making the effort to visit more often.

"Give it some thought sweetie. We would love to see you."

"Thanks, Mom. I'll let you know. Tell Ted I said hello."

"Will do. Love you."

"Love you too."

That evening, when Jason called to say goodnight, Sam told him about the conversation with Elise. Surprisingly, he was all for the idea.

"That sounds fun. What's not to like about Florida?"

"I would agree with you most of the year, but summer, really?"

"Why not? We could look at it as an end-of-summer getaway before we both have to go back to school."

"You mean wait until August?"

"Sure. We can probably find some cheap flights, and your mom said we could get a good rate on a condo. It'll be great."

Sam wished she could share his enthusiasm. Of course, he didn't know her mom.

"Think about it, Sam. Long walks on the beach, lounging by the pool, Florida sunsets, you in a bikini the entire time…"

"Hah," she said with a laugh. "I don't think so. Not with my mom and Ted around."

"We wouldn't have to hang out with them the entire time. C'mon, it'll be our last chance to get away before the school year starts."

Sam couldn't argue with that logic. It would be nice to go away with him again. "You're going into the wrong profession, do you know that?"

"What profession should I be going into?"

"Sales. You just sold me."

"Can I sell you on spending the day with

me tomorrow?"

"That's an easy sell. What do you have in mind?" Sam felt the smile spread across her face.

"I'll bring breakfast over in the morning, and then we can go golfing. Do you golf?"

"I know how to golf, but I haven't been since…"

"Brad," he finished her sentence as her silence hung in the air. "Do you have a set of clubs?" he asked.

"Yes, they're in the back of the garage somewhere. I would love to go golfing with you tomorrow," she added as reassurance.

She could practically feel his relief flow through the phone. "I'll be over around eight, then. Don't bother getting ready; let's eat first, and then we can shower together."

Sam felt a rush of heat flow through her at the implication of his words. "So, you want me dirty, then?" She taunted him with the double meaning.

"Dirty is fine with me." His voice sounded husky. "I only plan to make you dirtier."

"Hmm… sounds intriguing."

"It's been a few days. Forgive me if I attack you the minute I walk in the door."

"What about eating first to give us energy?"

"Who needs food? Oh, that's right, you

do!"

"Hey, you like to eat too."

"If we continue this conversation, I'm not going to be able to wait until tomorrow." Sam could hear him shifting around and conjured up an image of him lying on his bed across the street. She wondered what he was wearing, pajama bottoms, boxers, nothing at all? Ok, I've got it bad, she thought, trying to reel herself back in. "Are you in bed?" she whispered.

"Yeah, I'm in my room. I never got a chance to show it to you, but I'd like to." His voice lowered, becoming more intimate.

"I'd like to see it sometime. Are you wearing pajamas?" Sam couldn't believe her own ears. What had she turned into? Whatever it was, it felt delicious.

"It depends on how you define pajamas," he teased. "I'm wearing boxer briefs." He was obviously enjoying this as much as she was. "What are you wearing?"

"A white tank top and some gray knit shorts."

"Yum. I love when you wear a white tank top to bed. It's so sexy."

Sam felt her stomach clench with desire. "Why do you like it so much?" She asked the question, knowing full well what the answer would be.

"I like that I can see your nipples poking against the fabric. I can visualize that right now.

Am I right?"

Sam glanced down at her chest. Her nipples were pressing hard against the fabric in response to their suggestive conversation. "Yes." She could barely speak.

"There's something else pressing against fabric right now." His voice hitched. "I'm burning up for you."

Sam could feel her own heat building too, her every sense on high alert. "Imagine me lying next to you right now, kissing you, touching you."

"Are you naked in this scenario?"

"Yes."

"Keep talking."

"I'm lying on top of you, my bare breasts pressed against your chest."

"Awesome." His breathing was becoming raspy. "What next?"

"I slowly guide you inside of me and…"

Jason let out some loud, guttural sounds and went silent. Sam sat back, feeling strangely proud of herself. She'd been able to pleasure him via phone; another first for her! She wished he could see her smug, satisfied smile. "Are you still there?" She let out a soft laugh. "Are you alive?"

"Wow. That's all I can say right now. That was so hot."

"Yep, I'm pretty pleased with myself right now."

"You should be. That was unbelievable."

"Rest up, big guy, because you still have work to do tomorrow." Flirting with him was becoming easier every day. She loved the person she was becoming with him.

"Ok, sassy pants. I look forward to it."

"Sweet dreams." She giggled, shut off the phone, and snuggled down to sleep.

Chapter 15

Sam and Jason fell into a comfortable pattern as the summer weeks drifted by. Whenever he wasn't working, they found time to spend together. Sam was in better shape at age forty than she was ten years ago thanks to all the physical activities they did: hiking, biking, golfing, swimming, and tennis. Her appetite increased along with all the activity, and they enjoyed picnics in the park, intimate dinners at home (never meatloaf though!), and a variety of restaurant meals. They spent the evenings watching movies, talking, and making love. Jason spent the night with her whenever his parents were out of town. He even stayed a few times when his parents were home, if he was feeling particularly rebellious.

Sam brought Jason over to Jaime's house for pizza one Friday night, and it was a huge success. Her nephews took to him right away and were thrilled when he played basketball with them in the driveway. Her sister refrained from calling him a stud to his face, but she whispered to Sam that he was "seriously hot." Steve was the only one who seemed wary at first, but after watching Jason interact with the boys, he loosened up. At the end of the evening, Jaime made them promise to come over soon, with added endorsements from her nephews. Jason was still trying to win his mom's approval, but so far, she hadn't budged.

Sam hadn't been back to Jason's house other than one weekend when his parents were out of town and he invited her over to see his bedroom. They stayed long enough to make love on his bed and left quickly afterward to avoid his parents' unexpected return. During the month of July, neither of them mentioned the upcoming school year, but it hung over them like a cloud. Sam was all too aware of the dates as she marked off her calendar. They also made plans to visit her mom and Ted in mid-August. They found an inexpensive air fare, and when Sam called Elise to tell her, she was ecstatic. Sam looked forward to the week away with Jason, but she dreaded the fact that the following week he would have to leave for Central. She kept herself busy, buying new bikinis, shorts, sandals, and dresses, to keep her mind occupied. She was determined to enjoy their end of summer getaway rather than focus on what was coming after.

Sometimes, when she was alone, Sam reflected on how much her life had changed in such a short period of time. She attributed it all to Jason. He had opened up her world, and she literally felt born again. Even Leslie had to admit that Sam had a "glow" about her. One afternoon, she met Leslie and a few other teacher friends for lunch, and they all made similar comments. Leslie looked at Sam expectantly, silently encouraging her to share the news about Jason, but she didn't. The people she was closest to knew about him, and that was good enough for now.

In the midst of all the good she was experiencing, there were two events that left her feeling deflated. One Friday evening, Jason invited her to meet up with him and his basketball buddies for a beer at a local bar. She was reluctant at first, but he prodded her until she finally gave in. He had been such a good sport about meeting her family, how could she refuse him.

After fretting over what to wear, she finally settled on a teal blue wrap dress and wedge sandals. She put her hair up in a loose ponytail, hoping it would make her look younger. She decided to drive the Corvette for extra bonus points. Thankfully, Jason came out to greet her when she pulled into the parking lot. She hadn't been looking forward to entering the bar alone. He hugged her tightly and gave her a quick kiss before telling her how gorgeous she looked. Just being in his arms gave her the courage she needed, and they walked into the bar hand in hand. Jason led her to a table at the back of the bar where four guys and two girls were already seated. All eyes were upon her as he made the introductions. The guys approvingly sized her up, but the girls were another story. She could feel their stares boring into her as she tried to maintain her composure. The waitress came over to their table right away and took everyone's drink order, which gave her a few moments reprieve.

"So, Samantha, Jason mentioned that you work at Brandon Elementary. Are you a teacher there?" This came from one of Jason's closest friends, Scott.

"No, I'm the librarian," she replied, thinking how lame that must sound to this group.

"I hate to read," one of the girls spoke up. "It's soooo… boring."

"I only read if I have to for school," added the girl with the long straight blonde hair.

This is so awkward, thought Sam, struggling to come up with a witty response. Luckily, Jason jumped in to try and save her. "You girls are missing out; there's a lot of good stuff out there to read for pleasure."

"Yeah, right, like maybe Fifty Shades of Grey," the blonde said with a toss of her hair.

The girl with the sleek black bob laughed loudly. "I loved those books, and Chad did too, right honey?" She winked at her boyfriend, who turned a bright shade of crimson in response.

"Speaking of Fifty Shades, check out the

two hotties who just walked in." This came from John, one of the two unattached guys at the table. "Let's go talk to them, Brian," he said, nudging his friend.

Sam sat there drinking her beer, wishing she could disappear. She suddenly felt much older than her forty years. She was sitting amongst a group of horny teenagers who wouldn't know good literature if it slapped them in the face. Jason must have read her mind because he gently squeezed her hand under the table. She wished they had a code for get me out of here, now! Instead, she kept sipping her beer and smiling numbly at whatever the girls were saying, something about tanning beds and waxing!

"Do you guys want some appetizers?" Jason asked, not really waiting for the answer. "C'mon Sam, let's go up to the bar and order some food." He practically dragged her out of the chair and across the room to the bar. He picked up a menu and pretended to intently study it as he asked if she wanted to leave.

"I'm sorry, Jason, is it that obvious?"

"Yeah, I would say so. Look, I know the girls are a little ditzy, but I really wanted you to meet my guy friends."

"I understand, but I feel very uncomfortable here. I feel like the crazy aunt who thinks she's a lot younger than she actually is, hanging out at a bar with a group of college kids."

"Crazy aunt? Where do you come up with these things?" Jason shook his head, but he smiled at the same time.

"Your friend Scott seems really nice. Maybe we could invite him over for dinner sometime. It would be easier to get to know him one-on-one." Even as she said it, Sam knew it was just an excuse. She didn't see how she would ever fit in with his college friends. They were in a completely different stage of life than she was. How strange that she didn't see Jason that way, at least not until tonight. He was just as at ease with his friends as he was with her sister and brother-in-law, who were much older. He seemed to have no problem making the transition, so why did she? She had never been a party girl, though. She was always more of the serious, quiet type, and so was Brad. Jason had definitely broadened her horizons, but apparently, it wasn't quite enough.

"If we leave now, it'll seem rude. Can you at least stay and have some appetizers with me? After that, you can leave whenever you want." Jason glanced over to where his friends were gathered and then back at her pleadingly.

"Ok, fine, I'll stay for a little longer, but let's order something. I'm starved!"

"That's my girl," he said with a chuckle.

Sam stuck it out for another hour after that, just long enough to drink another beer, eat some unsatisfying finger foods, and listen to his friends talk about college. When the two girls got up to use the restroom, Sam stood up too. "I think I'm going to head home now. Nice meeting everyone."

Jason walked her out to the parking lot and helped her get into the Vette. He rested his arms along the window frame and leaned in for a kiss. "Thanks for sticking around. I know it wasn't easy for you."

"It's not like I was being tortured," she said. "Are you going to hang out much longer?" She hated to sound like a nagging girlfriend, but she was hoping he would come home with her.

"Just for another hour or so. Do you want me to come over after?"

Doing a quick calculation in her head, Sam realized she would probably be asleep by then. "You know us old folks, we can't stay up much past ten o'clock." She laughed, but it sounded hollow to her own ears. She knew that Jason hated when she made comments about her age.

"Stop it Sam. That's not even funny. You're only as old as you feel."

"Well, right now, I feel pretty damn old." She felt resentment rise up within her at the thought of him scolding her. Oh my God, she needed to get out of here fast before she said something she didn't mean.

Jason straightened up from the car and

gazed at her disappointedly. "Whatever, Sam. I'll call you tomorrow." With that he turned around and walked away, leaving her chilled and alone in the parking lot.

The next day, she knew he didn't have any jobs lined up, and they had planned to spend the day together. She went through the motions of making breakfast, showering, and dressing, all the while aware of the ticking of the clock. He usually called her by eight or nine at the latest, and it was after ten and still no call. Fine, if that's the way he wants to play it, then fine. She stomped around the house doing odd jobs like cleaning window sills and dusting under knick knacks that hadn't been moved in forever. She replayed the conversation from the previous night over and over in her head and found herself getting angrier with every swipe of the dust cloth. What did he expect anyway? She had to be true to herself; she wasn't about to act like someone else to fit in with his friends. Instead of him being angry with her, she should be angry with him for forcing her to meet them all at once like that. In a bar, on top of it! They never even went to the bar on their own, let alone with a big group of people. It was a mistake from the start; she never should have gone.

A persistent knock on the front door jolted her back to the present. As was her habit, she peered through the peephole to see him standing there, head down, hands in his pockets. She took a deep breath and swung the door open. When their eyes met, it erased all of the negative thoughts she had just been having. He looked tired and uncertain standing in her foyer, both of them unsure of what to say or do. "Can we talk?" he finally said.

"Sure," she said, leading him toward the living room.

They sat on the couch, farther apart than usual, avoiding eye contact; tension lay thick in the air. Jason ran a hand through his rumpled hair while she shifted uncomfortably in her seat.

"I'm sorry. I thought about it a lot last night, and I don't know what else to say. I'm sorry," he repeated.

His apology threw her off guard. "What are you sorry for? You didn't do anything wrong." With him sitting beside her looking so dejected, her anger was slipping away. Wanting her to meet his friends hadn't been wrong; her reaction was what was wrong.

"I'm the one who should be apologizing."

He sat tipped forward at the waist, elbows resting on his knees, head down. "No, you shouldn't. All along you've been telling me that I have an idealistic view of our relationship. I haven't wanted to believe that, but last night, for the first time, I understood what you were talking about."

Sam's heart pounded wildly. "No, Jason,

no." She hated to see him this way, so resigned. He was usually the one propping them up, keeping things positive. She tried to fight the panic from washing over her. She struggled for the right words while he continued his train of thought, undeterred.

"I haven't wanted to see the difficulties we might face because I'm in love with you, Sam. I love you, and it scares the hell out of me because I don't want to lose you."

Sam's eyes widened as a thousand emotions flooded her body. Fear, relief, surprise, joy, she felt them all, and it overwhelmed her.

"Last night, I felt you slipping away from me, and I hated it. I wanted to come after you right away, but I wasn't sure. I lay awake half the night thinking, and I realized that you were right. It won't be easy for us, but that doesn't change the fact that I love you."

Sam felt the first tear trickle down her cheek, followed by another and another until a full stream erupted. Jason's head was still down, and he started to say something else, but she blurted out, "Stop talking. I love you too."

He jerked his head in her direction. He placed his hands gently on her tear-stained cheeks, pressed his forehead to hers, and then gathered her tightly in his arms. They rocked back and forth together, consoling each other, unwilling and unable to let go. "I love you so much, Sam," he whispered, pulling back to gaze directly in her eyes.

"I love you too. I'm so sorry about last night. I feel so bad..."

"Shh, it's ok now. We're going to be ok." With that, he pulled her firmly back into his warm embrace.

Sam floated through the next few days in a haze of peace and contentment. Even the household chores were less daunting as she set out to clean up her flowerbeds one beautiful weekday morning. She was so busy pulling weeds and humming softly to herself that she wasn't aware of a presence until she stood up and practically crashed into Jason's mom.

"Oh, Janet, you startled me." Sam self-consciously tucked a strand of hair behind her ear. This was the first time she'd seen Janet since their dinner weeks before, and of course, Sam was covered in dirt and dripping sweat!

"Can I talk to you for a few minutes?" Janet's tone was all business, along with her stony expression.

"Ok, do you want to sit on the back deck?" Sam tried to squelch the feeling of dread that creeped up her spine.

"That will be fine."

Sam peeled off her gardening gloves as she led the way. Janet followed behind in awkward silence.

Janet didn't waste time; her interrogation

began the moment they were seated. "I know you and Jason have been spending a lot of time together. I was just wondering if he told you about his internship offer?"

Sam eyed her warily, trying not to act surprised even though she had no idea what Janet was talking about. When she didn't respond immediately, Janet plunged ahead. "There's a school in Denver that has approached him about being an intern there for the winter semester. If he accepts, there's a good chance he could be offered a permanent position after graduation."

Sam knew she had to say something instead of sitting there like a mute. "No, he didn't mention it, but I'm sure he was going to," she said finally.

Janet inhaled deeply and leaned forward in her chair. "Look, Samantha, I realize that we got off to a bad start. I was quite shocked when Jay told us he was seeing you. (That was an understatement, thought Sam.) Anyway, I'm guessing that you want what's best for him, am I right?" The question dangled in the air between them. "I hope you'll do the right thing and encourage him to take the internship."

Sam finally found her confidence. "Are you suggesting I would try to discourage him?"

"Maybe not intentionally. He's obviously attached to you, and I don't want it to affect his decision. This is a great opportunity for him.

Surely you can understand that."

Sam was stunned. First that Jason hadn't told her about Denver and second that his mother believed she would stand in his way. She was certain that Jason wouldn't be pleased with the direction of the conversation. "Janet, may I call you Janet? Good," she said without waiting for a response. "What leads you to believe that Jason would listen to either one of us when it comes to making decisions about his future? Last I checked, he's a grown man who's perfectly capable of making his own decisions. I, for one, don't intend to influence him one way or the other. Can you say the same?"

Janet glared at her intently for a moment. The vein on the side of her neck bulged in anger. "I realize that I don't know you very well, but I'm curious. Why would a forty-something-year-old woman be interested in a twenty-three-year-old man? Enlighten me."

Sam felt her hackles rising, blood rushing to her face. "You're right, you don't know me at all, nor have you taken the time to. You've come to your own conclusion about me, haven't you? I'm the neighborhood slut who stole your son away when you weren't looking. Am I right?" Sam stood up and continued in an even, controlled voice. "From now on, if you have any questions about our relationship, ask your son. This conversation is over." Sam stalked away, leaving Janet to stare after her in stunned silence.

That evening she rehashed the whole ordeal with Jason over dinner. He was furious about his mom's behavior and contrite about having kept the news from Sam.

"How long have you know about it?" She questioned, trying to keep her voice steady.

"I got the letter a few weeks ago," he admitted sheepishly.

"I don't understand why you didn't tell me." She put her salad fork down and waited for his explanation.

"There are a few reasons. One, I'm not sure I want to take the position, and two, I didn't want to give you something else to worry about. *If* I go, it won't be until January, which is still a ways off."

"Why wouldn't you go? Is it because of us?"

"Well, of course that makes the decision harder. If we weren't dating, I would probably go."

"There's your answer, then. I can't be the reason you don't take the job. That would only cause resentment in the long run."

Jason sat back in his chair and sighed. "Why would I resent you, Sam? If things were the other way around, I wouldn't want you to go."

"You wouldn't want me to go, but you would probably accept it if I did, right?"

"Ok, there are too many 'what ifs' in this

conversation for me. The fact remains that I'm not sure I want to up and move to Denver. Can we leave it at that?"

Sam wasn't finished with her interrogation yet. "Let's say you take the internship. How long would you be there for?"

"Almost six months."

"What happens after that? You would come home right?"

He squirmed uncomfortably beneath her intense gaze. "That depends."

"On what?"

"The letter stated that there's a possibility I could be offered a full time position if I do well as an intern. I would start with the new school year next September."

Sam took a moment to absorb what he was saying. "So it's possible that you could move to Denver permanently." It was more of a statement than a question.

"Yes, if, and only if, I choose to accept the internship."

"You said earlier that you would probably accept it if we weren't dating. That tells me that you're interested, and I don't want to be the one holding you back. I disagree with your mom's methods, but what she said was true; this sounds like a good opportunity for you."

"Another option is for me to take the internship but decline a full-time position. The internship would give me the experience I need to find a job elsewhere, somewhere closer to home. Anyway, I have until November first to make my decision."

Sam fiddled with her hair, which she did whenever she was nervous or uncomfortable. Jason recognized the sign right away and stood up from the table. He held out his arms to her. "Come here," he urged. She stood up and moved into the circle of his arms, letting the warmth of his body soothe her. "Now can you understand why I haven't said anything? I don't want you to worry about this from now until January."

"But you can't keep big things like this from me, Jason," she protested. "I didn't particularly enjoy getting the news from Janet."

"Ok, ok, I'm sorry." He ran his hand along the back of her hair and rested his chin gently atop her head. "From now on I'll tell you anything and everything that might affect us."

"Thank you," she said, feeling slightly better.

"For example, right now, I have something to say that affects both of us." He paused looking down at her with sparkling eyes and a wide grin. "I would like to make love to you, if you'll have me."

Sam's heart melted as it usually did where he was concerned. "I would love to have you," she teased. And with that, she grabbed his hand and led him up the stairs.

Chapter 16

They stepped off the plane in Tampa and into the bright Florida sunshine. Elise had offered to pick them up at the airport, but Sam had insisted they lease a rental car instead. Jason loaded their bags in the back of the black convertible Mustang they had rented (his idea) and headed off in the direction of the Delray condominium complex. Jason put the convertible top down right away, and they cruised along the highway, Sam's ponytail blowing gaily in the wind. She felt her entire body relax, letting the Florida feeling take over, as the car hummed along. Jason seemed relaxed too as he reclined in the leather seat, one hand on the wheel, the other on the stick shift guiding the sports car easily in and out of traffic. She studied him with open admiration (amongst other feelings), his long, lean frame clad in navy cargo shorts and a simple white tee. The wind made his typically messy hair even messier, and she thought he looked especially masculine and sexy behind the wheel of the Mustang. Once they arrived, she knew they would have to spend some time with her mom and Ted, but she planned on having Jason all to herself as soon as possible. Maybe a dip in the pool and then...

He disrupted her thoughts as they pulled off the expressway onto the exit ramp. "Penny for your thoughts, beautiful." He smiled widely, but she couldn't see his eyes behind the aviators.

"I was just thinking how happy I am that we're here together."

"Is that all you were thinking?" he asked. His ability to read her mind was uncanny.

"I was also thinking that I can't wait to get you alone later." Six months, no wait, three months ago, Sam never would have imagined herself saying such a thing. Now it was becoming second nature.

Jason chuckled huskily. "I was thinking the same thing."

"We probably need to spend some time with Elise and Ted first."

"Well, yeah, but as soon as you give me a sign, we're out of there."

"What should the sign be? It can't be too obvious."

"Darn. I was thinking we could just say, excuse us, we need to go make love now."

Sam hit his arm playfully. "Yeah, right."

"Let's just go with the flow. We'll know when the time is right to make our escape." A few minutes later they were pulling into the driveway of condo number 115. They were barely out of the car when her mom and Ted emerged to greet them.

Elise was exuberant as ever as she rushed over, arms outstretched, and wrapped them both in a warm hug. Sam never ceased to be amazed at how comfortable her mom was with complete strangers. Elise had never met Jason before, yet here she was, hugging him like she had known him for years.

"It's very nice to meet you...," Jason began.

"Just call me Elise," she filled in. "You must be Jason. Welcome, welcome, come on in, you two." Elise continued to gab as she led them into the house. Ted shook Jason's hand and smiled warmly. "Welcome to Florida, son."

The condo was decorated in true Florida style, mint greens, corals, and blues with nautical accents. Pictures of sailboats, dolphins, and ocean scenes adorned the walls. "Why don't we sit on the patio," Elise suggested. "Ted, will you bring out some lemonade for everyone?" Now came the part that Sam was expecting, the question and answer period.

"So Jason, tell us about yourself. What do you do again?"

Oh no, here we go, thought Sam. "I already told you that Jason is a student, mom. He doesn't have a full time job yet." She struggled to keep the irritation out of her voice.

"It's ok, Sam," Jason interjected. "I'm studying child psychology at Central Michigan, Elise. I expect to graduate in the spring."

"Child psychology, huh," Ted chimed in. "What made you choose that field? Not that there's anything wrong with it."

"I like working with kids, but I wasn't interested in teaching. I like the idea of being able to give kids the added support they need as they navigate their school years." Sam's face lit up with pride as he spoke. She loved that he was passionate about his career choice and that he was holding up well under the scrutiny of her mom and Ted. He looked perfectly at ease sitting on their patio sipping lemonade under the hot summer sun. Her heart swelled with love for him.

"Are there a lot of jobs available in that field? Maybe you can work at Sam's school. Wouldn't that be wonderful?" Elise was always painting perfect scenarios for her daughters. Next thing you know she'll have us living in a cute little house on a hill surrounded by a white picket fence. Sam found herself smiling at the image.

I'm not sure where I'll end up, Elise. I have an opportunity to go to Denver in January, but I'm not sure if I'll take it or not." He glanced over at Sam. She felt so wound up, she could swear he noticed the tension in her shoulders. "I would be leaving a lot behind if I went there," he added.

Elise gave Ted a nudge. "Isn't that sweet, honey? He doesn't want to leave our Sammy."

Sam winced at the nickname.

"Sammy?" Jason smirked with satisfaction. "I didn't know your nickname was Sammy."

"It's not anymore," she emphasized. "I haven't had that nickname since I was a kid." She glared pointedly at her mom. Elise ignored her and continued her questioning. Finally, Ted interrupted and said, "What are you kids going to do while you're here? Do you play golf, Jason?"

"Yes, sir. I try."

Ted let out a loud rumbly laugh. "Don't we all! Let's play a round or two while you're here. I can get you on the course right here for half price."

"Sounds good to me," Jason replied. Sam didn't mind being left out of the conversation. She was just glad that Elise and Ted had taken a liking to Jason.

"Would you mind showing us to our unit now?" Sam inserted. "We'd like to get settled in and maybe take a dip in the pool before dinner."

"Sure thing." Ted stood up, and the rest of them followed suit.

"We insist on taking you out to dinner tonight," Elise said, sounding reluctant to see them go so soon.

"Maybe the lovebirds want to have dinner alone tonight, dear," said Ted.

"We'll have dinner with you tonight,"

Sam conceded, "but I'm going to want to show Jason around the area, so it might not be every night."

"Of course, sweetie, I understand. We'll see you later." Elise winked knowingly and closed the door behind them.

Ted opened up their garage door and pulled out a golf cart. "Your unit is down the street a little ways. Just follow me."

Their unit looked a lot like Elise's except it was poolside. They could walk right from the patio to the sprawling in-ground pool and hot tub. They hauled their bags to the master suite, and Sam plopped backward onto the king sized bed. "Ah, peace at last!"

"Oh, it wasn't so bad. I like your mom and Ted." Jason laughed, sprawling out next to her.

"I love them, but I can only take them in short spurts. It always feels like my mom is trying too hard and Ted's job is to bring her back down to earth."

"Parents have a way of bringing out the best and worst in us. It's just the way it is." Jason leaned up and rested his head on his hand, gazing down at her. She grew warmer from the intensity in his eyes alone. They weren't even touching, but she could already sense his hands on her body, his lips on her mouth...

Her lips parted in anticipation as he reached out to brush a stray hair away from her face. Then his hand trailed down the side of her body and up the inside of her thigh. She was wearing a tank-style knit dress which provided him easy access. His fingertips skimmed the top edge of her panties, sending waves of pleasure directly between her thighs. She felt her nipples harden against the skimpy lace of her bra. Jason continued his exploration under her dress and finally leaned over to brush her lips with his. It was a soft, fluttering kiss, but it set off mini explosions inside her. Had she ever felt like this with Brad? She couldn't recall this level of intensity. Sure, they'd found pleasure with each other, but it had been different, not as passionate. Jason slowly moved his lips down her neck, placing warm kisses against her throbbing pulse. His head dipped further down, grazing the tops of her breasts as they pushed above the neckline of her dress. Supporting the bulk of his weight with his arms, Jason moved over her and began a sensual rocking motion with his hips against hers. Sam responded by arching her back off the bed, amazed to feel this aroused even though they weren't skin to skin. She pulled him closer, feeling his back muscles contract with each motion. Her breathing was becoming shallow as he continued to place kisses along her neck and bare shoulders. Was he testing her stamina? If she was this close to bursting, surely he must be too. Suddenly he pulled them both up to a sitting position. "Arms up," he commanded. In one fluid motion, her dress was removed and tossed to the floor. She sat before him in her black lace bra and tiny black panties. His eyes raked over her as if committing her body to memory. He pulled his t-shirt off hastily and unbuttoned his cargo shorts. She admired the hard planes of his chest and watched hungrily as he removed his shorts and boxers. He reached around and unhooked her bra before lightly pushing her back to remove her panties. Would it always be this good between them? The question was forgotten as Jason rolled her over on top of him and slowly linked their bodies together. They found their rhythm as he stroked her breasts, her hair, her face. Their kisses intensified, bodies colliding and finally collapsing with sweet release.

After relaxing in each other's arms for a time, they decided on a quick swim before dinner. Sam slipped into her new cherry red bikini and assessed herself in the full length mirror that hung on the bathroom door. When she tried it on at the department store, she felt sexy and daring, but now she just felt naked and longed for her conservative one piece. Jason assured her that she looked "hot," a word she would never use to describe herself, and pushed her out the door. They chose two deck chairs away from the other sunbathers, and no sooner had they laid their towels down than Jason shouted, "Last one in is a rotten egg," and cannonballed into the pool. Sam couldn't help laughing at his boyish behavior, but some of the older folks at the pool looked less than amused. She felt her cheeks flush as she realized all eyes were upon her standing at the pool's edge in her bright red bikini. Oh, who cares, she thought, and without further hesitation, cannonballed herself into the pool. She came up sputtering and wiped the water out of her eyes to find Jason doubled over with laughter. "I didn't really think you'd do it," he said once his laughter died down.

"It was either that or stand there while everyone stared at me." He gathered her in his arms, kissing her softly on the lips. Sam's eyes darted around, but no one seemed to be paying attention anymore. It felt good to be pressed up against him in the cool water; the last time they had been in the water together...

Jason must have been thinking the same thing. "Skinny dipping tonight?" he teased.

"No way, not with all these people around."

"None of these old folks will be here tonight at ten o'clock. It would just be you and me, baby." She couldn't be sure if he was joking or not. Knowing him, he would be game if she was.

"A secluded cove on Lake Charlevoix and a community pool are two very different things," she scolded him lightly. "We could get kicked out." She was speaking sensibly, but her body was warming with the possibility.

"I bet we could get away with it." She splashed him playfully and started to swim toward the opposite end of the pool. He overtook her in seconds, beating her to the pool's edge.

"We've scandalized the residents enough for one day," she said playfully. "It's time to get dried off and get ready for dinner."

Chapter 17

Elise and Ted picked them up an hour later, and they drove to a local Italian restaurant. In true "Italian" style, they were served fresh-from-the-oven breadsticks and heaping bowls of pasta. Sam and Jason drank a beer while her mom and Ted enjoyed a glass of red wine or two or three. Sam lost count as she felt Jason's hand gently caress her inner thigh under the red and white checked tablecloth. She was back in her tank dress with a fresh pair of panties on. She tried to focus on Elise's tales of various Delray residents, but Jason's hand tracing warm circles on her thigh was extremely distracting. He seemed to be enjoying himself immensely as he laughed at Ted's jokes and inserted comments whenever Elise paused to take a breath. Sam was feeling warmer by the second, and she was sure that her cheeks were rosy red by now.

"Are you ok, dear?" Elise asked. "You look flushed. Did you wear sunscreen today?"

Forty years old, and her mom still treated her like a child. "Yes, Mom, I wore sunscreen, but I'm not used to this heat yet." Her excuse sounded lame to her own ears. Jason just chuckled and continued to tantalize her under the table. At one point, she brushed his hand away, but he resumed his exploration a few minutes later. Finally, it was time to leave, and she shot him a warning look as they climbed into the back of Ted's Buick sedan. Jason was not to be deterred, and since it was dark when they left the restaurant, he felt free to continue his teasing on the drive home. After they said their goodbyes and were behind closed doors again, Sam feigned anger at Jason's behavior. "You are so bad!"

"I believe you meant to say, so good," he corrected, with emphasis on the word good.

She started to walk away, but he pulled her arm and twirled her back around. "It's your fault for wearing that damn dress. I couldn't help it when I knew what was underneath."

Sam reached her arms around his neck. "Thanks for loving me."

Jason kissed the end of her nose. "You're easy to love." And with that he pulled her into the bedroom.

The next day, they decided to divide and conquer. Jason would go golfing with Ted, and Sam would spend some quality time with her mom. Ted honked the horn on the golf cart promptly at nine a.m. Jason kissed her briefly and winked at her on his way out the door. "Don't worry, it'll be fun."

"Speak for yourself," she said grimly as he walked out to meet Ted.

Sam picked Elise up in the Mustang a few minutes later. They were going shopping and out to lunch, a typical ladies day out. Sam wished she could view it as fun, but it felt more like a chore. A psychologist would probably have a field day analyzing her relationship with Elise. It definitely changed after her dad died. It was almost as if he was the anchor that held Elise in place, and without him, she was floating aimlessly. Ted was a nice man, and her mother seemed happy enough, but Sam couldn't be sure who her mother had turned into. It was like she had adopted a role for herself that didn't quite fit. Sam recalled her saying years ago that she would never move to Florida with all the old folks; what did they do all day? Elise couldn't fathom the idea ten years ago, yet here she was, completely immersed in the Florida lifestyle. Sam attributed her mom's change of heart to meeting Ted. Sam was skeptical about their relationship at the beginning, but she couldn't deny that her mom did seem happy here. Maybe that's what love does; it makes you take risks and step outside your comfort zone. After all, isn't that exactly what she was doing with Jason? Maybe she and Elise weren't so different after all. She pushed her musings aside as they entered the parking lot of an outdoor shopping mall.

For the next two hours they went in and out of boutiques, chatting about nothing in particular. Sam bought another tank dress in a bright pink that she thought Jason might like. She smiled at a flashback of the previous night in the restaurant. She loved the way Jason flirted with her and made her feel sexy. She had a decent self-image, some days better than others, but he made her feel beautiful every day. Her added confidence made Sam slightly more daring with her clothing choices, showing a little cleavage and buying sexy lingerie. Brad seemed perfectly content with her minus the frills and lace, but she discovered that she enjoyed when Jason looked at her like he wanted to devour her. Yes, she definitely had it bad, or in his words, she had it good!

At lunchtime, they chose an outdoor café that sold sandwiches and cold drinks. The temperature hovered around 90 degrees but a gentle breeze made things bearable. Elise wore a large floppy hat, and Sam had on her Charlevoix baseball cap and sunglasses.

"That hat looks cute on you," Elise offered. "I thought you didn't like wearing hats."

"I didn't, actually. Brad didn't think I looked good in hats," she added and then instantly wished she could retract her statement.

"Really? Did he come out and say that?"

"Yes, he did once. I stopped wearing

them after that."

"Ahh, so I take it Jason likes you in hats."

"Yes, in fact, he picked it out for me."

"Jason seems like a very nice young man. I can tell you're smitten with him."

Her mom liked to use words like smitten. "I love him, Mom," she corrected.

Elise took a long sip of her lemonade and shifted forward in her chair. "Is it love or gratitude? Sometimes the two can get mixed up." She wore a neutral expression, but Sam wondered where she was going with this.

"I think I'm old enough to know what love is, Mom. I was married for a long time, remember?"

"No need to get angry, dear. I'm just saying that maybe you're grateful to Jason for bringing you back to life, so to speak."

Sam had certainly thought that herself, but hearing her mom say it cheapened things somehow. "Sure, I'm grateful to him for a lot of things, but I also love him. I love the person he is and the person I am with him."

"Do you see a future with him?" Elise took a big bite of her chicken salad sandwich, and Sam watched as a portion dribbled down her chin.

Sam wasn't sure how to answer the question. She was still concerned about them being in two different stages of life.

"I would like there to be one," she finally

answered. "I'm not exactly sure how things will work once he goes back to school."

"What does he have to say about that?"

"He says that every relationship takes work and we can make it work."

"Smart kid." She took another large bite of sandwich.

"He's not a kid, Mom, please don't call him that." Sam still bristled at any reference to their age gap.

"It's just a figure of speech, dear. No harm meant."

Sam sighed, "I know, sorry to snap at you."

Elise flapped her hand dismissively. "No need to apologize. I'm sure you've taken enough flak for being the 'older woman' and all."

Sam chuckled. "True, although, mostly from Jason's mom."

"I'm sure she's just looking out for her son. Parents do that, you know." She looked up at Sam pointedly. "We don't like it when our kids get hurt. It doesn't matter how old they are."

"Point taken." Sam tucked into her turkey reuben. Her mom backed off after that, but Sam pondered the conversation the entire way home. As they pulled into Elise's driveway, Sam thanked her for the outing.

"I enjoyed it too, sweetie." She smiled,

waved, and went inside, leaving Sam feeling strangely unsettled.

Since Jason was still out golfing, she decided to get some reading time in. She changed into yet another new bikini, this one in a bright flower print, grabbed her book and some sunscreen, and headed to the pool. There were only a few other sunbathers braving the heat, so she found a quiet chair and settled in. She tried concentrating on her novel, but her mom's words kept replaying in her mind. Was Elise worried she would get hurt? Was she just being a protective mother like Janet? Or was she voicing Sam's own concerns about their age gap? Sam shook her head to break the worry cycle. It was too gorgeous outside to get caught up in her own head. She opened her book and lost herself in the story until sometime later when she became vaguely aware of droplets of water hitting her forehead. She must have fallen asleep, and awakened to find Jason standing over her playfully flicking water droplets onto the top of her head. "Hey, sleepyhead," he teased. He was dripping wet, and she watched as water traveled in rivulets over his hard chest and down his muscular thighs to puddle around his feet.

"Hey, yourself," she said, smiling in return. "I must have fallen asleep reading."

"Obviously. I came out to join you, but you were sleeping, so I decided to take a dip first." He used a pool towel to dry his hair, which immediately and adorably sprang right back up. She sighed, realizing there was never a time when she hadn't been attracted to him.

"How was the golf outing?"

"Fun. Ted's a good guy. He beat me, but he lives on a golf course, so no surprise there. How was your shopping trip?"

"Not bad. I bought a new dress that you might get to see me in later." She winked at him suggestively.

"Good, because I'm taking you out tonight."

"Where are we going?" She loved when he made plans for them.

"Since I know you don't like surprises, I'll tell you. We're going on a dolphin dinner cruise."

"When did you have time to set that up?"

"I talked to Ted about it, and he drove me to the pier so I could sign us up. We got the last opening for the seven o'clock cruise."

"Jason, that sounds awesome. I've never been on one before."

"Me neither, but I thought it sounded romantic."

"It does." Sam was touched by his thoughtfulness. "What time do we have to leave?"

"We basically need to get dressed and go. Can you be ready in an hour?"

"Absolutely." She stood up and collected her things while he finished drying off and threw his towel into the poolside bin. She could already feel the anticipation building. She was excited that they would be alone tonight and on a sunset cruise, no less. Since Jason had just been in the pool, he left her to take a shower while he got dressed. Sam asked him to wait in the living room so she could make a grand entrance in her new dress. She took a quick shower but spent extra time styling her hair until it lay in soft waves around her face. Her face already held the glow of the sun, so she wore minimal makeup with a shimmery lip gloss. She slipped into her new dress and admired the hot pink color against her skin. She added a delicate necklace and earrings and slipped into a pair of neutral toned wedges. She stood back to survey her appearance and was quite pleased. She partially attributed her glow to the Florida sunshine, but the rest she attributed to him. Jason gave her this renewed energy, the stronger sense of self that she had been missing for some time. She smoothed down her dress and strolled out to the living room.

"Do you like?" She spun around in a slow circle in the middle of the room.

Jason let out a low whistle. "I don't just like, I love." He walked toward her and pulled her into his embrace. "Umm... you smell good too," he whispered seductively.

"Thanks." She looked into the brown pools of his eyes that were now hooded with desire. "Oh no, mister," she wagged her finger back and forth. "We don't want to be late."

"Where are we going again? Oh yeah, a dinner cruise." His feigned ignorance made her giggle girlishly.

"Come on, you." She grabbed his hand and pulled them toward the door. "There'll be time for other activities later."

Jason gave an exaggerated sigh of defeat and followed her out to the car. They drove with the top down on the short drive to the pier. As they cruised down the highway, Sam took in Jason's appearance. He wore a tailored pair of khaki shorts and a striped polo shirt. His boat shoes and aviators rounded out the look, casual and confident, just like him. She caught a whiff of his cologne, which was fresh and masculine, and admired his profile as he concentrated on driving. How did I get so lucky, she pondered. He could have any girl he wanted, but he chose me. She sighed contentedly as they pulled into the parking lot at the dock.

Once checked in, they had a short wait before boarding the cruiser. Sam glanced around at the other couples who would be joining them. The couples varied in age, but they all wore similar expressions, hopefulness, excitement, love? It appeared that she and Jason were the only couple with a big age gap, but at that moment, it didn't bother her. She was as much in love with him as the gray haired lady standing to her left seemed to be with her man. Sam watched as the lady leaned in and gave her husband (or boyfriend) a seductive smile and shared a private laugh. Jason noticed it too and pulled Sam closer to his side. Finally, it was time to board the boat, and they were immediately ushered into the main cabin where the dining room was. The captain's voice came over a speaker, urging everyone to get comfortable as dinner would be served shortly. A crewman guided Sam and Jason to a table for two next to a window and pulled out the chair for Sam. He assured them that a waiter would be out shortly to take their order. As soon as everyone was seated, the cruiser pulled away from shore. Onlookers waved as the boat slipped into the bay.

Jason reached for her hands across the table. "What do you think so far?"

A huge smile spread across her face. "I love it."

"I love you." His eyes seared into her, making her feel like they were the only two people on board.

"I love you too," she replied softly.

They ordered the seafood special, which seemed appropriate given the setting, and a glass of white wine. This didn't seem like a beer type of venue. "I would like to make a toast,"

Jason said, holding up his glass. "To the most beautiful woman in the world. You've captured my heart and my soul. I will always love you, Sam."

Jason's heartfelt words struck a chord in her, and she could feel the tears prick the corners of her eyes, threatening to spill over.

"That wasn't supposed to make you cry." Jason chuckled softly.

She dabbed her eyes with the linen napkin. "I'm sorry, I'm such a dork." She gathered herself together and raised her glass to him. "I would like to toast the man who brought me back to life. Thank you for everything you've done for me and just for being you. I love you, Jason."

He leaned across the table and lightly kissed her lips. They clinked glasses and took a deep sip of wine. Sam felt her body relax as she gazed out the window at the setting sun. They enjoyed their meal immensely and chatted comfortably as they ate. When the plates had all been cleared, the captain came back over the speaker. "We would like to invite everyone to explore the vessel; there are some awesome views from the upper deck. Please watch your step as you make your way around, and thank you for cruising with us."

Sam and Jason followed the other couples as they dispersed to the upper deck. They found a private corner and leaned against the railing.

Before long, someone spotted a pod of dolphins a short distance in front of the boat. It was thrilling to see them jump in and out of the water so gracefully. The setting sun provided a gorgeous background, the sky lit up with reds, oranges and yellows. Jason squeezed her closer against him, and she felt goose bumps rise on her forearms. It certainly wasn't cold, but the wind, combined with his closeness, gave her a chill. It had been a magical evening, and it wasn't over yet. A little while later, the cruiser pulled back into shore, and they thanked the captain and crewmen as they debarked. They held hands in contented silence as they walked back to the Mustang.

"What an awesome experience," Sam enthused on their drive back.

"It was, definitely," he answered distractedly.

"What's on your mind?" She was expecting playful Jason not ruminating Jason, especially after the great time they'd just had.

"I was thinking about having to go back to school and how much I'm going to miss you."

Sam sighed. "I've been trying not to think about that too much, but it's hard not to."

"I wish there was some way for me to commute instead of living on campus, but it would be kind of difficult."

"Living there makes the most sense, as much as I hate to admit it." Sam had turned this around in her head so many times that she was finally resigned to the idea. She couldn't see any way around it.

"I hate the thought of not being able to see you and touch you and hold you." He glanced over at her. "You have to promise me you'll come up and visit."

"I will," she assured him, mustering up a half smile. "As often as possible."

"Let's not talk about it for the next few days, ok? I just want to enjoy the time we have left here. Agreed?" He turned to her with the smile she knew and loved.

"Agreed." They pulled into the drive, and Jason came around to help her out of the car. He didn't let go of her hand as they entered the condo, and the minute the door was closed, he pushed her up against it. They began hastily shedding clothes, their breath coming in short bursts. The only light in the house came from the sliver of moonlight through the windowpanes. In seconds, they were naked, and in one swoop, Jason lifted her and carried her to the bedroom. She nuzzled into his neck, soaking up his fresh, masculine scent. The heat from his body instantly warmed her as they fell together in a mangled heap on the bed.

"I can't get enough of you," he whispered breathily in her ear. His hands ran up and down the length of her body as he gently rolled over on top of her. It was hard to see his expression in the dim light, but she didn't have to. She could feel the heat emanating off him as his hardness pressed against her. Oh God, how she would miss this.

"Kiss me," she demanded, and he promptly pressed his lips to hers. Their tongues met in desperation. She ran her hands up and down his back, feeling the muscles tighten beneath her fingers. She marveled at the way their bodies fit together so tightly, so perfectly. He entered her slowly at first and then quickly picked up the pace as she lifted her hips in response. Their breathing was labored, their skin damp with perspiration as they clung together, desperate for closer contact. Never before had their lovemaking held this much urgency; it was like they were trying to stamp this memory permanently on their brains. Sam gave herself with full abandon, reveling in his touch, his scent, his kisses. Jason's energy was relentless, his hands and lips never stopped moving until he gasped, "I'm going to explode."

She grabbed his hips, rocking harder against him, and that was all it took. They exploded together, releasing their combined passion, then glided back down softly, contentedly, still wrapped in each other's arms.

Chapter 18

True to their word, they didn't talk about school for their remaining three days in Florida. They used the time to play golf, swim, sunbathe, and visit with Ted and Elise. On the day of their departure, Elise insisted on making lunch, which they enjoyed on the patio. Ted engaged Jason in a lively discussion about golf while Sam and Elise cleared the dishes. While they were inside at the kitchen sink, Elise turned to Sam and took her daughter's hands in hers.

"Thank you so much for coming dear. It meant so much to me and Ted."

Sam hugged her mom tightly. "We enjoyed it too, Mom. Thanks for giving us a place to stay."

"Any time, and I mean that. I wish you and your sister would come down to visit more often."

It was the first time they'd mentioned Jaime since Sam had been there. "It's not as easy for her with the kids and the dog." Sam knew it was a flimsy excuse, but she didn't know what else to say. Jaime had remained quite stubborn on the topic of visiting her mom; she felt that Elise should be the one coming to visit them.

Elise waved her hand dismissively. "That's not the reason, and you know it. She's still mad at me for moving and marrying Ted."

Sam sighed, not wanting to admit that Elise was right. "Call her, Mom. Ask her to come down before school starts. When's the last time you called?"

"I called her when I found out you were coming. I thought it would be fun if both my girls were here at the same time."

"She never mentioned it to me."

"Oh well. You probably need to get ready to go; you don't want to miss your flight."

Sam made a mental note to talk to Jaime when she got home. She hated to see Elise looking so dejected, but she was right; it was time for them to leave. Ted and Jason walked in from the patio looking like best buddies. Sam and Elise instantly brightened up at the sight of them.

"Elise, thank you so much for your hospitality," Jason said warmly. "We had a great time."

"It was a pleasure to meet you, Jason. You take good care of my Sammy now." She hugged him as Jason glanced at Sam and winked.

"I promise to take good care of Sammy."

Sam just rolled her eyes at him. "Ok, enough of the love fest. We need to leave now."

They walked outside together, and Elise

waved until the Mustang was out of sight. Sam felt a tear prick her eye, but she stubbornly refused to let it fall. Jason reached over and squeezed her hand, not letting go until they reached the airport.

A few hours later, they landed in Detroit and followed the throng of passengers to the baggage claim area. Jason pushed his way through the crowd to retrieve their bags from the carousel before they made their way to the shuttle pick-up area. As they were waiting for a bus, Sam saw a young woman studying Jason intently. Jason was facing the other way, so he didn't notice. The woman was petite, with long, straight blonde hair and brilliant blue eyes. She was dressed in a tight-fitting pair of blue jeans and a cropped top that showed off her lean midriff. She had a polished, confident look about her, the kind of girl who was attractive and knew it. Sam was used to women ogling Jason even though he always seemed oblivious. Her worst nightmare started to come true when blondie advanced toward them.

"Jason? I thought it was you!" Blondie said, tapping him on the arm.

A look of confusion and then comprehension flashed across Jason's face. "Hi Rebecca," he replied simply.

Oh no, his college girlfriend, in the flesh. Sam shifted uncomfortably behind him, and he suddenly remembered she was standing there.

"Uh, Rebecca, this is Samantha." His discomfort was obvious as Rebecca gave Sam the once-over.

"Hi," she said dismissively and then turned her attention back to Jason. "How've you been?"

"Good, really good. How about you?"

"Ok, I guess. I just returned from visiting my sister. You remember Beth, right? She just had a baby girl."

Sam silently prayed that the shuttle would show up any minute to whisk her away from this uncomfortable scene.

"Sure, I remember Beth. How's Gary?"

The forced smile on Rebecca's face suddenly disappeared. "We broke up." A look of satisfaction crossed Jason's features, but he quickly regained his composure.

"That's too bad. Sam and I just got back from Florida; we had a great time."

Sam cursed under her breath. Please don't drag me into this, she thought angrily. Don't flaunt me in front of your ex-girlfriend like a trophy.

Rebecca glanced briefly in Sam's direction and then back at Jason. "Oh well, it was nice running into you. I need to go make a phone call. See you around."

"See you around," he replied quietly as she turned and walked away.

"Well, that was interesting," Sam said

once Rebecca was out of sight.

"Yeah, what are the chances of running into her here at this exact time."

"Apparently quite good. She's a pretty girl." Ok, why did she just say that?

"She's all right." Hmm, not the response Sam was looking for. She was hoping for something along the lines of "not as pretty as you."

"Why did you introduce me as Samantha? You never call me that."

"I don't know, it just came out that way."

He was obviously shaken up by the encounter, but Sam wasn't ready to let it go yet. She was still trying to read his reaction. "Did it upset you to see her?"

"Upset me? No, I don't think so. I was just surprised, that's all."

"Were you surprised that she broke up with Gary?"

"Not really. He wasn't the marrying type of guy anyway."

"Hmm… well, she seemed to be quite happy to run into you."

"Why do you say that?"

"She couldn't take her eyes off you, for one. She was staring at you long before she approached us." Ok, that may have been a bit of an exaggeration, but Sam was pretty worked up by now.

"Sam, stop this. I can see where you're

headed, and I want you to just stop."

"Why? Are you still attracted to her?"

"Oh my God, Sam. I just asked you to stop."

Sam felt the blood rushing to her head. His answers weren't comforting at all. She probably sounded like a jealous lunatic, but she had to get to the bottom of this. She had to know if Jason still harbored feelings for his ex-girlfriend.

"Why can't you just answer my questions? You keep deflecting them instead of giving me a straight answer."

The shuttle bus finally pulled up to the curb, and they found themselves surrounded by people pushing to get on board. "We'll finish this conversation in the car." Jason scowled at her as they boarded the bus. They rode in uncomfortable silence until they were deposited in the car park next to Jason's Jeep. He threw their bags in the back, jerked open the driver's door, and waited impatiently as Sam climbed in the passenger side.

As they exited the lot, Sam picked up where they left off. "I don't think it's wrong of me to ask questions, Jason. You obviously were in love with her not that long ago, and if she hadn't fallen for your roommate, you might still be together."

The vein in Jason's neck pulsed rapidly, and his fingers dug into the steering wheel so hard she thought they might leave permanent impressions. He looked like he was about to explode, and she realized she might have pushed him too far.

"What about Brad? If he hadn't died, we wouldn't be sitting here having this ridiculous conversation right now, would we?" He practically hissed at her, and she felt the blood drain from her face.

"Brad's dead. It's not like he's going to come strolling back into my life someday."

"That's not the point. The point is, we've both had past loves, there's no denying that. The key word here is past, not present. Yes, I loved Rebecca. Yes, I found her attractive, and maybe we'd still be together if she hadn't left me for Gary. But she did leave me, and Brad did die, and we're together now, right?" His eyes bored into hers, silently pleading with her to let it go.

"Yes," she said quietly. "I just…"

"You just thought that because I loved her once, she's still a threat to you. And I'm telling you that she's not. I'm not interested in reliving the past. I'm only interested in the present, and you are my present."

Sam felt herself start to relax. She still felt shaken, but Jason's words were starting to take hold, and the farther they drove away from *her*, the better she felt. She had to ask one more question, though. "Is it possible for you to run into her on campus or have a class with her?"

"Sure it's possible, but it's a pretty big campus, and we don't hang out in the same crowd anymore."

"Will you do me a favor please?"

"Anything."

"Please tell me if you run into her again. Don't keep it from me. I don't want any secrets between us."

"Ok, I promise." His voice had returned to normal, and his grip on the wheel loosened up some.

"Oh, and one more thing."

Jason sighed, clearly exasperated. "What else?"

"Don't ever introduce me as Samantha to your friends. It makes me sound old, and it's too formal. I'm your girlfriend, not your aunt."

"Agreed. I don't know why I did that. I'm sorry."

It was late by the time Jason pulled into her driveway, and Sam felt exhausted from the *Rebecca incident*. Jason carried her bag up to the house and waited while she unlocked the door and turned the lights on. They assessed each other for a few minutes before he cautiously put his arms around her. "I love you," he whispered. "Do you want me to stay?"

"I'm exhausted," Sam replied, catching the hurt that flashed in his eyes. "Why don't we get a good night's sleep and see each other tomorrow?"

Jason nodded in defeat and dropped his arms to his sides. "Ok. I'll see you tomorrow, then?"

She nodded. "See you then." She felt empty as he turned and closed the door behind him.

Sleep did not come easy that night. She tossed and turned, rehashing their conversation about Rebecca and Brad. The past and present blurred together in her mind. Jason's comment about them not being together if Brad hadn't died struck a chord in her. Of course he was right. She never would have looked twice at Jason if Brad were alive. Sure, she may have acknowledged his good looks, but that's all she would have done. She never would have imagined herself with anyone else, let alone someone so young. Who was she kidding? Rebecca probably found it pathetic; a middle-aged lady trying to hold on to a hot young guy like Jason. Was she trying to recapture her youth? Was it gratitude, as Elise had alluded to? What would have happened if Jason had been alone when he ran into Rebecca? Would they have gone for coffee, talked, re-kindled their failed romance? Would Jason have discovered that he had a lot more in common with Rebecca than with a widowed librarian? How could she expect them to stay together once he returned to school? There would be parties and football games and bar nights and… her mind whirled on and on. What if he took the internship in Denver? How often would she see him then? Janet's words came flooding back to her: "Surely you want what's best for him." If Sam stayed in his life, he might turn down the internship, and then what? Would he resent her for it? Wasn't it selfish of her to ask him to stay?

At the same time, Jason lay in bed with his own troubled thoughts. Why doesn't she believe that I love her? What more can I do or say to make her believe me? I haven't so much as glanced at another woman since we've been together, nor do I have the desire to. Why can't she see what I see when I look at her? A gorgeous, sexy, loving, intelligent woman who any man would be proud to be with. Sure, running into Rebecca at the airport caught me off guard, but that was all there was to it. She looked good, but I'm not attracted to her anymore. Besides, why would I take her back after what she did to me?

He lay in the dark and stared up at the ceiling, recalling the awesome time they'd had in Florida. The cruise, the lovemaking, the closeness. Here he was dreaming about a future with Sam, but she couldn't seem to get over the past. They were so good together, in so many ways. Why couldn't she see that? He thought they were finally moving forward, but tonight felt like a giant step back. Soon he would be leaving for school. Would she stay with him or use it as an excuse to slip away?

Finally, exhaustion took over, and they both drifted off into a restless sleep.

Chapter 19

The following morning, after choking down breakfast, Sam dialed Jaime's number. It was only nine o'clock, but she knew Jaime would be up with the kids. "Hey, sis," Jaime answered cheerfully. "How was your trip?"

"Good and not so good," she answered, still feeling groggy after the rough night she'd had.

"Spill it," her sister said.

Sam recounted the highlights, including her shopping trip with Elise and the dolphin cruise. She concluded with the story of their run-in with Rebecca at the airport.

"Ah-ha, the ex-girlfriend resurfaces. I hate when that happens." Jaime was trying to make light of the situation, but Sam wasn't in a jovial mood. She ignored her sister and continued on with her list of concerns until Jaime interrupted.

"Are you done yet? It sounds like you need to sit down and have a heart-to-heart with him. Lay all your cards on the table."

"I feel like I've already done that," Sam replied. "He's probably beyond tired of hearing it."

"I don't know what else to tell you. Life has a way of working itself out. Whatever is meant to be will be. You can choose to go along for the ride or hop off."

Sam felt her heart wrench at the thought of not having Jason in her life. "I love him, James."

"I know you do. Listen, I hate to do this to you, but I'm expecting my book club ladies to ring the doorbell any second. Can we talk more later?"

"Sure."

"Talk to him, Sam."

"I will." Sam dialed Jason's number after she hung up with Jaime. She hated the way they left things last night, and she was desperate to clear the air. His phone went right to voicemail, so she left a brief message asking him to call her. She tried to remember if he had anything scheduled today, but couldn't think of anything. Sam busied herself by unpacking and doing some laundry. Jason still hadn't called by eleven o'clock, so she tried his number again. When she heard his voicemail message, she disconnected the phone. Deciding he must be mowing someone's lawn, she grabbed her book and went outside to read for a while. Noon came and went, and still no Jason. She made herself a ham sandwich and ate it outside on the deck. It was very unlike him not to call or text her, and she started to have a sick feeling in her gut. Finally, around two o'clock, she couldn't take it anymore; she decided to walk across the street and knock on the door. The worst thing that could happen would be Janet giving her the cold shoulder, and that she could handle. As she approached Jason's house, she noticed his neighbor was outside, but she had no idea what the elderly woman's name was. Sam walked calmly up the Grant's driveway as the woman eyed her suspiciously from her front porch rocker. "Can I help you with something?" called out the elderly neighbor.

"No, I was just coming over to talk to Jason."

The woman looked her up and down and said, "He's not home. His family is at their summer cottage in Charlevoix this weekend."

Sam tried to trample the fear that creeped up the back of her spine. "I just saw Jason last night, so maybe you're referring to his parents?"

"No, no, his parents left yesterday, but Jason went peeling out of here this morning to join them."

Sam tried to hide her confusion. "Did you talk to him this morning?" Maybe the woman just assumed he was going Up North.

"Yes. I came out to get the newspaper, and he was in the driveway loading a suitcase in his car. Said he was going up to Charlevoix for a few days and asked me to collect their mail."

Sam was dumbfounded. Why would he

leave without telling her, and why was he in such a hurry? "Ok, thanks, I'll just talk to him when he gets back, then." She turned around to walk away, but the woman wasn't done with her yet.

"Are you a friend of the family or just Jason?"

Sam didn't think it was any of her business, but she chose the safest response. "A friend of the family," she replied with a tight-lipped smile. "Have a good day." She walked back to her house as quickly as possible before the nosy neighbor could ask any more questions. She could not understand why Jason would leave without telling her. He was leaving for Central the following weekend, and she had hoped they would spend the entire week together. She thought that's what he wanted too. She decided to try his cell one more time, and once again it went right to voicemail. This time she left a longer message explaining that she'd found out from a neighbor that he had gone Up North. She added that she really wanted to talk to him and to please call as soon as possible. Sam knew that if she sat at home the rest of the day, all she would do was worry, so she decided to go out and get some exercise. She took a long bike ride and worked up a good sweat. When she got back, she showered, dressed and went out to pick up a pizza for dinner. She sat in her empty kitchen eating pizza and gazing forlornly out the window. The ticking of the clock seemed especially loud to her, and she kept glancing at her phone, willing it to ring. Her fear turned to anger as the sun began to set. "How rude that he can't take one minute out to call or text me," she muttered aloud. She was practicing what she would say to him when suddenly the phone rang. She sighed in disappointment when the caller id read unavailable. Deciding that it was probably a sales call, she swiped ignore on her phone. A minute later her phone rang again, the word unavailable glaring at her. This time, Sam decided to pick it up with the intention of getting rid of the caller as soon as possible. "Hello," she answered impatiently.

"Hey, Sam," Jason replied, sounding very tired and very far away.

"Hey. I've been trying to call you all day. What's going on?" Now that she was finally talking to him, she didn't have the heart to be angry.

"I know, I'm sorry about that. I had to leave in a hurry this morning, and I forgot my phone charger. My phone died hours ago."

That still didn't explain why he left, but before Sam could ask a follow-up question he continued.

"My dad's in the hospital Sam. He had a minor heart attack."

"Oh my God. What happened, how…?"

"I guess he was on the golf course with his buddies, and he just collapsed. My mom called me in a panic this morning and asked me to get here right away. I didn't even think about grabbing my phone charger."

"Of course not. How is he now?"

"Stable. They're monitoring his vitals, and the doc wants to keep him here for a couple more days."

"I'm so sorry, Jason. If you would have called me this morning, I would have gone with you."

"I know, but it was so early I didn't want to wake you. I just grabbed a change of clothes and flew out the door."

"How's your mom doing?"

"She was a wreck when I first got here, but she's calmed down now. The doc said it was a minor heart attack, but Dad needs to change his diet and start on some medication. It could have been a lot worse, I guess."

Sam let out the breath she had been holding and tried to ease the tension in her shoulders. "I was really worried about you," she admitted. "I even went over to your house, but the neighbor lady stopped me before I got to the door."

Jason chuckled softly. "Marie? She's a little odd, but she's good about watching our house when we're gone."

"Well, that's for sure. She glared at me

like I was about to rob the place!"

"Sam, I have to go. My mom's coming down the hall with the doctor. I'll call you later ok? I love you."

"I love you too," she answered, but he was already gone.

Jason stayed in Charlevoix for two more days and nights while his dad was in the hospital. He called Sam a few more times, but he had to use his mom's phone, so they didn't talk for long. She didn't realize exactly how much she missed him until he showed up at her door on Wednesday morning holding a bouquet of pink roses in one hand.

She hurled herself into his arms, flowers and all, as he pulled her in close. She breathed in his fresh scent and instantly felt relaxed. His grin stretched from ear to ear as he set the flowers on the counter to give her a proper greeting. "I missed you so much," he said in between kisses.

"I bet I missed you more," she teased, sliding her arms up around his neck. He leaned his forehead against hers and kissed the tip of her nose.

She reveled in the feel of his large masculine hands rubbing up and down her back and his broad chest pressing against her breasts. It felt like forever ago that she'd last been in his arms, and she wasn't about to let him go. He placed soft kisses on her cheek and trailed down to her neck, where his warm breath caused her to sigh with pleasure. He dipped his head down further to kiss the little bit of cleavage that was exposed above her scoop neck tee shirt as she pulled her fingers through his hair. She melted into him, and luckily his arms were holding her up, or she might have fallen over.

"Maybe we should get the flowers in some water," he breathed huskily in her ear.

"The flowers can wait, but I can't," she whispered back. Her words seemed to ignite something in him, and the next thing she knew she was being lifted up onto the kitchen counter. Jason's eyes were hooded with desire as he instructed her to lift up her arms. In one swoop, her t-shirt was off and tossed to the floor. His eyes widened at the sight of her purple see-through bra, her nipples clearly outlined through the material. He brought his lips up to hers while his hands travelled beneath her skirt. Sam's body was on fire for him; she quivered at every touch, every breath, every kiss. He broke away to pull her skirt up around her waist and whistled at the sight of her matching purple see-through panties. "You're killing me here," he said huskily.

He dipped his head down and placed tender kisses along the insides of her thighs, darting his tongue out to trace a line up one thigh and down the other. Through her fog of desire, Sam registered that he was still fully clothed, and she swelled with the sudden urge to rip his clothes off. "You need to take something off," she demanded.

"Ok, ok, bossy pants," he teased and stepped back from her to remove his shirt and shorts.

Wow, she thought, taking him in. I will never get over the awesomeness of this man's body. The hard planes of his chest were now tanned a coppery brown from their trip to Florida. His tousled hair, shimmery brown eyes, and brilliant smile made the package complete. Not to mention his tight buns and muscular thighs.

"Better?"

"Much."

He picked her up off the counter, cradled her in his arms, and carried her to the living room couch. She lifted her hips so he could pull her skirt off, and then he stretched out beside her. They lay together, gazing into each other's eyes, his hands stroking up and down her body. Sam felt the anticipation building inside her as she warmed beneath his hands.

"I want you, Sam," he sighed, dipping his hand inside her panties.

"I want you too," she breathed as he bent down to kiss her lips. She turned on her side and ran a finger down his chest, over his abs, and into his boxers, causing him to gasp at the contact. They continued exploring each other as if it were the first time, nibbling, licking, touching, flicking until they were burning up inside. They hastily removed the rest of their clothes and joined together, Jason's hands on either side of her face, eyes locked on hers as they found sweet release and collapsed, spent and sated on her living room couch.

Chapter 20

The dreaded day had finally arrived, and the weather matched Sam's mood, dark and dreary. Jason's Jeep was packed to the hilt with his belongings and various supplies he would need for his apartment. They'd decided ahead of time that Sam wouldn't accompany him so she wouldn't have to drive home alone. Better to say their goodbyes here, in her kitchen on this ugly Saturday morning.

"So let's synchronize our calendars one more time," Jason said with forced cheerfulness.

Sam tried desperately to keep herself together while choking out words around the lump in her throat. "I'm driving up the third weekend in September, and you're coming home the third weekend in October."

"Don't forget about Thanksgiving and Christmas breaks."

She nodded. "I know," she mumbled.

"And we can call each other whenever we want except during your school hours. Not to mention texting, emailing, and face time. "

Jason's positive attitude was not helping her this time. It wouldn't be the same without him there every day to talk to, see, and touch.

She felt an empty hole inside that threatened to swallow her up. He pulled her into his arms and hugged her so tightly it hurt. The physical pain was nothing compared to the ache in her chest. All morning long, she had been telling herself not to cry, but she felt the first hot, salty tear slide down her cheek and onto his shirt. Jason pulled away from her and wiped the tears gently from her face. "Please don't do this. I can't stand to see you this upset."

"I know, I'm sorry," she muttered. "It's just hard because we've been seeing each other just about every day, and now..."

"Now we're going to be apart for short periods of time. It's hard for me to think about too, but this is my last year, and then we can be together as much as we want."

One year sounded like a lifetime to Sam, but she didn't dare say it. She lifted up on her toes to kiss him lightly. "I had a wonderful summer, the best I've had in a long, long time."

"Me too, but don't make it sound like it's our last."

She rubbed her finger over the frown lines on his brow. "I didn't mean for it to sound like that. I just wanted you to know how much this summer meant to me. How much you mean to me."

His mouth turned up at the corners. "I love you so much, Sam. You mean everything to me."

They clung to each other for a few more minutes in silence until they were interrupted by the kitchen clock chiming ten. "I should go," he whispered.

She nodded and walked him to the back door. "Call me after you get settled."

"I will. What are you going to do today?"

"I'll probably call Jaime and see about meeting her for lunch."

"Good, I don't want you to sit here alone all day."

"Don't worry about me. I'm used to being alone." She said it matter-of-factly but realized it probably made Jason feel worse.

"You're not alone anymore, Sam. This is only temporary."

"I know. I love you. Now get going." She pretended to shoo him out the door.

He gave her a sexy grin, winked at her, and said, "See you then."

"See you then," she whispered and closed the door softly behind him.

Sam drifted through the next few days in a fog. She found herself unable to concentrate on anything for very long. Even her favorite pastime, reading, wasn't satisfying. The only thing that gave her temporary relief was exercise, that and the phone calls, texts, and emails that arrived in a steady stream. The empty feeling in her chest was reminiscent of the early days when she'd grieved for Brad, which brought back uninvited memories of his death. Her favorite time became nine o'clock at night, when she and Jason would talk for an hour or so before she went to sleep.

Sam was quite relieved when Labor Day passed and it was time to go back to work. She woke up early that Tuesday and arrived at Brandon Elementary an hour before the students did. She couldn't wait to delve back into her work at the library and was anxious to reconnect with the teachers that she hadn't seen all summer. Of course, Leslie was there too, and they shared a coffee in the lounge before the bell rang. Leslie didn't ask about Jason, and Sam was glad; she didn't want other staff members overhearing and bombarding her with questions. There was one staff member in particular whom she wanted to avoid, Mark Gibson, the physical education teacher. Mark was a divorced father of two who had flirted with her shamelessly over the past few years. He was a good-looking, forty-something-year-old man, but she hadn't wanted to get involved with a co-worker then, and she certainly had no interest now. He had asked her out at the end of the last school year, but she'd pretended she hadn't heard him and walked away. She spent the first school day organizing and rearranging library materials in preparation for the classroom visits that would occur later in the week. Various staff members poked their heads in to say hello, but for the most part, she was left alone. The day passed quickly, and before she knew it, the last bell rang. She headed to the teacher's lounge to find Leslie and instead bumped right into Mark.

"Hey Samantha, how's it going?" He smiled down at her, a flicker of interest gleaming in his eyes. To an outsider it would appear as though he was just being friendly, but Sam knew he had other intentions.

"Doing well, how about you Mark?" she responded casually.

"Real good, real good. How was your summer? I was hoping to see you at a couple of the teacher get-togethers, but no such luck."

"Yeah, I was pretty busy this summer." She didn't elaborate as he looked at her expectantly.

"Well, maybe we can get together for coffee or something after school one day."

Before she had a chance to reply, Leslie walked in. Saved! "Hey Mark," Leslie said, glancing between the two of them. "I'm surprised you're still here." She laughed loudly, causing his face to redden with embarrassment. Mark was known to leave right after the final bell rang. The other teachers teased him mercilessly about not having any lesson plans to write; it was just gym class, after all. It irked him to no end. He just sneered at her and walked out.

"Thank you," Sam exhaled loudly. "You saved the day."

"Oh, he won't give up that easily. He was quizzing me about you at the summer picnic. He kept asking if you were seeing someone."

"Really?" Sam couldn't believe the gall. If he wanted to know, why didn't he just ask her. "What did you tell him?"

"I didn't know about Jason at the time, so I said you were still single. Don't worry, I didn't encourage him, though. I said that you were perfectly content with your life the way it is."

"Thanks, Les. What would I do without you?"

"How's it going with Jason, by the way?"

"He went back to school on Saturday. I miss him." Sam realized how funny it sounded to say that her boyfriend went back to school. She waited uncomfortably for Leslie to say something.

"Is he really worth waiting for, Sam? I'm sorry, but you could have your pick of men..."

Sam cut her off angrily. "Men like Mark Gibson? No thank you. The guy gives me the creeps."

"Some people would say it's creepy that a college kid went after a middle-aged woman."

Sam could not believe her ears, and this was supposed to be her best friend! She felt the anger well up inside her until she was about to explode. She didn't want to cause a scene at work, so she gathered her strength and marched past Leslie to the door. Before she opened it, she turned and spewed, "I should have known you would never understand. Don't ever speak to me about Jason again, do you hear me? Never again." She slammed the door on her way out and huffed back to the library to collect her purse. She was shaking as she left the building and stomped through the parking lot to her car. If it wasn't bad enough already, Mark was there, leaning casually against her car door, waiting for her.

"What do you want, Mark?" She was done being polite. The guy was seriously getting on her nerves.

"I want to know why you won't give me the time of day."

How to answer that? She could think of a dozen reasons but none that he would enjoy hearing.

"Mark, you're a fine person, but I'm not interested in dating you. I'm sorry."

"Is it because we work together? I can be discreet."

Her frustration was rising again as she realized she wasn't going to fend him off that easily. "No, it's not that. It's because I'm seeing someone. Now kindly move aside so I can leave, please."

"Whoever he is, he's a lucky guy," Mark conceded, and when she didn't respond, he turned and walked away.

Sam used the drive home to breathe deeply and restore her calm as much as possible. What a hellish end to her day. If only Jason were home waiting for her. Her eyes welled up just as her cell phone buzzed in her purse. She was at a red light, so she took the phone out and sighed with relief at the sight of Jason's name on the screen. "Hello," she answered shakily as the light turned green.

"What's wrong?" he asked instantly.

His voice caused the stress of the day to come bubbling out of her, and she burst into tears.

"Sam, if you're driving right now, please pull over."

Sam did as he suggested and pulled into a drugstore parking lot. She found a space in an empty row and parked the car. She regained her composure and said, "I'm parked now."

"Good. Now what's wrong, what happened?" His concern flowed through the phone and seeped into her.

She relayed her conversations with Leslie and Mark, relieved to get it off her chest. Jason listened patiently until she was finished. "That bastard better not bother you again," he hissed. "I can't believe the nerve of that guy."

She could hear the jealousy in his voice and rushed to reassure him. "I don't think he'll bother me anymore. Now that he knows I'm taken, he'll probably back off."

Jason huffed, and part of her was flattered that he felt so jealous. Up until now, he had no one to be jealous of, other than Brad's ghost. "What about Leslie? Do you think you'll still be friends?"

Sam honestly wasn't sure. Leslie was entitled to her opinion, but her words stung. "I don't know. Friends are supposed to support you not criticize you."

"I know, but maybe you should talk to her, Sam. I'd hate to see you lose a friend because of me."

"I'll think about it, but right now I'm too angry to talk. I'll wait until I cool off some."

"Good idea. I'm so sorry you had a bad day. I wish I were there to hold you right now."

"Just the sound of your voice helps," she sighed.

"Maybe we should try to get together before the third weekend of September. I don't think I can wait that long."

Sam smiled for the first time in the past couple of hours. "Don't worry about me, Jason. I just had a bad day, that's all. Everything will be better tomorrow." She didn't want to distract him from his studies so soon after he had left for school. "I can wait."

"Well, maybe I can't," he said, chuckling gruffly. Her emotional outburst had made him emotional too.

Before she could respond, she heard a guy's voice (presumably his roommate) in the background asking Jason if he was ready to go shoot some hoops. "We can talk more later; it sounds like someone's waiting for you."

"It's just Max, he can wait. I love you Sam."

"I love you too. Call me later."

"Count on it." And Sam knew she could.

Chapter 21

The next morning, as Sam was sorting through some new library books, Leslie poked her head in the door. "Can I talk to you for a minute?" she asked timidly.

"Ok," Sam said, motioning her in.

"I'm really sorry about yesterday. I don't know what came over me. Please don't hate me."

Sincerity and concern were etched on Leslie's face. Sam let her guard down and gave her friend a half-smile. "I don't hate you, but I wasn't very happy about what you said. Jason is a wonderful person, and there's nothing creepy about our relationship."

"I know, I believe you. I know you would never be with someone who wasn't a good person. I just worry about you."

"Because of Brad."

"Yes."

"Instead of worrying about me, try being happy for me. I'm happy for the first time in a very, very long time."

"I can see that, and I promise to keep my big mouth shut from now on." Leslie made the elaborate motion of zipping her lips shut, coaxing a giggle out of Sam. The first bell rang, so they agreed to talk more at lunchtime. Sam was glad to get through the rest of the week without running into Mark. She caught glimpses of him in the halls on occasion, but he seemed to be avoiding her too, which suited Sam just fine. The first week of school sailed by, and she faced her first weekend without Jason. They talked on the phone regularly, and he sent her sweet texts throughout the day, but it wasn't satisfying. She loved the sound of his voice but missed being able to look in his golden brown eyes while they were talking. She missed his arms around her and his wide smile. When she went to bed at night, she found herself hugging a pillow as a replacement for him until she finally drifted off to sleep. When they talked on Saturday afternoon, he mentioned that he and his friends were going to a bar that evening. She tried to squash her feelings of trepidation, but he knew her too well, so she finally relayed her concerns.

"You have nothing to worry about," Jason assured her.

"I beg to differ. There will be plenty of girls there who are looking for a big, strapping, guy like you."

He cracked up at her description but then turned serious. "Nobody could steal my heart away from you."

Sam melted in her chair. "Smooth talker.

You always know the right thing to say."

"I mean it, Sam. I'm not looking for anyone else. My friends on the other hand…"

"That's exactly what I'm afraid of. Girls tend to flock together and…"

"You have a very active imagination, you know that?" He was half teasing, half serious. "You really should write a book someday."

"Maybe I will. I could write a romance novel and call it 'My Strapping Stud.'" They both laughed at this, but before she knew it, Jason said he had to go.

"I'll call you before bed," he promised, blowing her a kiss through the phone.

"I love you," they said simultaneously, and Sam hung up smiling.

The next couple of weeks went by rather quickly, and finally Sam was heading up to Mt. Pleasant for the weekend. They made arrangements to meet at a Chili's restaurant where they would have dinner with Max. After dinner, Max was driving to Gladwin to spend the weekend with his parents so Jason and Sam could have the apartment to themselves. Sam was still wearing the royal blue wrap dress and black pumps that she'd worn to work that day. She'd planned on changing, but Jason had asked her not to; he'd mentioned something about taking her dancing later. She wasn't sure what he had cooked up; she only knew that she couldn't wait to see him. Her heart pumped double time when she pulled into the Chili's parking lot a couple of hours later. She sent Jason a text letting him know she had arrived, and the next thing she knew he was walking toward her, arms outstretched, and then drawing her into a bone-crushing hug. She let herself be enveloped in his arms and breathed in his masculine scent.

"Oh, I missed you so much," he said, stepping back to take her in. His eyes appraised her hungrily, and she felt the familiar flutter in her stomach.

"I missed you more," she said, smiling up at him. He took her hand in his and led her into the restaurant.

"Max is waiting at our table," he explained almost apologetically.

She was so happy to be back in Jason's presence that she didn't mind having to share his company for a while. She hoped it was a short while, though! Max stood up as they approached and gave her a bright, boyish smile. "Well, it's nice to finally meet you," he said extending his hand to shake hers. "Jason hasn't stopped talking about you these past few weeks."

Jason slid into the booth, pulling Sam in next to him. She was certain her smile was just as wide as Jason's. "It's very nice to meet you too. Jason's told me a lot about you, as well." Sam took a liking to Max right away. She could tell that he was warm and sincere and seemed to have a genuine affection for his roommate. They teased and joked with each other throughout dinner, and Sam felt relaxed and comfortable as they enjoyed their meals and a few beers.

"I hope we're not kicking you out this weekend."

"Not at all," Max said with a grin. "I had planned to be away this weekend anyway, and now you can keep my boy Jason company."

Jason squeezed her knee under the table, and she felt the warmth of his hand travel up her body. They were pressed close together in the booth, and her nerve endings tingled with anticipation. "I'm sure we'll find a way to keep busy," Jason teased, squeezing her knee once again. Sam felt her cheeks flush as she swatted Jason's arm playfully.

Finally, they paid the bill and stood up to leave. "It was really nice meeting you, Sam," Max said. "I hope to see you again some time."

"You too," she said and meant it. Sam and Jason held hands as they walked toward her Corvette, which she had driven purposely for him. He didn't bother to suppress a big grin as she handed over the keys.

"So, what is this about going dancing?" she asked a few minutes later. Jason had been concentrating on the road ahead but finally glanced her way. The look in his eyes made her stomach flip again. She could see the intent there and found his desire intoxicating.

"We've never danced together before." His voice sounded gruff. "I want to slow dance with you."

Sam swallowed the lump in her throat. "I'd like that," she managed as they pulled into the parking lot of his apartment complex. He pulled the Vette up to a single garage door in a line of many, hopped out, and punched a code in a box next to the door. The door lifted, and he pulled the Vette safely inside. He came around to open her door, offering his hand for assistance. She loved the feel of his large, warm hand enveloping her small one. He then popped the trunk and extracted her bag from inside. She followed him in silence through an entrance way and up a flight of stairs until they stopped in front of a door marked #223. She felt her heart race as Jason inserted a key into the lock and turned the door knob. She couldn't tear her eyes away from him as they entered the apartment and he set her bag down.

She stood in the middle of a very small living room while Jason went over to a table that held an iPod docking station and a set of speakers. The only light in the room came from a small table lamp next to a well-worn blue couch. She slipped her coat off and laid it across a matching blue lazy boy chair as Jason flipped through the iPod to select a song. They hadn't spoken at all, but the air was charged between them. Sam swallowed nervously and tried to keep her heartbeat steady. Jason finally found the song he was looking for, and the sweet sound of Faith Hill's voice came over the speakers. Sam recognized the song instantly and recalled telling Jason that it was one of her favorites. The sexy melody of *Let's Make Love*, sung by Faith and her husband Tim McGraw, filled the living room. When Sam and Jason were first getting to know each other, they had discovered a shared love of country music. Jason reached her in two steps and pulled her into his arms.

"Is this where we're dancing?" she giggled.

"Mmm-hmm," he replied, nestling his mouth in the hollow of her neck.

Sam's temperature rose a few degrees as she pressed closer to him. Jason's hands were clasped together at the small of her back, and hers were clasped tightly around his neck. They swayed back and forth in time to the music and turned in a slow circle on the makeshift dance floor.

"This is nice," she whispered, sinking into him.

"Mmm-hmm," he said again.

Sam wasn't sure if it was the beer she'd had at dinner or the music or the fact that they hadn't seen each other for three weeks. Whatever the reason, she found dancing with him to be extremely sensual and romantic. She let the music take over and focused on the warmth of his hands against her back, the way their hips pressed together, the rustle of her dress as they spun around, his hot breath on her neck. The song ended way too soon, and then Rascal Flatts kicked in with another of her favorites – *I Melt*.

Jason pulled away from her slightly and gazed at her with adoring eyes. "I knew dancing with you would feel this way."

She gazed back with equal adoration. His hands moved around to the front of her waist where the wrap dress was tied in a neat bow. Without breaking eye contact, he slowly and carefully untied it, letting the dress fall open. Sam watched as his eyes took in her matching royal blue push up bra and panties. Her breath caught as he trailed a finger up her rib cage to the curve of her breasts peeking over the edge of her bra. He bent his head down and placed a series of warm, gentle kisses where his hand had been. She buried her hands in his thick, soft hair and massaged his scalp as he continued to graze her breasts with kisses. His hands encircled her waist and pulled her closer. Sam trailed her fingertips down his muscled forearms to land at his hips. Jason was wearing a light blue oxford shirt, which she untucked from his jeans. He grinned at her as she unfastened the buttons somewhat hastily. "There's no way I'm standing here naked while you're fully dressed," she explained in response.

His deep chuckle filled the room. "That does seem to happen a lot, doesn't it?"

She just smiled as she shoved the shirt off his shoulders and reached down to his belt buckle. Rascal Flatts continued to serenade them as they removed the rest of their clothes. Once they were naked, they stood motionless for a few beats until Jason took her hand and led her to his bedroom. The window blinds were still open, and the orange glow from the sunset provided the perfect mood lighting. Sam noticed that Jason's bedside table held a framed picture of her that he had taken in Florida the night of their dinner cruise. In the picture, she was smiling directly at the camera, and happiness radiated from her. They tumbled onto Jason's twin size bed and began caressing each other softly, kissing and whispering as the sun went down. Jason traced the outline of her face, his gaze intense and heated as Sam ran a finger down the middle of his chest. She noticed the flex of his muscles and sharp intake of breath as she dipped lower. They teased and tickled and licked and nibbled until urgency overcame them. When their hunger and need finally found release, it was all-consuming and delicious.

As their breathing slowed and they curled into each other's arms, one word floated into

Sam's mind — home. With Jason, she was home.

Sam jolted awake a few hours later, naked and cold. Jason was still wrapped up in the blankets, breathing rhythmically. She slowly moved off the bed and padded out to the living room where she had left her overnight bag. The table lamp still burned, allowing her to see inside her bag to retrieve some pajamas. She was parched and felt the beginnings of a headache at her temples, probably due to the beers she'd had at dinner. She scolded herself for not drinking water before bed as she quickly slipped into her tank top and pajama bottoms. Sam found a plastic cup in the kitchen cupboard and filled it with water from the tap, hoping that she wouldn't wake Jason. Next, she padded down the hall to the bathroom in search of something for her headache. She slipped inside, not bothering to close the door all the way, and perused the counter for an aspirin bottle — nothing. A mirrored cabinet hung above the sink, but she hesitated before opening it. Her persistent headache made the decision for her, and she pulled open the door. A value sized box of condoms practically jumped out at her, and she stepped back in surprise. A million thoughts ran through her mind as she stood there, frozen on the spot.

"Those belong to Max," Jason stated matter-of-factly.

She turned around slowly to read his

expression, which was neutral and relaxed. Sam was on the pill, so birth control had never been an issue for them. She'd been on the pill while Brad was alive and had stayed on it out of habit.

"I wasn't snooping. I came in here to find some aspirin for my headache."

Jason moved in front of her and shifted things around in the cabinet until he came up with a bottle of Tylenol.

"Did I wake you?" she asked as she poured out a couple of tablets and swallowed them down.

"No, I turned over and realized you weren't there, so I came to investigate."

"Does Max have a lot of girls over?" She tried to sound casual but knew that Jason could see right through her.

"Not a lot, no. He just likes to be prepared." Jason sighed and gathered her in his arms. "Don't worry, Sam. We don't have a parade of girls coming in and out of our apartment. Max had a girl over a few nights ago, and I just stayed out of their way."

Sam conjured up an image of Max and Jason out at the bar the other night. Max was good looking in his own right, although not as hot as Jason. She recalled his flop of blonde hair and sparkling blue eyes. Max was a few inches shorter than Jason, with a broad chest and muscular arms. In her college days, she probably would have fallen for either one of them. For that matter, she was well beyond her school years and had still fallen for a college guy — go figure.

"Sam, what are you thinking?"

"Sorry, I zoned out for a minute. My head is really pounding right now."

"Let's go lay back down." She let him lead her back to bed and tuck her in tight beside him.

They held hands in the dark and were silent for a few minutes. "I promised not to hurt you, and I won't." His tone was strong and soothing.

"I know that," she whispered. "It's just hard for me sometimes when we're apart..."

"And you don't always know what I'm doing."

"Exactly."

"Then I'll tell you what I'm doing. I'm going to class and daydreaming about you. I'm counting down the days, the hours, the minutes until I can be with you again. I'm staring at your picture and remembering all of the great times we had this summer. I'm bragging about you to my friends..."

"Ok, ok, I get it." She laughed and leaned her head on his shoulder.

"What about you? How do I know what you're doing at home?"

"You know because we talk or text ten times a day! In between that, I'm thinking about you, missing you, and wanting you."

He gave her a squeeze, and she could sense his smile in the dark. "I have plans for us tomorrow."

"Of course you do." She felt her body relax further into the bed.

"I'm going to show you around campus and take you out to lunch and…"

Sam cut him off with a deep kiss as she rolled over on top of him. "I have plans for you too," she giggled. They made love slowly and tenderly this time, whispering promises in the dark.

The next morning, Jason made them a breakfast of scrambled eggs and toast. "Don't get used to it," he teased. "This is about the extent of my cooking prowess."

Sam was famished and polished off the meal with her usual relish. "These are the best scrambled eggs I've ever had!" They really were just eggs, but the fact that Jason had made them for her gave them extra value. Sam cleaned the kitchen while Jason disappeared into his room. He returned a couple of minutes later and handed her a shopping bag with CMU printed in large letters across the front.

"What's this?" she asked, wiping her hands on a towel.

"Just a little something for our day. Open it."

Sam reached in and pulled out a college

sweatshirt and baseball cap in the school's colors, maroon and gold. "Thank you," she said. She leaned over and kissed him lightly on the lips.

"Now you'll fit right in when I take you on a tour."

Sam doubted that she could pass for a college student, but she didn't want to ruin Jason's fun, so she just smiled and thanked him again. He reached for her hand and pulled her toward the bathroom.

"What are we doing?"

"Taking a shower," he replied matter-of-factly. And what a shower it was. They took turns washing each other, slowly and methodically soaping every naked inch. Jason even shampooed her hair, massaging her scalp gently, and she went weak in the knees. She leaned back against his chest and sighed, enjoying the warm spray of the water against her skin. He wrapped his arms around her waist and placed soft kisses along her neck and shoulders.

"As much as I want to ravage you right now, I think we should get going," he whispered breathily.

"What's the rush?" She was enjoying just being with him and wasn't in any hurry to leave.

"I have things planned." He rubbed his hands up and down her arms, causing goose bumps to break out.

"Well then, you have to stop doing things like that," she scolded playfully.

"Like what?" he asked with feigned innocence.

"You know what. Stop being a tease."

He laughed, the sound deep and vibrating in the small shower stall. "I'm a tease? I thought we were just washing up."

"Yeah, right," she giggled and splashed his face with a handful of water.

He jabbed his fingers into her sides, where she was especially ticklish, and she broke out in a fit of laughter. Finally, he stopped torturing her and reached around to turn off the water. "That's what you get for calling me a tease!" He stepped out of the shower and handed her a towel, then wrapped one around his waist. In between drying off, she kept glancing over at him, studying his grooming routine with interest. She admired his muscular arms and chest, his masculine hands that, despite their large size, could be so gentle. He squirted some hair product into his palm, rubbed his hands together, and pulled the product through his soft brown hair, creating the perfect tousled effect. Lots of women would kill to have his hair, she mused. She gazed upon his defined abs as he gave himself a spritz of cologne. Suddenly, his towel fell to the floor, and Jason turned toward her with a huge grin. "That's what you get for staring at me," he teased as he turned and strolled toward the bedroom.

"Was not," she yelled.

"Were too."

"Was not," she repeated for good measure, giggling as she stepped out of the shower. She wrapped the towel around her, twisting it securely above her breasts, and began combing her hair. Jason returned a few minutes later completely dressed in jeans and a CMU sweatshirt that matched hers. He held her clothes in his hands.

"You can get dressed in here so you don't get cold."

Sam took the clothes and leaned in for a kiss. "You are too good to me."

"I think it's the other way around." He smiled and walked out, leaving her to finish getting ready. Shortly after, they were holding hands as Jason played the role of an enthusiastic tour guide, showing her around campus. He pointed out the buildings where his classes were, the library, and the bookstore. It was Saturday, so the campus wasn't teeming with students, and Sam was secretly glad. They passed a few people walking or jogging on the paths, but for the most part, they were alone. It was a crisp yet sunny fall day, and she enjoyed the simple act of walking with him hand in hand. They talked and laughed the day away, returning to the apartment around dinner time.

They decided to have a pizza delivered and settled in to watch TV while they waited. Jason flipped through the channels impatiently while Sam studied his profile. His mood had changed drastically, and she was just about to ask him why when he suddenly pressed the off button on the remote.

"My advisor called a meeting with me this week," he began. "He needs an answer from me about Denver by October 15. "

Sam's heart plummeted. "I thought you had until November."

"I did too. I wasn't prepared to give him an answer at the meeting. Plus, I wanted to talk to you first."

Sam swallowed nervously, unsure of how to respond. "What does your gut tell you to do?" She was trying to be objective, but the look on his face said she missed the mark.

"I was hoping you would tell me not to go. I don't want to make this decision, Sam."

She suppressed a brief flare-up of anger. "I can't make this decision for you, Jason. I would miss you like crazy, but it would be selfish of me to keep you here. I told your mom that I wouldn't try to influence your decision, and I meant it."

"My mother has nothing to do with this. It's about us. It's about our future."

Sam felt a prick of fear, fear of him leaving and fear of the word future. Did they really have a future together? Was she ready to commit to him? She knew she loved him, but could she see them together forever? She wasn't ready or able to answer these questions right now, but she was certain that she couldn't jeopardize his career.

"I think you should go," she whispered, the words hanging ominously in the air. Jason stared at her in disbelief for what felt like forever before speaking.

"You're afraid, aren't you? I can see it all over your face. You're not sure if you can envision a future with me." His words sounded harsh even though his voice was still soft.

Sam dug her nails painfully into her palms as she attempted to calm her breathing. "I don't know what to say, Jason. I'm afraid that no matter what I say it may not be exactly what you want to hear."

"Well, I'm not afraid, so let me tell you what I want. I want to marry you someday, I want to have kids with you, I want to grow old with you…"

His words tugged at her heart, but she couldn't reciprocate. "Jason," she interrupted, "please don't do this right now."

"When, then? When is it a good time for me to share my true feelings with you, Sam? I'm sorry that I'm not on your schedule." The last sentence was spoken with anger, and Sam found herself unable to look him in the eye.

"I don't know how the conversation got to this point. I was just talking about your career and how I don't want to stand in the way of it. Suddenly, you're talking about marriage and children, and I'm not there yet. I'm not sure I ever will be. I'm sorry."

Jason's icy glare cut right through her. He stood up abruptly and stomped out of the room. His bedroom door slammed so hard she felt the floor shake. Sam put her head in her hands and sobbed, her shoulders shaking violently as wave after wave of tears poured out of her. When she finally stopped crying, she went to the bathroom to wipe off her face and blow her nose. She stood just outside Jason's closed bedroom door and listened for any sounds within—nothing. She reached her hand up as if to knock, but quickly pulled it back to her side. He probably wasn't ready to talk yet, and truthfully, neither was she. How did this happen? They were having such a good time, and everything was flowing so well between them. How did something so wonderful turn into something so painful in a few moments time? He'd totally caught her off guard with his talk of the future. Sam honestly hadn't thought that far ahead. She wasn't even sure that marriage and children were what she wanted anymore. That ship had sailed with Brad. Yes, she had enjoyed being married, but did she want to become a wife again? Jason had brought out her spirit of adventure; he made her feel like she could do anything, be anyone. Did that include being his wife? She admitted that she was so busy having fun with him that she hadn't stopped to think about the depth of his feelings. She knew that he loved her, but that wasn't a guarantee that they would always be together. He wasn't even out of school yet. Why was he already thinking about things like marriage and children? Sam felt horrible about their argument, but she wasn't sure how to resolve it. She couldn't say things she didn't mean just to make him feel better. It was probably best to give him some space for now. She went into the kitchen and tore a sheet of paper off the magnetic notepad hanging on the refrigerator. There was a pen lying on the counter, and she used it to write him a short note.

Jason—I'm sorry that the weekend ended this way. I didn't mean to cause an argument. Maybe we should take a breather for a few days. I'm not sure what else to say right now, but I do love you. Sam

Her overnight bag was still in his room, but there wasn't anything she really needed from it. She put on her coat and shoes, grabbed her purse from the chair, and left the apartment, closing the door softly behind her.

Sam cried on and off the entire way home, and by the time she pulled into her driveway, she was spent. Her phone was on the passenger seat, and she kept glancing at it, willing it to ring, but it lay dark and silent. She replayed their conversation over and over trying to figure out what went wrong. How could it have ended differently? She vacillated between sadness and anger. Jason had told her repeatedly not to worry about the future, to just be in the moment, and she thought she had achieved that. Now, he was talking about their future as if it was a foregone conclusion. She was just coming to grips with the idea of dating him, and now he wanted to talk about marriage? It was all too much, too soon. Why couldn't he understand that? Why did he walk out of the room and slam the door on her? She finally came to the realization that she wouldn't get any answers tonight. Her phone stayed silent, and she was absolutely exhausted. When she finally tumbled into bed, she fell into a fitful sleep and woke the next morning with a pounding headache. She went through Sunday in a fog, trying but failing to distract herself by reading or watching TV. Her phone rang once, and when she saw Jaime's name on the screen, she ignored it. She wasn't ready to talk to her sister yet, or anyone else for that matter. At various times throughout the day, she sat in front of her laptop attempting to draft an email to Jason. The words failed to come, and the page remained blank.

Chapter 22

In the meantime, Jason sulked on the couch in his apartment after giving Max an abbreviated version of what had happened.

"Man, you need to call her."

"I don't know what to say to her."

"Tell her that you love her and that you're sorry for being an ass." Max was never one to mince words.

"Why am I the ass?" Jason's anger flared. "She's the one who left without saying goodbye."

"I don't blame the lady. You walked out in the middle of a conversation, and then you hid in your room like a sissy."

"Who asked you anyway?" Jason sneered at him across the room.

"Ok, that's it. You either call her or come out to the bar with me."

Jason weighed his options and decided to go to the bar. He wasn't ready to call Sam, and he really didn't want to be alone. He stood up and pulled on his Converse. "Let's go."

They went to a popular local bar and sat at a high-top table. Jason generally believed in moderation when it came to drinking, but tonight was a different story. He was ready to get shit-faced drunk. The beer kept coming, and he kept slugging them down. A few of their other friends showed up and joined them at the table. Jason welcomed the fuzzy haze that took over his brain and enjoyed the distraction of being with his buddies. He hardly thought of Sam at all. The guys eventually moved over to the pool table to take up a game, leaving Jason alone in his drunken stupor. He was nursing his sixth beer when *she* strolled into the bar, surrounded by a group of girlfriends—Rebecca. She was obviously dressed in her look-at-me clothes, a tight denim mini skirt and t-shirt that showed an ample amount of cleavage. Her long blonde hair was straight and shiny, and her lips glistened with pink gloss. His head wasn't the only one turned in her direction; she always made quite an entrance. Rebecca was facing her best friend, Kaley, and they were giggling about something. He had to admit that she looked good, really good as a matter of fact. Her head suddenly turned in his direction, and their eyes met across the crowded room. A look of surprise crossed her face, which she quickly replaced with a slow, sexy smile. Oh, what that smile used to do to him. She whispered something to Kaley and then started walking in his direction; strutting was more like it.

"Hi," she said. She smiled and leaned over to kiss his cheek. The scent of vanilla shrouded her.

"Hey," he muttered in response.

"What are you doing here all alone?"

"My friends are playing pool," he said, slurring his words. She hopped up on the stool next to him and leaned forward, offering her perky breasts for his viewing pleasure.

"You don't look so good."

"Thanks a lot."

"What's wrong? Where's your new girlfriend?"

Nothing like pouring salt on his wound. "She's not here." No further explanation was necessary.

"Did you break up?"

"Not exactly." He took another swig of his beer. "We're on a break."

"Hmm, that's too bad."

Yeah, right, he thought. She was like a shark sizing up her prey. Her hand reached out to cover his.

"I miss you, Jay."

Nice play, using his familiar nickname. He stared at her through the haze and saw that she meant it. At that moment, Rebecca was warm and real, and she smelled good. He was pretty sure that she would go home with him if he asked. Her hand slid further up his arm. "It looks like you could use some company tonight."

Bingo. He picked up the beer mug and

swallowed the last drop, then hastily wiped his mouth with a napkin.

"Do you have a car?"

They drove back to his apartment in silence, his head leaned back and eyes closed. He felt like he could fall asleep if only his head would stop spinning. Rebecca weaved her arm through his as she guided him up the stairs, and he must have handed her his keys because the next thing he knew he was sprawled out on the couch. She kicked off her black pumps and went into the kitchen, emerging a few minutes later with a tall glass of water.

"Here, drink this," she demanded. He drank it down in one long gulp, and she went back to refill the glass. "Is there ibuprofen in the bathroom?" she asked. He nodded yes and swallowed the pills she brought out to him. She took the glass from his hand, set it on the side table, and, in one fluid movement, swung her legs over to straddle him. Jason was having trouble focusing, but he could feel the weight of her warm body on his legs, and then she was grabbing his hand and placing it underneath her mini skirt. He felt her bare butt cheek against the palm of his hand and registered that she wasn't wearing any underwear. Strangely, that fact didn't arouse him. She leaned forward until her boobs were practically in his face and pressed her lips against his. He must not have responded because, in the next second, she moved off of him and glared at him accusingly.

"What?" he managed to ask.

"You are an ass, do you know that?" she spat.

He vaguely recalled someone else calling him that earlier, but who was it? She didn't wait for his response and launched into a tirade. "What do you see in her anyway? She's a dried up old lady, for God's sake."

Jason felt his own anger start to rise but couldn't find the energy to stand up.

"I practically threw myself at you tonight, and you just sat there like a dummy. Most guys would kill to be with someone like me."

"I'm not most guys," he whispered while she banged around the room collecting her shoes and purse.

"Enjoy the rest of the evening—alone!" She slammed the door so hard that Jason's ears rang. He slid further down on the couch, covered himself with the handmade quilt Max's mother had made, and fell instantly asleep.

The next thing he knew someone was shaking him roughly, jolting him out of a deep slumber. "What, what is it?" He sat up slowly, eyes adjusting to the bright light streaming into the room.

"It's time to get up, Sleeping Beauty, you have class in an hour." It was Max leaning over him with an annoyed expression on his face.

Jason sat up, rubbing his eyes vigorously

in an attempt to clear them.

"Go jump in the shower, and I'll make you some breakfast. "

Jason didn't argue as he shuffled off to the bathroom. As the warm spray hit him, he started to feel more alert, and the previous evening's events came flooding back to him. Rebecca in his apartment, no panties, kissing him before leaving in a huff. She must have been the one to drive him home, though he barely remembered it. Thank God he'd had the sense not to sleep with her. In his drunken state, he probably wouldn't have been able to perform anyway, nor had he wanted to. He scrubbed his face and body harder than necessary as if to wash away the memories. A few minutes later, he was dressed and sitting down to a plate of scrambled eggs and toast. "Thanks man," he said as Max rinsed out the egg pan.

"What happened last night Jay? I saw you leave with Becca. You didn't..."

"No, I didn't," he replied around a mouthful of egg. "She gave it her best shot, but I kicked her out."

"That's the first smart move you've made in days."

"Thanks. Are you going to call me an ass again?"

"No, I think you probably feel like one all on your own."

"I do."

"Call Sam, dude. I mean it. Get yourself together and call her."

Jason didn't respond. He finished his breakfast and grabbed his backpack. "See you later," he tossed over his shoulder as he left the apartment. It was a short walk to his first class, but he thought about Sam the entire way. Here he was, a psychology student, and he had exhibited all the classic symptoms of denial and rejection. He'd felt rejected when she'd told him to go to Denver, but she'd only been trying to be supportive. She was right about not wanting to stand in the way of his career. Second, he'd surprised her with the marriage and kids bombshell, and he understood why it was overwhelming to her. He had practically begged Sam to take their relationship one day at a time, and here he was dumping all these expectations on her. What was he thinking? They had only been dating for a few months, why did he feel the need to push it? He reasoned that he was looking for confirmation that she would still be there for him after his stint in Denver. He was the one who was scared now, not her. He was deathly afraid of losing her. Hell, the marriage topic had come out of his mouth without him really thinking about it. Sure, he wanted to get married someday and have kids, but it didn't have to be decided right now. He knew one thing for sure — he missed her like crazy. It had only been two days, but he felt like weeks had gone by since he'd talked to her, held her, laughed with her. He felt a bubble of panic rise in his chest. "I hope I didn't blow it," he said aloud to the empty air.

Jason could hardly concentrate during class. As soon as it was over, he found a bench in the corridor and typed out a text.

We really need to talk. I'd like to come home this weekend and see you.

It would be Sam's lunch hour, and he waited a few minutes, praying she would respond. After what felt like an eternity, her answer appeared.

Ok.

He was hoping for a little more enthusiasm, but he deserved this. He typed again.

I can be at your house by 4:30 on Friday.

The reply came back instantly this time.

Ok.

Him: *See you then.*

Her: *See you then.*

Jason sighed with relief and trepidation. She certainly wasn't making it easy for him, but it was wrong to expect otherwise. He had been an ass after all. He tucked the phone in his pocket and headed back to the apartment.

Chapter 23

Sam went through the next four days in a fog. On one hand, she was glad Jason had contacted her, but on the other, she still wasn't sure what to say to him. Luckily, she had a busy week, which included work, yoga, and dinner at Jaime's on Thursday night. She wasn't able to say much to Jaime about what had transpired over the weekend because Steve and the boys were nearby. She promised her sister she would call on Sunday night to give her the scoop. Sam was actually glad for all the distractions because the week went sailing by, and Friday came before she knew it. She started to get butterflies when she pulled out of the school parking lot at four o'clock Friday afternoon, knowing Jason would be there to greet her when she got home. She employed her deep breathing skills as she drove and promised herself it would be ok, no matter what happened. As she drove down her street, she noticed Jason's Jeep in his parent's driveway and felt a brief wave of disappointment. Maybe he'd decided to visit them first. Then, as she pulled into her drive, she glanced at her porch, and there he was, pushing himself out of the wicker chair and heading toward her. Her nerves flared up again, and she took one last deep breath as she opened the car door.

"Hey," he said. The uncertainty was evident in his expression and his voice.

"Hey," she replied and gave him a watered down smile. She noted the stiffness between them as he followed her into the house. What she really wanted to do was fling her arms around his neck and kiss him, but it didn't seem like the right time. Jason was holding back too, which saddened her. "Would you like something to drink?"

"No thanks," he shook his head.

He followed her into the kitchen as she poured herself a glass of water, hoping it would remove the rather large lump that was lodged in her throat. Jason stationed himself on a bar stool and watched her carefully trying to gather courage.

She came around the counter to sit at the stool beside him.

"I'm sorry for being such an ass," he blurted out.

She almost laughed at his bluntness but kept her expression blank.

"I felt rejected when you told me to go to Denver, but now I understand why you were doing it. I've been afraid of leaving because I don't want to lose you, Sam."

Sam let his words sink in for a moment

before responding. "Why are you afraid you'll lose me?"

"I don't know, probably because we're going to be on opposite sides of the country!"

"I was the one who used to worry about that, remember? You were the one telling me not to. It's just temporary and…"

"I know, I know, I'm sorry."

"Jason, do you trust me?"

He looked confused. "Yes, of course. Why?"

"Because if you trust me and believe in me, you would know that I'm not looking for an excuse to get out of this relationship. I'm not waiting for you to go to Denver so I can break up with you."

"You shared your feelings. Now it's my turn. When you brought up marriage and kids, I freaked out a little. I'm not saying that it can't happen, but I'm just not thinking about that right now. It's not that I can't envision being married to you. It's about me finally finding my footing after Brad's death, mostly due to you. I'm in a good place right now, and I'm not anxious to change it up just yet. Can you understand that?"

"I totally get that. To be honest, I'm not ready either. It was just my way of expressing my commitment to you, to us."

"I'm committed to you too, and I thought you knew that."

"I do know, but all I could hear in my head was you telling me to leave, and it was a blow to my ego."

"Tell your ego that I always want to be with you, but it would be selfish of me to keep you from your goals. You've worked hard for this degree, and you need to see it through to the end. If that means going to Denver, then I'm here to support you."

Jason felt himself starting to relax. It was so comforting to stare into her gorgeous brown eyes and see the love shining through. He desperately wanted to lean over and kiss her, but he knew the hard part was yet to come.

"Thank you for explaining all that to me, and know that I'm really sorry for shutting you out that night. I guess I was just nursing my bruised ego."

The corner of Sam's mouth twitched up in a smile, but she quickly turned serious again. "Jason, if there's one thing I learned from being married, it's that communication is key. We need to be able to tell each other anything and everything without holding back."

He cleared his throat noisily and said, "I agree. There's something else I need to tell you about that weekend."

Oh no, now what? "What is it?"

"I went to the bar with Max Sunday night and got pretty drunk."

Sam kept her expression neutral and

waited for him to continue.

"Rebecca showed up and offered me a ride home."

Her face fell, and her heart felt like it would pound right out of her chest. "What happened then?"

"She came on to me, but I didn't respond. I swear to you, nothing happened. She gave me a glass of water and then left in a huff."

Sam thought the story sounded plausible, but she couldn't squash the ugly green monster that reared up inside her. "Is that all? Did you touch her?"

"She tried to get me too, but I wasn't interested. She kissed me at one point, but I know I didn't kiss her back because the next thing I remember is her slamming the door on her way out."

Sam exhaled, but she still felt shaky. "Did you know she was going to be at the bar that night?"

"I had no idea. Max convinced me to go out with him, and then some of our other friends showed up. They started playing pool, but I was too far gone, so I just sat at the table. Rebecca came in with her friends and approached me."

"Why didn't you ask Max to drive you home? You know she still has feelings for you. Why would you even get in a car with her?"

"I was drunk, Sam. I hardly knew what I was doing. I know it sounds like a bad excuse but…"

"You're right it does. How would you feel if it were the other way around? What if I went to a bar, got drunk and ended up in Mark's car?"

Jason flinched at the sound of Mark's name. "Has he been after you again?" he growled.

"No, I'm just trying to make a point. Look how mad you get at the mere mention of his name. Imagine how I feel knowing that Rebecca was in your apartment."

Of course, she was right, and it made him feel like an ass all over again. "Believe me, I wish it never happened. I wish you and I hadn't argued, I wish I hadn't gone to the bar, and I definitely wish I hadn't run into Rebecca."

"It would have been acceptable if you'd just run into her. It's not acceptable that you let her take you home. Is there anything else you need to tell me?" She hoped like hell that was the end of the story.

"Not really. She made it very clear that she would sleep with me if I wanted to but I didn't. I promise you with my whole heart, Sam, I didn't feel anything toward her. She was only there for a few minutes, and then she stormed out. All I remember feeling afterward was relief, and then I fell asleep."

Jason's phone buzzed, and they both glanced at the display. It was his mom calling, and Sam motioned for him to go ahead and answer. While he was on the phone, Sam took the opportunity to regain her composure. He sounded remorseful, but she still felt angry. She continued ruminating until Jason ended the call and turned his attention back to her.

"How's your dad doing?" she asked, partly to change the subject.

"He's doing ok. Still a little tired, I guess. My mom was calling because my car is in the driveway but I haven't been home yet. She was just wondering where I was."

"What did you tell her?"

"That we were talking, and I would be home soon to have dinner with them."

"Oh, ok." She shouldn't be surprised; of course he would want to see his parents while he was here.

"I'm not sure what else to say, Sam. I understand if you're still angry because I'm angry at myself too. I made a lot of mistakes last weekend, and I'm very sorry."

She nodded her head in acknowledgment.

"Would you please let me try to make it up to you? I have some ideas about what we can do tomorrow if you're free."

Sam felt the corners of her mouth twitch into a reluctant smile. "Of course you do."

He smiled back at her, a wide grin spreading across his face. "Can you let me surprise you this time? I know you don't like surprises but…"

She could at least give him that. "Yes."

"Great. I'm going to head across the street and spend some time with my folks, but can I pick you up tomorrow morning?"

"What time?" She felt herself softening, but she still held back a little.

"How about ten?"

"Ok," she nodded, feeling slightly disappointed that he wouldn't be staying with her tonight.

"See you then?"

"See you then," she said, walking him to the front door. They hadn't kissed or touched at all, and she found herself aching for his arms to go around her. Jason simply leaned down to gently kiss her cheek before walking out the door. She almost called out to him as he started across the lawn but stopped herself. Things were still unsettled between them and it was probably best to take it slow. She hated that it felt like starting all over again after they had been so close, but he was trying to be respectful of her feelings, and she couldn't really fault him for that. Hopefully, things would return to normal between them tomorrow. Until then, she would go to bed wondering what he had in store for her…

Jason lay in bed that night desperately wishing that Sam was wrapped up in his arms. He knew she was still upset with him, and she had every right to be. He cursed himself for being such an idiot. Tomorrow will be a better day for us, he vowed. I have a lot to make up for, and I have every intention of doing just that. He switched off the light and willed himself to sleep.

Chapter 24

At ten the next morning, Sam heard the sound of the Harley purring in her driveway. A joyful smile spread across her face. It was a perfect fall day, and she was anxious to get on the bike with Jason. She went outside to greet him and was taken aback, as usual, by his gorgeousness. He stood next to the bike, helmet in hand, wearing faded jeans, a CMU t-shirt, and a varsity jacket. His grin was infectious as he held out a helmet to her.

"Morning, m'lady," he teased, bowing slightly. "Your chariot awaits."

Sam giggled in response, tugging her helmet on and securing the strap. "I would be honored, m'lord."

He held her steady as she straddled the bike before hopping on himself. Sam snuggled close to him and slid her hands around his waist, relishing the feel of his warm back against her chest. "So, I suppose I can't ask where we're going."

"You can ask, but I'm not telling. Just relax and enjoy the ride."

Sam was determined to do just that. After the rough week they'd had she was ready to simply enjoy herself. He took the side streets, and as they travelled northeast, the busy suburbs gave way to rolling farms and wide open spaces. Forty minutes later, Jason pulled into the parking lot of the Stony Creek Cider Mill.

"We're here," he said, taking off his helmet and giving her a hand off the bike. "It's not fall in Michigan until you've been to a cider mill."

Sam hadn't been to a cider mill in several years, but the sights, sounds, and tantalizing smells instantly came back to her. "You're right," she agreed enthusiastically. Jason grabbed her hand and led her toward the open door of the mill store. He still seemed a little hesitant with her, but the familiarity of his warm hand clasping hers was comforting. They ordered a half dozen donuts and a pint of cider and carried them out to a nearby picnic table. Jason poured the cider in small plastic cups and handed her a sugared donut on a napkin.

"I used to come here every year as a kid," he mused. "It was our family's fall tradition."

Sam recalled that Brad hadn't cared for cider mills because of the crowds and the bees. He'd taken her a few times during their marriage, but she'd always enjoyed it more than he had. A few bees were buzzing around nearby, but Sam ignored them as she bit into the sugary donut. "This is delicious," she said, licking the sugar crystals off her lips. She looked up to see Jason staring at her intently. "What? Do I have sugar on my chin?"

"No. I'm just watching you savor your food."

She chuckled self-consciously. "I can't help it, everything tastes so good!"

They ate quietly for a few minutes until Jason broke the silence. "I love you, Sam."

He sounded so serious, almost reverent when he said it. "I love you too," she breathed, gazing into his glistening eyes.

"I'm really sorry about last weekend."

"I know. You don't have to keep saying it." She tried to be reassuring, desperate to break the barrier between them.

"It won't happen again. I want everything to be good for us."

Sam wondered which part he was referring to, the arguing or Rebecca. She didn't want to spoil their outing, so she just nodded her head. "Let's just put it behind us. Every couple argues. It's normal."

"I know it's normal but…"

"Just stop, please. I'm having a wonderful time with you today, and I don't want to ruin it. Let's just concentrate on the fun day you have planned. What's next on the agenda?"

"I thought we could go Stony Creek Metro Park for a picnic. The last time we tried to have a picnic, we were interrupted, remember?"

How could she forget? It was the first time Jason had kissed her, and more might have happened if they hadn't been interrupted. "Of course I remember," she said. She smiled flirtatiously. "That was the first time you tried to take advantage of me."

"Take advantage? What? I think it was the other way around, woman."

"You wish. I clearly remember you leaning over to kiss me."

"Hmm... kind of like this?" He slowly leaned across the table, locking her eyes with his, and gently kissed her lips. The kiss was tender yet filled with promise. Sam didn't want it to end, but the cider mill was getting busier, and she didn't want to put on a show.

"Looks like we've been interrupted again," she breathed.

"Let's go to the park. We can find a more private spot there."

Sam heard the desire in his voice, and her heart skipped a beat. She was anxious to be alone with him too. They took care of their trash and headed back to the bike. On the way to the park, they stopped at a Subway and bought sandwiches and water for their picnic. Jason parked the bike in a lot near a walking trail. From the pouch on the side of the Harley, he pulled out a small backpack that contained their lunch and a blanket. They headed out on the trail, passing a handful of people who were also taking advantage of the warm fall day. After a while, he led her off the official trail up a narrow dirt path to a high spot in the park. He stopped in a clearing among the trees to lay down the blanket.

"Do you have a secret map of the parks around here?" she teased, plopping down on the blanket.

Jason chuckled, eyes sparkling. "I don't know what you're talking about!"

"Well, it seems like you know every private spot there is in these public parks."

"I've honestly never been up here before. I saw the path and thought it looked like it might lead to a secluded place." He plopped down next to her and leaned back on his elbows.

"What a beautiful day," Sam commented, looking up at the crystal-clear blue sky.

"What a beautiful woman," Jason replied.

She turned toward him. "What a smooth line that was!"

"It's not a line, it's the truth. You are a beautiful woman."

Sam knew that he meant it, and felt her heart flutter in her chest. It suddenly felt like an eternity since they had been intimate, but she was still waiting for him to make the first move. She didn't have long to wait, as Jason leaned toward her and placed his lips in the hollow of her neck. He traced a line down her bare arm with his fingertip, causing her to shiver in anticipation. He dipped his head down to kiss the swell of her breasts that peeked over the edge of her t-shirt.

She tilted her head back as he continued his exploration. "Should we be worried about anyone seeing us?" she asked, slightly out of breath.

"No," he answered between kisses. He tugged her t-shirt out of her jeans and slid his hand underneath. Sam was rendered speechless; she was mesmerized by all the sensations assaulting her body. His hand moved around to unclasp her bra, and then he gently eased her down to the blanket. In one motion, Jason lifted her top and bra to expose her breasts and then closed his mouth over her pebbled nipple. A sigh escaped her as he licked and suckled at first one breast, then the other. She squirmed with anticipation as his lips left her breasts and trailed over her abdomen down to the edge of her jeans. She made an attempt to sit up, but he shook his head, and she collapsed back down.

"Am I tickling you?" he asked throatily, his fingers resting on the snap of her jeans.

"You could say that," she said, her voice filled with desire.

He chuckled as he slowly unzipped her jeans. Sam arched her hips up and watched as he eased her jeans and panties off, tossing them carelessly to the side. She was now completely bared to the elements, not to mention any hiker who happened by. The sensible side of her should have put a stop to it, but the sensual side of her wanted to keep going. She lost all sense of her surroundings when Jason's head dipped between her legs, and she opened up to him with abandon. She was flooded with the sensation of his warm lips and the cool breeze lapping against her skin simultaneously. His movements sped up in response to her arching hips as the fire grew within her. Jason's tongue was relentless, and she closed her eyes as the climax took over, her arms raised above her head in complete surrender. Jason gently lowered her hips down and kissed his way back up her body until he reached her lips. She smiled up at him contentedly and then, in a swift movement, pushed him over onto his back. His look of surprise was replaced by a knowing grin as her hands went to his belt buckle.

"Why is it that I'm always the one who's naked first?" She laughed as she unzipped him.

Jason just shrugged, unable to tear his eyes away as she undressed him. Once he was naked, she straddled him, slowly rubbing back and forth against his hardness. His body was tight with arousal. She leaned up a little to grasp him with one hand, and he exhaled loudly as she guided him inside. Sam was determined to give him as much pleasure as he had given her, and it seemed to be working. She rode him slowly at first, increasing the intensity to match his.

"I want to kiss you," he panted between thrusts. She lowered herself until she was flush against him and kissed him passionately as he wrapped his arms around her. He cupped her head with one hand while the other squeezed her butt cheek. His climax came crashing down on them, and he grasped her tightly until the last bit of energy was spent. She rested on top of him for a few minutes longer, waiting for their breathing to return to normal. They quickly got dressed, marveling at how lucky they were not to get caught.

"Now I get to cross off having sex in a public place from my bucket list!"

Jason caught her up in a bear hug and kissed the tip of her nose before setting her back down on the blanket. "Isn't that on everyone's bucket list?"

"Well, if it isn't, it should be!"

"Let's eat," he said.

She ran her fingers through her hair in an attempt to give it some semblance of order as Jason arranged their lunch on the blanket. They sat cross-legged across from each other and devoured the sandwiches contentedly.

"This has been a wonderful day," Sam said as they were cleaning up.

"It's not over yet."

"You have more things planned?" she

asked incredulously.

"That depends."

"On what?"

"On if you'll let me spend the night with you."

Why was it that a simple sentence from him could cause such an intense reaction in her? "I would love it if you spent the night."

"Good, then our wonderful day can turn into our wonderful night."

They walked hand in hand back down the dirt path to the parking lot. As they rode out of the park, Sam reflected on the day. All of the uncertainty of the last few days had disappeared and, in its place, was the love and intimacy she craved. She was sure that Jason felt it too as his body was relaxed and pliant in her arms. Sam was also relieved that Jason had suggested spending the night. She wanted to soak up every minute with him before he had to go back to school. When they were together this way, she felt that their love was indestructible. Nothing and nobody could come between them.

When he pulled into her driveway, he helped her off the bike but kept the motor running. "I need to take care of a few things before tonight, ok?"

"Ok," she answered, trying not to let her curiosity get the best of her.

"I'll be back in an hour or so."

"Do I need to prepare for anything?" she

asked, fishing for clues.

"No, not really; just get comfortable. Wear your sweats and a tank top. We'll be staying in."

There went the shiver of anticipation again. Would she never tire of this? "Ok, see you then."

"See you then," he said and gave her a quick peck on the cheek. Sam watched him drive away on the Harley, missing him already. She was dying to know what he was up to but resigned herself to having to wait. She decided to take a shower and freshen up in his absence. After a warm shower, she slathered herself with cherry-scented lotion and put her hair in a high ponytail. As instructed, she pulled on her grey sweats and a white tank top, minus a bra, knowing that Jason would love it. There was a slight chill in the air now that evening was approaching, so she donned a zip-up hoodie over the tank. She applied moisturizer and lip gloss and then curled up in her favorite chair with her latest novel. An hour or so later, the doorbell rang, and she practically ran to answer it. Jason was loaded down with an overnight bag and several grocery store bags.

"Supplies for our dinner," he explained as they headed toward the kitchen. He unloaded a six pack of Bud Light and all the ingredients for a homemade pizza. "Beer and pizza, man's best friends!"

Jason cracked open two beers as she brought out the mugs. Once their drinks were poured, Jason took her hand and led her into the living room. They sank down on the couch and enjoyed the cold beer in silence for a few minutes. Jason suddenly sat up, as if he'd just remembered something, and said, "I have a gift for you."

Sam felt a brief moment of panic as she recalled their recent marriage conversation but quickly dismissed the idea as foolish. He had admitted to not being ready for marriage, so it couldn't be an engagement ring.

Jason fished in his jeans pocket and pulled out a teal blue satin bag. Sam sat up straighter on the couch, recognizing the trademark of a prestigious jewelry store. "It's not my birthday," she said nervously as he held the bag out toward her.

"I know, but can't a guy give his girlfriend a gift whenever he feels like it?"

Sam felt touched by his sentiment as he handed her the bag. She opened the drawstring and pulled out a silver chain-link bracelet with a silver heart charm dangling from it. "It's beautiful," she gushed, turning the bracelet from side to side.

"Look on the back of the heart."

She hadn't noticed at first glance that the heart was engraved. The words read: See you then. Love, J.

Sam's throat closed up as she choked back a sob. She threw her arms around him and said, "I love it. Thank you so much."

"It's like a promise, you know? When we can't be together, you'll know I'm always thinking about you until we see each other again."

Sam knew he was referring to the upcoming internship, but it also meant so much more than that. She knew it was his way of promising to always be there for her, no matter what. She was overwhelmed with emotion and couldn't find the words to thank him enough. Finally, she sat back and held out her wrist so he could clasp the bracelet on her. It was delicate and feminine yet heavy enough that she would always be aware of its presence. "I can't express how much this means to me, Jason. You always know what's in my heart and how to make me happy. I will cherish it forever."

Jason was visibly relieved as he leaned over to gently kiss her lips. "I'm glad you like it. Are you ready to eat yet?"

"Not quite, but by the time we make it, I'll be ready." They worked side by side in the kitchen, preparing the pizza and talking about all kinds of things. Sam reflected on what a perfect day it had been and how complete she felt with Jason there. Up until recently, she had purposely tried not to think about the future. She had taken his advice about living in the moment, but their recent talk about marriage and children had her pondering it again. Would her future include all those things? She had all but given up on love during the years after Brad's death. She knew women who'd had children in their forties, but she also knew the risks went up with each passing year. Jason hated when she talked about her age in negative terms, but she was just being realistic. Maybe she was past the point of being able to get pregnant. She recalled a few teachers who had gone through fertility treatments in their thirties with mixed results. Two of them had become pregnant and given birth to healthy babies, and one of them had given up the fight after several years of trying. Sam had a hard time visualizing herself going through all that in order to have children. She wanted to talk to Jason about her fears, but she wasn't sure now was the right time. He still had to finish school and…

"What's on your mind, Sammy?"

She swatted him on the arm. "You know I hate that nickname."

"I know, but I had to resort to something drastic to stop you from ruminating."

Rather than hide it from him, she decided to broach the subject. "I was just wondering what my chances are of becoming pregnant at my age."

Jason choked on his swig of beer, and a fine spray misted in her direction. "You aren't pregnant, are you?" His voice wavered a bit, but there was no fear in his eyes.

"No. It just popped into my head since you mentioned it last weekend."

"I'm no expert, but I'd say as long as the woman is healthy, the chances would be pretty good."

They continued setting the table, maintaining their composure as if they were talking about the weather. "I have a physical every year, and so far, everything's been fine."

"Is it something you would consider?" he asked nonchalantly as he set out the silverware.

Sam hesitated before answering. "Maybe. I haven't thought about the possibility in a long time. I would want to talk to my doctor about the risks."

"Of course."

They continued to move around the kitchen as if in a strange dance, avoiding eye contact. "Is having kids really important to you?" She was almost afraid of his response, and he cleared his throat before answering.

"I would like to have one or two someday, but if it's not in the cards, I could deal with that."

She could always count on his honesty, and since they were being open, she decided to continue the conversation. "I don't think I explained myself well when we talked about marriage before."

Jason stopped fussing with the place settings and motioned for them to sit at the barstools. He looked at her expectantly, waiting for her to speak.

"When I was your age, getting married and having children were definite goals of mine. I always knew I would work with kids someday, and I accomplished that goal soon after college, around the same time I married Brad. When he died, my goals changed to include, at the top of the list, daily survival. I had to find a way to live in the world without him, and I wasn't looking for some guy to rescue me. My goals were to do the things I love, be around good people, and try to find peace. I honestly didn't give much thought to getting married again or having children. I kind of resigned myself to being on my own. And then..."

"And then I came along," Jason stated simply.

"Yes, and as you know, it took me by surprise. Not just our age difference, but everything about us. I didn't expect to fall in love again."

"That's the beauty of it, don't you think? Love doesn't follow a formula or a set of rules. It just sneaks up on you."

"You've taught me that, yes."

"Have I been a good teacher?" he asked teasingly.

"Very good."

"I sense that there's a problem here, but I don't see it. I'm waiting for the inevitable *but*..."

"The *but* is that, just when I was getting comfortable with our relationship the way it is, you brought up marriage and children, and it spooked me."

"I didn't mean to. I was just being honest about my feelings, Sam. I agree that it's way too soon, but I can see myself with you for the long haul, with or without kids. I was fishing to see if you felt the same way."

"I know that I love you. I know that I feel at home when I'm with you. I know that you make me smile and laugh. I know that you've made me more adventurous and you've brought out the passionate side of me that was dormant for so long. I know that I'll miss you like crazy when you go to Denver."

"But you don't know if you want to get married again." He said it so plainly that Sam flinched and immediately moved to correct him. Jason held up one hand to hold her off. "It's ok. I'm ok with that for now. I just want to be with you, and it sounds like you want to be with me, so I can wait on the rest. We'll take it one day at a time, like I said in the beginning."

Sam leaned over and wrapped her arms around his neck, pressing her cheek against his. "Thank you," she breathed, relief flooding through her. He hugged her tightly in return until they were interrupted by the oven timer.

The rest of the evening passed quickly, and Sam awoke the next morning wrapped up in Jason's arms. The first thing she thought of when her eyes cracked open was that he had to leave today. She watched his chest expand and contract with his slow rhythmic breathing as she tried to carefully extract herself from his hold. She slipped quietly out of the bedroom, pulling her robe on as she crept down the stairs. Sam tried to push away her melancholy mood as she set about making a breakfast of French toast and bacon, the comforting aroma of which drifted through the house. She heard the creak of the stairs before she saw his magnificent form and gazed up at him with adoration. Jason was bare chested in his navy blue boxers, hair ruffled up from sleep, a huge grin on his face.

"Morning, beautiful," he said, bending down to gently kiss her lips.

"Did I wake you?"

"No, but I must have sensed that you weren't beside me."

She wrapped her arms around his waist and laid her head on his chest. "I wanted to make breakfast before you have to leave."

He hugged her tighter and simply said, "Thank you."

She motioned him toward the table where a glass of freshly made orange juice was waiting for him. "You spoil me," he said as she set a plate of French toast and bacon in front of him.

"I enjoy it," she said, taking the seat next to him. They ate in silence except for the sighs of satisfaction Jason made as he savored each bite. Sam felt melancholy as she watched him eat, but she was determined not to let it show.

"So, what time are you leaving?"

He shifted uncomfortably in the chair. "I need to get an early start because I have a lot of homework waiting for me. After I clean up, I'll head across the street and say goodbye to my parents and then take off."

"Sorry for keeping you away from your studies this weekend."

Jason put down his fork and pulled his chair closer to hers. "There's no place else I'd rather be than right here with you."

"I know," she sighed, gazing into his caramel eyes.

He brought her hand up to his lips and placed a tender kiss on the back of it. The gesture was right out of her romance novels.

"Wear the bracelet and think of me."

"I will. I'll wear it every day."

"I'm planning on coming home in a few weeks for my mom's birthday. You know you can always come up and visit between now and then."

He was trying everything to make her feel better, but none of it was really working. The fact remained that he was leaving and she would be alone for the next few weeks. She should probably try harder to get used to it, but it felt worse each time. "I know. My nephew's birthday is next weekend, so I won't be able to come then and…"

"It's ok Sam. We don't have to plan it all out right now. Let's just play it by ear."

She nodded in agreement as he stood up and cleared their plates from the table. "Shower with me?" His grin is impossibly irresistible, she thought, as he pulled her back up the stairs. After entering the bathroom, Sam turned the water on while Jason ran an electric razor over his face. The scene felt natural and intimate, as if they had been together for years instead of months. As the steam started to rise from the shower stall, Sam slipped off her robe and hung it on a wall hook. Jason stopped mid-shave to admire her naked body in the mirror.

"Like what you see?" she teased, doing a slow spin for his perusal.

"No. I love what I see," he corrected. He shut off the razor and turned to face her, slowly easing his boxers down his muscular thighs. When they hit the floor, he grinned and asked, "Like what you see?"

"No. I love what I see." She opened the shower door, and they stepped inside letting the warm water stream over them. Sam leaned her back against Jason's broad chest and reveled in the close contact. Jason took a bar of soap from the shower ledge and rubbed it vigorously between his hands, creating a rich lather. Sam was mesmerized by the motion of his masculine hands rubbing the soap.

"Move out of the spray for a minute," he directed. She did as she was told, sighing as his soapy hands started caressing her body. He started with her neck and shoulders and slowly and methodically worked his way down, over her breasts and rib cage, down her legs, to her toes. He motioned for her to turn around, and then he concentrated on her back, running his hands down her spine, over her hips and down the back of her legs. She was in such a relaxed state that it took her a minute to register that he was done. She turned back around to face him and was met with his sparkly eyes, twinkling with desire.

"Time for your hair," he said gruffly, reaching for the shampoo bottle on the ledge behind her. Sam watched the stream of water run down the middle of his chest and over his very full, erect manhood. Jason appeared not to notice her gaze as he poured some shampoo in his palm and returned the bottle to the shelf.

"Are you done gawking yet?" His voice broke her trance.

She let out a nervous giggle. "I wasn't *gawking*," she insisted.

"Well, what do you call it, then?"

"I call it admiring."

Jason gave a gruff chuckle and motioned

for her to turn away from him again. He started massaging the shampoo gently but firmly into her scalp, and she let out a peaceful moan.

"That feels so good," she hummed.

"You feel so good," he breathed into her ear. "And by the way, feel free to *admire* me anytime." Jason rinsed the soap from her hair and squeezed out the excess water before she turned back to face him.

"Now it's your turn," she said with a smile.

"Oh no, you don't."

"What, why not?" She scowled in disbelief.

"Because I'll never leave if you start on me," he admitted huskily.

He leaned over and placed a gentle kiss on her furrowed brow. "Don't be mad at me, baby. You know I would stay all day if I could."

Sam let out a heavy sigh and wrapped her arms around his neck. "I know, but I'm not ready for you to go yet." She knew she was whining, but at the moment, she didn't care. Jason pulled her closer, his hardness pressed against her belly.

"Think about how great it will be the next time we see each other."

She was amazed and somewhat disappointed at his self-control. She was starting to wonder if her sexual appetite was surpassing his! The night before, they had made love twice before drifting off to sleep, and here she was all hot and bothered again this morning. She had gone years without having sex, and now, she couldn't seem to get enough of it. She was no longer worried that she couldn't keep up with Jason in this arena.

Sam took a step back. "You're right. I shouldn't try to delay you more than I already have." He soaped up his hands and scrubbed himself vigorously. She enjoyed the view as he leaned back to shampoo his thick brown hair.

Her heart was heavy as they hurriedly dried off and got dressed. They didn't speak at all as Jason packed up his belongings. They walked back downstairs, clutching hands as Sam braced herself for the inevitable.

Jason set down his duffel bag and pulled her into his arms. "I had a great time this weekend."

"Me too," she said, fighting back the tears that were threatening to spill out.

"I love you, Sam. I'll call you later, ok?"

As if that would take the place of his presence. "Ok. Drive safe."

"I will. Don't forget to wear the bracelet."

"I will." Silence hung in the air between them for a moment, and then Jason picked up his bag and headed to the back door.

They kissed good bye, but it felt much too short and much too chaste for her. Sam knew she couldn't prolong the inevitable anymore. "I love you, Jason," she said simply, eyes moist with sadness.

"I love you too. See you then?"

She smiled at the familiar phrase, the one that now adorned the bracelet he gave her. "See you then," she nodded and watched as he walked out the door.

A few days later, Sam was cleaning up her dinner dishes when the doorbell rang. A mixture of surprise and fear flooded through her as she opened the front door to Janet.

"Sorry to bother you, Samantha, but may I come in for a moment?" Her tone was polite, yet Sam was still wary as she motioned Janet inside. Sam didn't have to wait long to find out why she was there; Janet came right to the point.

"I came over to apologize. I realize we didn't get off to a very good start, and I'm sorry."

Sam hesitated for a moment before she said, "I accept your apology."

"Since my son is obviously crazy about you, I decided that I should try to get to know you better. You're all he talks about these days."

Sam doubted her sincerity, but she agreed that they needed to at least try to get along.

"Would you like something to drink?" she offered, realizing they were still standing in the foyer.

"No, thank you. I don't want to keep you. I just wanted to be the one to invite you to my upcoming birthday dinner. Has Jason mentioned it?"

"He said he would be home for your birthday in a few weeks."

"Yes, three Saturdays from now, we're having some friends over for dinner, and I would like it if you joined us."

Sam almost pinched herself. Is this for real? First she apologizes, and then she invites me over for dinner? "Sure," she heard herself say. "Thanks for inviting me."

Janet nodded and turned to leave. "Oh, and Samantha, thank you for convincing Jason that going to Denver is the right decision. I think he feels much better about it now that you're on board."

If she only knew how many reservations I have, she might not be thanking me, thought Sam. "Like I said before, I'm not trying to stand in his way."

"I see that now. Enjoy the rest of your evening, and we'll see you in a few weeks." Janet was out the door before Sam had a chance to say goodbye. Sam immediately picked up her phone to tell Jason the news.

He answered on the first ring. "Hey, sweetheart."

She loved when he used terms of endearment in place of her name. "Hey, handsome. I have some big news for you."

"Lay it on me!"

"Your mom just left my house. She came over to apologize and to invite me to her birthday dinner."

"Get out," he mocked.

"Did you put her up to it?"

"Not at all, that was all Janet. I had a feeling she might, though."

"Why's that?"

"Before I left on Sunday, we had a little chat. I told her that you are a very important part of my life and it would be nice if she could put forth some effort to get to know you."

Sam understood why Jason would want them to get along, but she was still skeptical about Janet's intentions. She obviously loved her son and wanted him to succeed, but could she really accept Sam in his life?

"Well, whatever you said to her must have sunk in because she was very contrite."

"Contrite, now that's a good word!" Jason's chuckle warmed her soul through the phone. She always loved the sound of his voice, especially when he was teasing her.

"Anything new with you today?"

"No, I'm just studying for my psych test while I have the apartment to myself."

"Where's Max?"

"He went out with some girl he met at the library."

"The flavor of the week?" Every time she talked to Jason, he told her about Max's latest dating escapades. For being such a nice guy, it seemed like he always chose the wrong kind of girl.

"The flavor of the day is more like it. I've tried lecturing him on the error of his ways, but he's not having any part of it. He's determined to have a variety of experiences before he settles down."

Once again, Sam was struck by how different Jason was from his college friends. It didn't seem to bother him at all that he was "tied down" to her instead of picking up girls with his buddies. He was an old soul in a hot, twenty-three-year-old body.

"Sam, you still there?"

She pulled herself back from her musings. "Yeah, sorry. I drifted off for a minute."

"What were you thinking about?"

"Just you and how much I love you."

"I love you more."

Oh no, this game was becoming a regular part of their conversations now that he was away. "I'm not doing this, Jason," she scolded half-heartedly. He always managed to get the last word in at the end of their calls.

"Poor sport. When am I going to see you next?"

"I don't think it will be until your mom's birthday. I have obligations over the next two weekends."

"I know about your nephew's party, but

what else is going on?"

"Leslie asked for my help painting her kitchen two weekends from now. She's helped me with a lot of household projects over the years, so it's only fair that I reciprocate."

"Can't her husband help?"

"He hates painting, and she says he's terrible at it. She's kicking him out for the weekend so we can get it done."

"Hmm. For the record, if you ever want something painted, I will be happy to oblige. You'll never have to kick me out for not doing my part."

Sam had no doubt that was true. He kept giving her reasons to love him more every day. "I know," was all she could say around the rather large lump that had just lodged in her throat.

"I understand you wanting to help her, although I miss you like crazy."

"I miss you too, and for the record, I'm dangerously close to crying right now, so I think it's time to hang up." She was always trying to spare him from the blubbery outbursts that overcame her at unexpected times. She blamed her oversensitivity in part to Brad's untimely death. She'd decided long ago, that being apart from the one you love most in the world is the hardest pain to bear. She tried to keep a grip on her emotions for Jason's sake, but it didn't always work. He was calm and patient with her whenever she expressed her true feelings, but she didn't want him to see her as needy or whiny.

"Don't cry, sweetheart. Happy thoughts. Are you wearing my bracelet?"

"Of course," she said, smiling through the haze of tears that clouded her vision.

"Good, then you know I'm right here for you. I'll always be here for you, Sam."

"I know," she said quietly, dreading the goodbye that was about to follow. Sometimes Jason let her be the first to say goodbye, probably in an attempt to make it easier. The only time he ended a call was if he was running late for a class. Even when he was in the middle of doing homework, he always took her call.

"I'll see you then," she said, a slight waver in her voice.

"See you then, beautiful. I love you."

"I love you too." She disconnected the call before the first tears rolled down her cheeks.

Chapter 25

The following Saturday, Sam showed up early to her nephew Jacob's birthday party to help Jaime with any last minute preparations. Her true hope was that she would have a chance to talk to her sister alone before all the party guests arrived. As usual, Jaime was very organized, and they actually had a few minutes to sit at the kitchen table and drink a cup of tea.

"Tell me all about last weekend. How was it?" Jaime was always eager to talk to her about Jason.

"Great. We had a lot of fun, but it went by way too fast."

"Details, details," Jamie said, taking a glance at the kitchen clock.

"Well, I guess the latest news is that we discussed marriage and having kids."

Jaime leaned in toward Sam, her eyes as big as saucers. "Are you serious?"

"Settle down sis, we're not rushing to the altar anytime soon. We just talked about it."

"In a general way, or is there a date I need to pencil in on my calendar?"

"I told him that I wasn't ready for all of that yet, but maybe someday."

"What did he say?"

"He's willing to wait it out, but he definitely wants kids, and I don't blame him. I'm just afraid that with my age..."

"Hold it right there, sister! No playing the age card. Tons of women your age and older are still having babies. Case in point, my neighbor Carrie is forty-five, and she just had a healthy baby boy."

"I know, but think about how old she'll be when he graduates from high school!"

"Who cares? As long as you take care of yourself, you'll be around for a long time."

Sam knew that wasn't always the case, but she didn't want to correct her sister and bring up her painful past. Brad certainly had taken good care of himself, but that hadn't prevented him from dying young. Jaime recognized the error in her statement but just plunged ahead.

"If it's meant to be, it will happen. Just promise me to be open-minded." She reached across the table and squeezed her sister's hand lovingly right as the doorbell rang. "Show time," she called as she made her way to the front door.

Later that night, while lying in bed, Sam replayed the conversation with her sister. Logically, she knew that women were having children later in life, but in reality she couldn't quite fathom it. She loved kids, but it was hard to visualize herself as a mom. She convinced herself that it was because she had been alone for so long, but she knew there was something else there too. She pushed her nagging thoughts out of her head and drifted off to sleep.

The week passed surprisingly fast, and before she knew it she was at Leslie's house bent over an open can of buttery yellow paint. She and Leslie had reached an unspoken agreement in their relationship. Sam rarely mentioned Jason, and Leslie didn't ask many questions. They stuck to safer topics in order to maintain their friendship. Sometimes Sam missed being able to confide in her best friend, but she still had Jaime and her mom on her side. Besides, Jason was her true confidante now.

"Thanks again for helping me with this," Leslie said as she stepped up a ladder, paintbrush in hand.

"No problem at all. You've helped me out plenty of times." Sam didn't say that it also helped her pass the time while Jason was away. They went on to talk about books, movies, their co-workers, and a variety of other topics as they worked companionably. They took a lunch break at noon, and Leslie served up soup and sandwiches. As they were eating, Sam heard her cell phone ring and knew by the tone that it was Jason. She had talked to him briefly that morning before leaving for Leslie's, so she was somewhat surprised that he was calling now.

"Aren't you going to get that?" Leslie asked curiously.

"No, that's ok. I'll call back later." She took another bite of her sandwich as Leslie eyed her closely.

"You don't have to do that on my account. It was Jason wasn't it?" Her tone was neutral, but Sam was still wary. The last thing she needed was to get in an argument with Leslie.

"Probably, but like I said, I can call him back later."

Leslie set her sandwich down and clasped her fingers together. "This is terrible, Sam," she said earnestly. "You shouldn't have to hide your boyfriend from me, or anything else for that matter. What's important to you is important to me."

Sam felt a tear prick her eye. Geez, what is wrong with me lately? I'm a blubbering idiot! Leslie sensed her discomfort and tried to make light of it.

"Don't get all teary on me, girlfriend! I'm just saying… I want you to be able to talk about him."

Sam finally found her voice. "Thanks, Les. He is very important to me, and I would like to be able to share some things with you."

"But not everything?" she teased, eyebrows raised knowingly.

"No, not everything!" Their combined

laughter cleared the air, and they finished their lunch in happy silence.

Sam could hardly wait to call Jason and did so as soon as she pulled out of Leslie's driveway a few hours later. First Janet and now Leslie, what was the world coming to? Jason answered on the first ring as if he expected her call.

"Hey, pretty baby."

She could feel his smile through the phone. "Hey, stud."

His boisterous laughter rang in her ears. "How was your painting party?"

"Better than expected."

"Really, how so?"

"I think Leslie has finally come to accept the fact that you and I are together. We talked about it, and she told me not to hide my feelings for you."

"That doesn't mean you're going to tell her everything, does it?" He emphasized the word everything.

"No, but it will be nice for me to bring up your name without her visibly flinching."

"Glad to hear it."

"What are you doing tonight?" she asked, always curious about how he spent his Saturday nights.

"Max's parents are coming over, and they offered to take us out to dinner. Max isn't too keen on it, but I said we should go."

Sam felt her body relax. She hated the thought of Jason and his friends out bar-hopping and was secretly grateful to Max's parents. "Why doesn't he want to go?"

"He thinks it's lame to spend a Saturday night with one's parents."

"But you set him straight, huh?"

"You know me, always the voice of reason." And he was, she thought. Just one more item on the list of things she loved about him. "I'd rather be with you instead."

"It's less than a week now, right? You're coming home on Friday." It was more of a statement than a question.

"You know it, and I'm heading straight into your arms."

Sam felt a shiver of delight at the thought of their reunion. "I can't wait," she breathed. Before he could respond, she heard the sound of the doorbell in the background.

"My hot date has arrived," he teased as the sound of Max's parents filled the room.

"Try not to have too much fun," she teased back.

He chuckled. "I love you."

"I love you too. Call me later."

"Guaranteed," he said and was gone.

In preparation for Jason's arrival, Sam found herself at the grocery store on Thursday night. She planned on making chicken stir fry for Jason's homecoming dinner, and she was perusing the frozen vegetables when a voice from the past interrupted her.

"Samantha, is that you?"

She turned around to an intense pair of deep blue eyes that had first caught her attention twenty years ago. "Tony?" It came out as a question to which she knew the answer. Tony Delvecchio, the handsome, enigmatic guy she'd met in college just after she had started dating Brad. They had "hit it off" right away in English Lit and become friends, although it had been obvious they were attracted to each other. The memory of Tony admitting as much came flooding back, and she felt her face flush in response. He'd known she was dating Brad at the time, but it hadn't stopped him from asking her out. Sam had been dating Brad for a couple of months at that point, and even though they'd never specifically said so, she'd felt that their relationship was exclusive. She recalled Tony's look of disappointment and her twinge of regret, when she turned him down. "We could have been so good together," he had said before walking out of her life.

"You look great. How've you been?" Tony's warmth and enthusiasm struck her as it had in college. It didn't help that he was easy on the eyes too. He had thick, cropped black hair and perfectly straight white teeth that seemed to glow against his olive complexion. He was a few inches shorter than Jason with a stockier build but still in great shape from what she could tell. She shook herself back to the present.

"Thanks, I'm doing good, and you?" She tried to sound polite without being overly friendly.

"Better now. I went through a rough divorce a couple years ago, but things are settling down again."

"Sorry to hear that. Any kids?" Sam found herself drawn in due to her natural curiousity and their past connection. She had genuinely liked Tony apart from finding him attractive.

"No kids, thank God. I don't mean that the way it sounded. I just meant..."

She shook her head in understanding. "I know what you meant. You're glad you didn't have to drag any kids through the divorce."

"Exactly. What about you, any kids?"

Sam swallowed nervously. Whenever she ran into someone she hadn't seen in a long time, she dreaded having to rehash the story of Brad's death. Most people stumbled for the right words, and then the rest of the conversation was awkward and uncomfortable. Sam thought she would be used to it by now, but it never got any easier.

"No. My husband Brad died before we were able to have children."

"Oh no, I'm really sorry to hear that. I knew that you guys got married, but I lost touch with most of my college friends after graduation."

For some reason, his reaction soothed her. He didn't ask any follow-up questions, but she found herself volunteering information. "It was about five years ago, and I know what you mean about college friends; I haven't stayed in touch with anyone either."

"I take it you live around here?"

"Yes, just a couple miles away. What about you?" Sam was starting to wonder where this conversation was headed. Had she already exceeded the appropriate amount of time allotted to talking to an almost boyfriend? She would probably say it was too long if Jason was talking to Rebecca. But that was different, right? After all, she and Tony had never officially dated. Still, she knew that Jason wouldn't like her talking to a man who had shown interest in her.

"I live in Davisburg, but I pass through Clarkston on my way home from work every day."

"Where do you work?"

"At a software development company in Auburn Hills. What about you?"

"I'm a school librarian in Brandon."

Tony nodded his head as if this was the answer he expected. "You always did love your books."

Sam was touched that he remembered

that about her, although it was a logical conclusion since they'd met in an English literature class. "I enjoy my job." Deciding it was time to wrap things up, she made a clear point of looking down at her watch and then...

"I'm sorry if I've kept you too long. It was nice seeing you, Samantha."

His blue eyes sparkled down at her, and she couldn't help but smile up at him. "You too, take care."

Instead of walking away, Tony reached into his back pocket and pulled out a black leather wallet. He extracted his business card and handed it to her. "If you ever want to meet for coffee or something, give me a call."

She took the card from him and slid it in her purse, but when she looked up to respond, he was already walking away.

Sam fretted as she drove home and unpacked the groceries. It was getting late and Jason would expect her call, but she was trying to gather her thoughts before she picked up the phone. I didn't do anything wrong, she repeated to herself. I happened to run into an old friend, and we talked for a few minutes. That was all. Oh, and he gave me his business card, big deal. People do that all the time, right? Tony hadn't said anything inappropriate; maybe he was just being friendly. Why would he give her his card unless he was hoping to talk to her again? Surely, that's what Jason would say.

Speaking of Jason, Sam scolded herself for not mentioning him to Tony. She could have slipped it into the conversation casually. When Tony asked how she was, she could have said, "My husband died several years ago, but I'm dating a really great guy named Jason." Ok, now I'm just being silly, she scoffed. None of this mattered because she had no intention of calling or seeing Tony again. She couldn't help pondering the coincidence that they had run into each other now that they were both technically single. If she hadn't been with Jason, she might have called Tony to meet for coffee; why not? He was someone she felt comfortable with who happened to be good-looking and employed, not to mention that they were the same age! Recognizing that her thoughts were spinning out of control, Sam forced herself to stop. This is crazy; I don't even drink coffee, for Pete's sake! That's it, I'm calling Jason right now and telling him the entire story. She took a deep breath, exhaled, and picked up the phone.

"Hello, gorgeous," his sweet, masculine voice filled her ears. "What have you been up to?"

It was an innocent question, but why did she suddenly feel guilty? "Not much, I just got home from the grocery store."

"Oh yeah, what are you making me for dinner?"

Sam giggled. "How do you know that's

why I went there?"

"Well, let's see, you like to cook, and I'm coming home tomorrow, so..."

"Naturally you thought I wanted to cook dinner for my man."

"You said it, not me!"

She decided to relieve her burden right away since they were on the topic of the grocery store. "I ran into an old friend while I was there."

"Makes sense, everyone needs groceries. Who was it?"

Sam plunged ahead. "His name is Tony. We had a couple college classes together way back when." She added the last part in order to soothe any reservations he might have. It didn't work.

"Was he an old friend or an old *boyfriend*?"

His direct approach could always be counted on. "I was dating Brad at the time, so we were just friends."

"I've always hated that phrase, 'just friends.' It implies that friendship isn't as important as, let's say, a romantic relationship."

"Hmm, I never thought of it like that." Does this mean he's not upset or that he's working up to it?

"What did you talk about it?"

"Oh the usual, our jobs mostly."

"Is he married?"

She shifted around on the barstool uncomfortably. "Divorced."

"Hmm," Jason said as if giving this point deep consideration.

"It was really no big deal. I just wanted to let you know. You've always been honest with me about girls from your past, so I'm doing the same."

"Is he good-looking?"

Was he giving her a taste of her own medicine? This line of questioning was beginning to wear on her, but hadn't she done the same to him? "He's not bad, but he doesn't hold a candle to you." Jason might have used that exact phrase on her before, but he wasn't buying it.

"Did he ask you out?"

"No," she said a little too abruptly. "We talked for a few minutes while I was picking out frozen vegetables for your dinner tomorrow. That's all there was to it."

"Thou doth protest too much," he replied, his voice lowering back down to a more even tone.

Sam sighed. "If you're trying to give me a dose of my own medicine, you're doing a good job. Can we please move on now?"

"Sorry, but I hate the thought of some other guy swooping in on my girl while I'm away."

"No one's swooping."

"Ok, fine," he relented. "So, what are you making me for dinner tomorrow?"

"How does chicken stir fry sound?"

"It sounds wonderful if you're making it. Will you be wearing an apron?"

"What? Where are you going with this?"

He chuckled deeply. "I was going to request that you wear an apron and nothing else while you're cooking."

"That could be a little dangerous, don't you think?"

"It depends on how much coverage your apron provides."

Sam belted out a loud laugh, and the sound filled her empty kitchen with joy. "Ok, mister, enough of this. I will make your dinner properly clothed so as not to burn myself, and you will eat it because you love me."

"I do love you."

"I know. Hurry up and come home."

"I'll be there as soon as you get home from school. Maybe I'll bring you a new apron."

"Good night, Jason. I love you, and I'll see you tomorrow," she said with mock exasperation.

"See you then," he sighed and waited for her to disconnect.

As Sam sunk down in a warm bubble bath, she found her thoughts drifting from Brad to Tony to Jason and back again. She pondered the circumstances that had put these three men in her path and wondered about God and fate. When people talked about "fate," it seemed like such an obscure concept, but now she was beginning to understand. Why had Tony suddenly reappeared in her life? Why did Brad die so young? Why had Jason been put in her path? There were no answers to these questions, but she marveled at the direction her life had taken. She could never have predicted the course of her life, but she was finally becoming more accepting of it. Was that because of Jason? Was life just one long learning process? Whatever was at work in her life, she decided that she would be ok. She had Jason, she had friends and family who loved her, and she had the future to look forward to. Life is pretty good, she thought as she snuggled under her comforter and drifted off to sleep.

Chapter 26
(Three Months Later)

The day had finally come, the day Sam would take Jason to the airport and leave him there to board a plane for Denver. She still couldn't quite wrap her head around it even though they had been talking about it for weeks. They had spent Christmas break wrapped in a tiny cocoon they'd built tightly around them, only popping their heads out for the required family gatherings. The last two weeks had been bittersweet; they were either laughing and loving or serious and sad. Last night, their lovemaking had been as fierce and passionate as it had ever been, with both reluctant to break the connection, uncertain of when they would be together again. They argued about whether or not she should take him to the airport. Jason thought it would make things harder, but she insisted. She wanted to be with him up until the very last second. They drove in silence as they approached the airport exit, the tension palpable between them. Sam was determined not to cry until the drive home, if there were any tears left at that point. Right now, she just felt flat and empty. During the first half of their drive Jason had tried to cheer them up by blasting music and singly loudly and out-of-tune to the latest pop songs. It had worked for a few minutes, but they'd both felt weary after a few songs. They'd finally turned off the radio and settled on holding hands for the remainder of the trip.

"I really don't want to say good bye in front of a bunch of strangers," he said, breaking the silence. "Let's pull into one of those cell phone lots and say goodbye there. Once we pull up to the airport doors, we'll be surrounded by people."

Sam hadn't thought of that, but to her, it didn't really matter where they said goodbye. Goodbye was goodbye; it would be devastating wherever it took place. "That's fine," she said bleakly.

Jason pulled into a lot with only a few parked cars. It faced a smattering of bare trees in a brown landscape. The day was as bleak as she felt: gray and dreary with a brisk chill in the air.

He shut the car off and turned toward her, resting his hands on either side of her face. "I don't know what to say that I haven't said a thousand times before."

"It's ok if you say it all again," she replied with a pained smile.

"I love you, and I'll miss you like crazy. I'll think about you every day, all day, and I'll call until you can't take it anymore."

She had to chuckle on that point because she knew it was true. Max teased Jason mercilessly about how often they talked on the phone. "I promise never to get tired of your calls."

"Talk to me again about when you might be able to fly out and visit."

They had discussed this a hundred times, but if it reassured him, she would repeat it again. "I'll fly out over mid-winter break in February. It will only be for four days, though."

"I know, but four days is better than nothing. Promise you'll keep checking the flight prices and buy a ticket as soon as the price looks reasonable."

"I promise." She held up her fingers in a scout's honor gesture.

"What will you do on New Year's Eve?" She had asked him this question before, but she couldn't think of anything else to say.

"Probably order a pizza, buy some beer, and sit in my hotel room wishing you were there."

Sam had already made plans to spend the night at her sister's house so she wouldn't have to be alone. It had been their tradition ever since Brad died; Jaime had insisted that no one should be alone on New Year's Eve if they could help it. They usually rented romantic movies, made popcorn, and curled up in the family room until they both fell asleep sometime after midnight. Steve and the boys hated watching "girlie" movies, so they usually stayed out of the way.

In the past, Sam had always looked forward to spending the time with her sister, but this year, she knew it would be different. Knowing the one you love is alive and well but out of reach brought on a whole new type of grief.

"Sam? I lost you for a second." He brushed a strand of hair gently away from her face. The gesture was sweet and loving, and it would be these simple things that Sam would miss the most.

"Sorry." She bent her head to his chest and just rested there for a time, breathing in his fresh, masculine scent and feeling the heat from his body radiate into her. Jason gently rubbed his hands up and down her back and didn't say a word. Finally, when her neck was beginning to hurt, she looked up and saw that his normally sparkly brown eyes were glossed over with moisture.

"I don't want to do this," he whispered, shaking his head from side to side. "This isn't right. I can't do this to you, to us."

Sam ran her hand over his messy brown hair and leaned her forehead against his. "You have to do this, Jason. We both know it's what's best for your future."

"How can it be the best choice when it feels this bad?"

"There were no other options. The internships in Detroit were taken, and the closest you could have been was Missouri. Missouri or

Colorado, it doesn't make much difference."

"At least Missouri would have been closer. I could have rented a car and driven home occasionally."

They both knew that wasn't practical, but Sam didn't bother refuting it. Instead, she glanced at her watch and said the inevitable. "I think you need to get going. You still have to check your bags and get through security."

"I know," he said gruffly. "Come over here and kiss me." He pulled her onto his lap, and she leaned in to kiss him. His touch instantly warmed her as she pressed her lips fully against his. One of his hands held the back of her neck with a firm grip as if daring her to pull away. Sam wasn't budging and met his demanding kiss with equal passion. He broke away only to kiss her cheeks, the tip of her nose, and her neck, leaving a trail of warm, wet impressions. She wrapped her arms even tighter around his neck and held him. Finally, after a few more minutes of soaking each other up, he released her. They silently switched seats so Sam could drop him off at the departure area. Sam adjusted her seat and mirrors and pulled out of the lot just as the first tear slid down the left side of her face. Jason was staring straight ahead, so she took the opportunity to quickly wipe the tear away before he noticed. When she pulled up to the curb, her heart was in her throat. Jason grabbed her hand and pulled her over for one last kiss, which was hurried due to the line of cars behind them.

"I love you," he said fiercely. "Don't forget that."

"I love you too, so much." She squeezed his hand as the car behind her honked.

"I'll call you," he said and then backed out of the door.

She watched in the rear-view mirror as he extracted his bags from the back and slammed the hatch. He blew her a kiss, turned, and headed into the terminal.

So much for not having any more tears left. She angrily swiped them away as she headed for home.

Chapter 27

Sam was glad to be back at work after the holidays and found herself arriving early and staying late to keep busy. By the time she went home and had dinner, it was time to talk to Jason on the phone, and then it was off to bed. She thought she was handling things fairly well until it happened again. She was wheeling her grocery cart slowly up and down each row on a Thursday night, and there he was in the cereal aisle — Tony. He was studying the ingredient list on a Lucky Charms box and didn't see her approach. Sam considered turning her cart around and heading the other way but dismissed the idea as foolish. Chances are, she would run into him in another aisle. She might as well say hello and move on. Just then, his head turned in her direction, and his eyes and face instantly lit up with pleasure.

"Well, we meet again!" He beamed at her and set the Lucky Charms back on the shelf.

"Hi. You don't have to pretend not to want those for my benefit," she said, chuckling and pointing to the cereal.

"You caught me. I try to eat healthy most of the time, but every once in a while, you just have to indulge."

"True," she said, suddenly glad that she hadn't avoided him after all.

"So, how were your holidays?" He asked the question innocently enough, but Sam felt a heaviness in her chest, thinking about Jason's departure. She decided that now would probably be a good time to mention her boyfriend.

"Good and bad. The guy I'm seeing had to go out of town for a while, so New Year's Eve was kind of tough. What about you?"

Tony appraised her for a few seconds before responding. "I spent some time with my folks in Pittsburgh, but I was ready to come home. How long have you been dating?"

Sam wasn't sure how much detail she wanted to share with Tony. He was obviously interested, but she was reluctant to say too much. "About six months now."

"Will he be out of town for long?"

"Until late April. He went to Denver, so it's not like I can see him much between now and then."

Tony nodded in understanding. "That would be tough. I figured you were probably seeing someone when you didn't call me."

She smiled apologetically. "I should have mentioned it the last time but…"

"No need to explain, it's alright. Maybe if you told your boyfriend that we're old friends, he wouldn't mind if we met for coffee. Coffee wasn't a code word for anything else, I promise."

She couldn't help but chuckle. "I mentioned that I ran into you, but I don't think it would go over very well if I told him we were having coffee since I don't even drink coffee!"

Tony chuckled this time and self-consciously ran his hand through his wavy hair. "Point taken. My loss, again," he sighed.

Sam felt torn—why couldn't she have a drink with a friend? Now that he knew she was dating Jason, there shouldn't be anything to worry about. What if it were the other way around, though? She wouldn't be enthused if Jason were having coffee with some woman from his past. Tony must have noticed her hesitation and added, "If you change your mind, call me. You still have my card, right?"

"I do. Have a good evening, Tony."

"You too." They both turned away at the same time and headed in opposite directions down the aisle.

That night, Sam pondered over the fact that she'd neglected to tell Jason that she'd run into Tony again. She slept horribly and went to work grumpy and tired the next day. Leslie asked if she was ok at lunch, but Sam didn't want to divulge the real reason for her sleepless night. Now that their friendship was back on track, she didn't want to give Leslie any reason to doubt her relationship with Jason. She was afraid that Leslie would try to convince her to have coffee with Tony, and she didn't want to hear it. There was only one person she could trust to be completely honest with her, and that was Jaime. Sam called Jamie on the way home from school, praying that she would be home.

"Hey sis, what's happening?" Jaime answered cheerfully.

"Help!" Sam pleaded and proceeded to spell out the problem.

"Wow, when it rains it pours. Now you have two men who want you — must be rough," she teased.

"C'mon, James, stop joking. What should I do?"

"This is a hard one because I really like Jason, you know that. However, it sounds like you're curious about re-connecting with Tony. I think you need to ask yourself why. Are you still attracted to him, or are you just lonely because Jason's gone? What is the real reason behind this, Sam?"

"Wow, since when did you become a psychologist?"

"Just answer the question, smart-ass."

"I'm not sure; maybe a little of both. I do find Tony attractive, and I am missing Jason."

"Are you having doubts about Jason? If you are, it's better to address them now before things go any further."

Sam had wondered the very same thing

herself the night before as she tossed and turned in bed. "I guess running into Tony reminded me that there are guys out there my own age who could be interested in me."

"I can't believe you're just now realizing that, sis. That's not the point, though. Just because some guy is your age doesn't mean you'll be perfect together. It doesn't guarantee a good relationship, like the one you have with Jason."

Sam was feeling more confused by the minute. "What if Tony is a better match? Don't I owe it to myself to find out? Why else was he put in my path again after all these years?"

"Who knows? Circumstance? Fate? I don't know. My advice is to give it some more thought before you do anything you might regret."

Sam hung up feeling as though nothing was resolved. She didn't regret telling Jaime, but now she was left with more questions than answers. That night, when Jason called, he sensed that something was off. After they took turns giving a synopsis of their workdays, Jason asked what was wrong.

"Just the usual—I'm missing you," she said truthfully.

"Besides that."

"Nothing. Some days are just worse than others."

He sighed, "It's hard on me too, baby.

What are you going to do this weekend?"

"I haven't really thought about it yet," she admitted.

"Maybe you should go hang out at your sister's."

"I think she's busy this weekend. I talked to her today, and it sounds like she has a lot going on. What are your plans?"

"A few of the teachers offered to take me into the city to show me around. We'll probably go out to dinner too."

Jason had mentioned a few teachers' names, including one woman, but Sam was pretty sure they were all older and married. "That sounds fun," she said distractedly.

"Sam, are you sure you're all right?"

"Yes, I'm fine," she repeated a little more adamantly this time. "Don't worry about me."

"I always worry about you because I love you," he said simply.

"I know. I love you too."

"Have you looked at flight prices lately?"

"Not in the past few days."

"That's something you can do this weekend," he suggested.

Sam didn't find any consolation in that prospect, but she nodded and replied, "Good idea." They hung up shortly after, having run out of things to say. There was no way that Sam was going to share her doubts with Jason while he was across the country. It would only exasperate them both. She needed to figure this one out all on her own.

The next day right before noon, Sam's home phone rang, a rare occurrence since most people she knew called her cell phone. She didn't recognize the number on the display, but it was local, so she decided to pick up.

"Hello?"

"Samantha? It's Tony."

Sam almost dropped the phone as sweat instantly broke out on her forehead and hands. "Tony?" How on earth did he get her number?

"You're probably wondering how I got your number."

"Yeah, kind of," she admitted, wiping her sweaty palm on her pant leg.

"I found it in the alumni directory. I hope you don't mind."

Sam wasn't sure how to respond to that, but before she even had a chance, he continued.

"I hope I'm not catching you at a bad time. I just called to see if you would like to have lunch today."

She could hear the nervous waver in his voice and realized that she probably wasn't the only one sweating right now. It took a lot of courage for him to call her like this. As she was debating the answer, he piped in again.

"It's only lunch, Samantha. I know you don't drink coffee, but I figured you'd probably need to eat today, so…"

"Ok," she interrupted before she lost her nerve. "Yes, I'll have lunch with you."

He gave an audible sigh of relief. "Great. Do you want to meet somewhere? What kind of food do you like?"

This was all happening so fast; Sam's head was spinning. She was surprised she was still standing let alone forming words. "How about the sports bar and grill on Dixie Highway?"

"The one that advertises a beer and a burger for five bucks?"

"That's the one." Sam knew because she and Jason had been there before, several times.

"What time is good for you?"

"How about 12:30?"

"That works for me. See you then."

"See you then," she said quickly and hung up the phone. It struck her that Tony had used Jason's phrase instead of the usual goodbye. "See you then," the phrase that was imprinted on her bracelet to remind her of his love and commitment. There wasn't enough time to give it any more thought. She needed to freshen up before meeting Tony.

She ran a comb through her hair and applied some clear lip gloss. She decided that her jeans and striped sweater were good enough for a casual lunch date and headed out the door. Sam was a bundle of nerves as she pulled into the parking lot. "Why am I doing this?" she said out loud, checking her appearance in the rearview mirror. It took her eyes a minute to adjust to the dim lighting in the bar as she scanned the room for Tony. He was seated at a booth against the windows and smiled broadly as she walked toward him. He stood up as she approached and offered to take her jacket.

"No thanks, I'm a little chilled right now," she said, her voice slightly shaky. A waitress approached their table and took their drink order—two light beers. Just like she and Jason would order.

"I have to admit, I'm surprised you agreed to meet me," Tony said.

If he was attempting to put her at ease, it wasn't working. Sam was warring with herself even as she spoke. "Like you said, it's only lunch."

The waitress brought their beers over and took their burger orders. When she left, Sam found Tony staring at her as if contemplating what to say next.

"Tell me about your boyfriend," he offered, an air of resignation about him.

"Is it that obvious?"

"Plain as the nose on your face," he answered, taking a long swig of beer.

"I'm so sorry," Sam breathed. "I'm not sure why I came here today."

"You must love him a lot if you're agonizing this much."

"I do, I really do. He's a great guy. He's funny and smart and sweet and…"

"So, when are you getting married?"

Sam shifted in her seat unsure of how to answer that. She was so relieved to be talking this freely that she decided on full disclosure. "I don't know, he's still in college."

The waitress came over again bearing plates piled high with hamburgers and french fries. They dug into their food for a few minutes until Tony casually asked, "How old is this guy?"

"Twenty-three. He's graduating at the end of this semester."

To Tony's credit, he didn't miss a beat. "So, this trip to Denver was for an internship, I take it?"

"Yes," she nodded, dipping a french fry in ketchup.

"I hope he loves you as much as you love him because you deserve the best."

It was Sam's turn to smile. "Thanks, Tony."

"If things don't work out between you two…"

She cut him off while stifling a laugh, "Don't even say it."

"I'm a glutton for punishment, I guess; first Brad, now this guy. What's his name anyway?"

"Jason. Jason Grant."

"How about a toast, then, to the future Mrs. Grant? May she be forever happy and forever in love."

They clinked beer bottles together and took a slug. Sam cleared her throat and set down the bottle. "Tony, what do you think about the age gap? Be honest."

"I think the heart wants what the heart wants. Love doesn't come with a rulebook. It is what it is, and you just have to be grateful for it."

They parted shortly after with a chaste hug in the parking lot, and Sam felt satisfied that they would probably never see each other again. Tony's words rang in her head and filled her with immense relief and joy. The heart wants what the heart wants, and now she knew without a doubt that her heart wanted Jason.

Chapter 28

Jason leaned against the window of the Boeing 737 and stared out at the empty sky. He could hardly contain the adrenaline that pumped through him as he imagined the surprise on Sam's face. It was all he could do yesterday to keep from sharing his news. He had told her the bit about sightseeing with the teachers to throw her off, and it had seemed to work. He hoped her excitement about his unexpected arrival would trump the little white lie. He also hoped that she'd be at home and not out with Leslie or Jaime. Just then, the pilot's voice came over the speaker: "Ladies and gentlemen, we are beginning our descent into the Detroit Metropolitan Airport. The skies are overcast and the temperature is 34 degrees. Flight attendants please prepare the cabin for landing."

Jason breathed an audible sigh of relief; this had been one of the longest flights of his life. He had tried reading a magazine and watching the in-flight movie, but nothing could distract him from his anxiousness to get to Sam. Something about their conversation yesterday bothered him, but he couldn't quite put his finger on why. It was probably just as she said—she was missing him. Well, she won't have to miss me anymore, he mused.

Jason made it through the maze of the airport and collected his luggage in record time. The next step would be to rent a car since he hadn't called anyone to pick him up. A short time later he was on the expressway in a white Chevy Malibu, cruising toward home.

In the meantime, Sam had just stepped out of the tub and was drying off hurriedly. She had tried calling Jason several times that afternoon, but the calls had gone right to voicemail each time. It wasn't like him to ignore her calls, and she was concerned. Supposedly he was out with some teacher friends exploring downtown Denver, but what if something else was going on? After all, she had been out to lunch with Tony unbeknownst to Jason; what was there to prevent him from being with some woman. She was sure her guilt was getting the best of her, so she quickly abandoned that idea. Maybe he was in a car accident and was lying in a hospital bed somewhere alone and helpless. She finally resorted to calling Jaime, who talked her down from all her worries. Jaime insisted that Jason was out having fun with his co-workers and he either didn't hear the phone or the battery ran down and he didn't have a charger with him. Sam decided that the latter explanation was very likely and then sank into the tub to wash her fears away.

It was now approaching nine o'clock, and she planned on curling up with her current romance novel before settling down for bed. She would call Jason one more time before she turned off her phone for the night. She got so caught up in the story that the sound of the doorbell startled her, and her book fell off her lap with a thud. She couldn't imagine who would be at the door at this time of night unless it was her sister coming over to console her. She peeked out her upstairs bedroom window, which had a view of the driveway below, and saw a white mid-size car that she didn't recognize. Sam tied her robe tighter and padded downstairs. An intruder wouldn't pull in the driveway and ring the doorbell, so it must be someone she knew. She switched several lights on as she passed through the house, just in case, and silently thanked Brad for insisting they have a peephole installed on the front door.

Sam stood up on her tiptoes and peered through the hole. No way—she must be hallucinating! She blinked her eyes a few times and peered through again. Her heart thumped wildly in her chest, and she let out a squeal that he must have heard through the door.

"It's me. Open up, beautiful."

It was the sweetest request she had ever heard. The warm, rich tone of his voice calmed and energized her at the same time, and she flung the door open. Jason was illuminated by the dim light, looking a bit rumpled but gorgeous, as always. His amber eyes sparkled with excitement. Sam struggled to find her voice while she opened the door wider and motioned for him to come in.

"Oh my God, it's really you," she exhaled and wrapped her arms tight around his neck, crushing him and almost tipping them over.

Jason pulled her even closer and buried his face in her neck. Finally, they pulled apart, and she led him into the living room. "What on earth is going on? Why are you here? Not that I don't want you here because of course I do but..."

"Slow down Sam." He laughed and settled himself next to her on the couch. "One question at a time!"

Sam shook herself to make sure she wasn't dreaming. She slid her hand down his forearm as if to assure herself he was real. "I just can't believe you're here. I thought you were roaming the streets of downtown Denver with your friends, and instead, here you are on my couch."

Jason entwined his fingers with hers. "The marvels of air travel, huh? I spent most of the day trying to get home to you."

"Why didn't you tell me you were coming home this weekend? I would have come to the airport to pick you up."

"I wanted to surprise you," he said with a

grin, "and it looks like I succeeded."

"Tell me everything. What else is going on?" Sam was just starting to understand that there was more to this story than an impromptu visit. Jason kept one of her hands locked in his and took a deep breath.

"I'm not going back, Sam. I'm home to stay."

She couldn't believe what she was hearing. He didn't have an ounce of distress on his face, but she was still confused. How could he just leave the internship behind? How would this effect his graduation?

He brought her hand up to his lips and placed a gentle kiss on her knuckles, sending a wave of desire through her. The gesture distracted her but only for a moment. She wanted answers before anything else could happen. "What about the internship? Did you just quit?"

Jason's thumb moved back and forth across the back of her hand, causing her to feel tingly all over. "Not exactly. Before I left for Denver, I asked my counselor to call me if any positions opened up in Michigan. Turns out an intern assigned to a middle school in Detroit got cold feet and quit the program. The counselor called me last week and asked if I could start on Monday, so here I am."

Sam gave his hand a squeeze. "Jason, this is awesome! I still can't believe it."

"Well, believe it because you're going to see a lot more of me, sexy lady."

She leaned in for a kiss, and he pulled her onto his lap. Their first kiss was soft and slow, almost tentative, neither one breaking eye contact. Sam suddenly felt overheated in her fuzzy white robe lying against Jason's warm, broad chest. Their kiss deepened, and Sam felt her eyes fluttering closed as she opened her mouth wider to meet his exploring tongue, stroke for stroke. She was vaguely aware of Jason's hand loosening the tie around her waist and then slipping it inside to cup her breast. He flicked his thumb back and forth over her nipple, and she felt it harden against her white tank top. Their movements became more urgent as Jason worked her robe down off her shoulders until it gathered around her waist. He moved his lips across her cheek to find the hollow between her neck and shoulder, and she leaned her head back to give him greater access. His hand moved from one breast to the other, teasing and tugging at her nipples through the fabric of her top. Jason suddenly swooped her up in his arms and walked toward the staircase, continuing to place warm kisses on her neck as he moved across the room. She kept her arms clasped tightly around his neck and laid her head against his muscular shoulder. He effortlessly moved up the stairs and gently laid her down horizontally across the bed. She propped herself up to get a better view as he removed first his long-sleeve t-shirt, followed by his jeans and boxers. She had left the reading lamp on in her bedroom and it now served as a backlight for his magnificent, hard body. She let her eyes travel down until they landed on his arousal.   He smiled as he crawled back on the bed and leaned over her, supporting his weight with his hands.

"I got naked first this time," he whispered, gazing down into her desire-filled eyes.

"So I see," she whispered back with a smirk.

"I missed you so much, Sam. I missed everything about you, including your touch."

Sam nodded her agreement, entranced by his words and his presence.   Their bodies weren't touching, but she felt her own arousal building inside her. He leaned closer and lightly pressed his lips to hers and then moved off to the side, a whoosh of cool air flowing over her in the process. She wanted to feel him against her, to feel his heat and his love, but she was trying to match his speed, which for the moment was slow and sensual.

"Get naked for me, Sam," he said, leaning up to rest his head in one hand. She didn't hesitate. Sam sat up on her haunches and pulled her arms out of her robe slowly, making sure to give him the proper show. She tugged the hem of her tank top out from her pajama pants and slid it up over her breasts and then over her head. Jason swallowed noisily as she got up on her knees and untied the drawstring of her pink striped pajama pants. She seductively pulled them down, along with her panties, and then leaned back to slide them over her hips and down her legs. She pushed the pile of discarded clothes off the bed with one arm while maintaining eye contact. She could read the pleasure in his expression as he perused her body, and she remained still under his intense gaze. In the next second, she was pulled over on top of him, and their passion exploded. They couldn't seem to get close enough; their bodies slid and ground together with impatience. Sam ran her hands up and down the length of his body, delighting in every hard angle and plane while soaking up his heat and his energy. They took turns kissing and licking and teasing each other until Jason rolled her over to her back and plunged inside her, filling her with his strength and his need and his love. They moved together until their release was complete, and they collapsed with matching grins of satisfaction plastered on their faces.

It struck Sam a little while later, as they lay side by side, hands entwined, that Jason was truly home and that she was truly home now too.

"So, was it a good surprise?" he whispered in the dark.

"The best ever," she replied with a smile. "I don't think you'll ever be able to top it."

"Don't be so sure. I plan on surprising you for the rest of our lives."

Sam snuggled into his side and closed her eyes. "Whatever else you have planned will have to wait until morning. I'm getting really sleepy."

"I can wait until morning," he said, pulling her closer.

"See you then," she replied contentedly.

"See you then, sweetheart. See you then."

Chapter 29
(Three Years Later)

"What name do you give this baby?" the nurse asked as she swaddled their brand new baby boy.

"Evan Bradley Grant," Jason answered proudly. The middle name was Jason's idea; he had insisted that this was an ideal way of keeping Brad's memory alive.

"That sounds like a good strong name for this little guy," said the nurse with a smile as she carefully placed Evan in Sam's arms.

Sam couldn't stop grinning as she stared down at their beautiful baby boy. "He's strapping, just like his daddy."

Jason scooted up on the hospital bed to be closer to his wife and son. He brushed Sam's damp hair away from her face and placed a tender kiss on her forehead. "You did great, beautiful."

His words filled her heart, and she thought she would burst with the love that she felt for these two wonderful men in her life.

"I think there are a few people in the waiting room who are anxious to meet Evan," the nurse said as she tidied up the birthing room. Jason had kept their friends and family informed during her labor, but Sam and he had insisted on privacy for the birth.

"We've probably kept them waiting long enough," he conceded, and Sam agreed.

A few minutes later, they were surrounded by their parents (Elise and Ted had flown in from Florida to be there), their sisters and brothers-in-law, and their best friends Leslie and Max. After all the "oohing" and "ahhing" and the discussions about who Evan looked like, the nurse finally kicked everybody out. "Mommy and baby need their rest," she said firmly. Why don't you all go down to the cafeteria and come back in a couple of hours." Once the reluctant goodbyes were said, the nurse left to complete some paperwork, and Sam, Jason, and Evan were alone again.

Sam stared down at Evan's tiny face and ran her hand over the tuft of caramel brown hair that stuck straight up from his head. He lay peacefully in her arms, and she watched as his chest heaved up and down in his sleep. Jason was just as enthralled as she was as he reached out to softly stroke the side of their baby's cheek.

"Now who had the best surprise ever?" she teased, grinning up at her handsome husband.

"Ok, ok, you win!" He threw his hands up in the air in defeat, recalling the day Sam had come home from what he'd thought was a routine doctor visit and told him that she was pregnant. He hadn't thought anything could top that day, but now, here he was, staring down at the most wonderful gift he had ever been given, next to his beautiful wife.

"We all win," she said softly.

32143435R00194

Made in the USA
San Bernardino, CA
29 March 2016